The Mercy Quilt

A WAXAHACHIE, TEXAS, QUILT MYSTERY, BOOK 2

Jeffree Wyn Itrich

Publisher: Amy Barrett-Daffin

Creative Director: Gailen Runge

Senior Editor: Roxane Cerda

Copy Editor: Second Glance Editorialx

Cover/Book Designer: April Mostek

Production Coordinator: Tim Manibusan

Photography Coordinator: Rachel Ackley

Front cover photography by Sharla Kay Salazar

Published by C&T Publishing, Inc., P.O. Box 1456, Lafayette, CA 94549

Library of Congress Cataloging-in-Publication Data is available upon request.

Printed in the USA

10 9 8 7 6 5 4 3 2 1

WAXAHACHIE, TEXAS, QUILT MYSTERY SERIES

Book 1

The Wedding Dress Quilt

Book 2

The Mercy Quilt

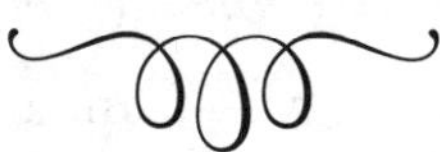

PRAISE FOR *THE WEDDING DRESS QUILT: A WAXAHACHIE, TEXAS, QUILT MYSTERY, BOOK 1*

"Loved this book and couldn't put it down!

This is a wonderful story with a little bit of everything. Excellent character development, suspense, budding love, a dream inheritance, mouth watering visions of food, humorous descriptions of quirky family members and perfect detail of a creative quilter, made this a story I absolutely could not put down. I loved every minute of it and truly hope the author writes a sequel to this sweet story, and I think it would make an excellent movie! I highly recommend The Wedding Dress Quilt by Jeffree Wyn Itrich."—Canda W. (Amazon)

"Very engaging book! I am enjoying reading this book. Can't wait to finish it! I love the references to specific locations as I am familiar with the area, and of course love any mention about quilting too! Great job! Hope there is another soon!"
—Betty F. (The Featherweight Shop)

"Came to the end and wanted more!

This read was exceptional. I have lived in Waxahachie for many years. So many in fact, I call it home. The story flowed easily from one chapter to the next. While reading, I felt the ease of living here in a smaller town, and I was able to relate to all the wonderful places she mentioned. The suspense was just enough to make me want to keep reading. In fact, once I began reading, I never put it down. When the end came, I so wanted more. In fact, I'd love to see a sequel or part two in a series offered up soon. I can't wait to see what might come next. I also had the opportunity of meeting the author in person. She was so easy to talk to. I could tell she loves what she's doing!"

—paul Corp (Amazon)

"Entertaining

The author's love of all things Texan and quilting combine to make an enjoyable story. Interwoven in the main character's quest to connect to her birth family are engaging characters, a budding romance and a mystery to solve. Texas culture and regional dishes add to the flavor and fun. The book's fast pace makes it a page turner. Definitely would recommend!"

—Amazon customer

DEDICATION

To Mr. Edgar Krepps,
my seventh-grade English teacher, who told me
that I had the talent to be a writer some day.
Thank you, Mr. Krepps, for your
encouragement and faith in me.

ACKNOWLEDGMENTS

For the wonderful people of West, Texas, who helped make the book cover possible. My thanks to Carla Sykora for letting me use The Oak House. Much appreciation to Tracy Carter Devers for loaning her antique rocking chair and Sarah Lee Blair for allowing us to use her dear mother's Grandmother's Fan quilt. Thank you also to Sharla Kay Salazar of Sharla Kay Photography for bringing the scene to life.

Content Warning: Please be advised that this book features a character who experiences post-traumatic stress disorder (PTSD) stemming from past combat. The narrative includes descriptions of their anxiety, flashbacks, and other symptoms of trauma. While the content is handled sensitively within the cozy mystery format, some readers may find these sections distressing.

Prologue

May 18, 1882

Lillian Clayburne was tending to washing and supervising the cleaning of the family's large, three-story Victorian house in Waxahachie, Texas. Ever since the fire on May 9 burned down fifteen buildings on the east side of the town square where the majestic Romanesque-style courthouse stood, ashes and soot had spread all over the small town. It seemed as though all anyone in town was doing was cleaning, cleaning, and cleaning some more. Every time Lillian was sure she and the family's housekeeper had thoroughly removed all the soot and ashes from the windows, furniture, and floors, within minutes the ashes and soot seemed to magically reappear.

"This is ludicrous!" Lillian announced in frustration, her fists planted on her hips.

"Yes, ma'am," the housekeeper agreed, wiping a window with vinegar, which only seemed to push the ash around into a streaky mess.

"What's ludicrous, Aunt Lilly?" Lillian's teenage niece, Adelaide, asked, walking into the kitchen.

Lillian pushed the strands of brilliant copper-red hair that had fallen out of her bun over her ears to give her momentary relief.

"All this soot and ashes from the fire nine days ago. Just when I think Hilda and I have cleaned it, in moments it reappears!"

"Auntie Lilly, come," she said, beckoning her aunt to follow her. "Look," she exclaimed, pointing north out a window to where flames could barely be seen licking the tops of buildings downtown. "You're not cleaning old soot and ashes, you're cleaning new."

Lillian was dumbfounded. "Oh no! Not again!"

As though on cue, Lillian's husband, James, bolted into the house with their son, Clarence. Their faces were covered in soot, and ash dusted their hair and clothing. They looked like raccoons peering out of a tree hollow. Their jackets and the hems of their pants were singed, reddened skin showing beneath. Lillian's hands flew to her face, covering her mouth.

"James, Clarence! What happened to you?" she cried.

"We were downtown at the mercantile when we smelled smoke," James said in a forced, breathy voice.

In fact, another fire had broken out in downtown Waxahachie, less than two weeks after the first fire. Everyone ran outside to see dozens of buildings engulfed in flames. The Salamander Fire and Hose Company brought their steam engine to the scene and made a valiant effort in pulling water from the creek to fight the fire, but it wasn't enough. The fire rapidly spread all over town. "Oh no!" Lillian lamented, "What can we do to help?"

"That's why I came home, dear. We need to set up an aid station here at the house. Other men ran home to do the same. There are a lot of injured people."

"Indeed, husband. You and Clarence go on back and direct as many people as possible here, just as we did during the last one." As they departed, Lillian turned to the housekeeper. "Hilda, cleaning is futile when greater duties await us. Please gather up the carbolic acid, clean cloths, honey, and all the bandages you can find."

"Ma'am, we have quite a lot. After the last fire, I replaced all the supplies to have at the ready the next time we would need them. I must admit, I never expected we'd need them so soon."

"Thank you, Hilda. Please bring everything into the kitchen. We will turn it into the treatment room."

In moments, women from neighboring houses rushed into the Clayburne home with additional supplies, helping to lay out what they would need in an orderly sequence. No one took the time to ask questions; they simply set themselves to task as they had done a few days previously. Just as they finished lining up chairs for the patients, men began bringing firefighters, shop owners, customers, and homeowners through the front door and into the kitchen. Some had suffered minor burns, others more serious.

The women carefully cut off burned fabric, cleaned the burns with antiseptic carbolic acid, and applied honey to prevent the subsequent bandages from adhering to the wounds. As each man was treated, one of the women led him into the parlor to rest in a comfortable chair and poured him a shot of whiskey to take the edge off his pain.

James brought another group of men into the home, and Adelaide saw that her uncle had suffered several burns. She whispered to her aunt and pointed to her uncle's wounds. Lillian rushed to her husband's side.

"I'm fine, Lil, truly I am. Please go on helping one of the more seriously burned men." He laid his hand, which she noticed was scarlet and inflamed, on her shoulder.

"No, James, the others are all being taken care of. I need to clean your burns now, before they get infected."

"Now, Lillian ..., " he began, towering over her, his head of thick hair unkempt and tousled.

"Don't you 'Now, Lillian' me, James Clayburne! You sit down in one of the treatment chairs right this minute or we will force you to sit." She planted her fists on her hips, still looking up at her husband. "Do I make myself clear?"

James heaved a sluggish breath and voluntarily sat in the chair, his knees nearly buckling, forcing Lillian and Adelaide to catch him and gently set him down.

Lillian and Adelaide cleaned, sterilized, and wrapped his burns. No sooner had they moved him to one of the parlor's large wingback chairs than James began to shiver. Lillian looked up at Adelaide and whispered, "Go get the new quilt." Adelaide nodded and skittered up the stairs to the linen closet on the second floor. She quickly found the Grandmother's Fan quilt and brought it downstairs.

"The new quilt, Lil?" he looked up at her. "You spent months making it and just finished it a few weeks ago." He turned to Adelaide. "Bring me an old, tattered quilt, not this one."

Adelaide looked at her aunt.

"No, leave the quilt be. It's new and it's warm, something he needs so he doesn't go into shock." She looked at her husband. "You deserve the best, my dear, and right now, this quilt is my best. You settle down and try to nap."

Not having the strength to argue, he settled into the chair and soon fell into a deep sleep. As the women continued to treat injured men and women, they learned that the town had lost 28 businesses and 25 homes that day, a staggering loss for a small town of their size. After the first fire nine days before, they had wondered how their little town would ever recover from such a tragedy. Now they wondered whether the town could recover from a second one.

Lillian thought, *What choice do we have? This is our home, and our livelihood.*

It wasn't until Lillian and Adelaide walked James upstairs a couple of hours later and removed the quilt that they saw that small drops of blood had seeped through the bandages and onto the back of the quilt.

Adelaide looked at her aunt, distress marking her face. "Oh, Auntie! Your beautiful quilt!"

Lillian laid her hand on her niece's arm. "It's alright. I made this quilt to be used, and it has fulfilled its purpose honorably."

"But, Auntie, it's ruined."

Lillian shook her head. "No, it's not. I'll admit that it's a little worse for the wear. Other than that, it has a long life ahead of it. You know how I tell you whenever I make a new quilt that the quilt will let us know its purpose, its role in our or someone else's life?"

Adelaide nodded.

"Today, the quilt showed us that it is a mercy quilt. It gave compassion and comfort to your uncle and will continue to do so for others in the years to come."

Chapter One

Present Day

Though it had been several months since her daughter, Savannah Mae, had found Emma Clayburne Jenkins in Georgia and brought her home to Texas after a 30-year absence, Emma still wasn't comfortable living back in her hometown of Waxahachie. She blamed herself. When her mother had forbidden her from keeping her baby and forced her to put Savannah Mae up for adoption, as well as divorce the love of her life, Jack McDonald, she fled to college in Boston, vowing never to return.

To punish them all, which ultimately only punished herself, she cut off communication with every member of her family and her friends, especially Stella, her best friend, who had been like a sister since they were babies. Though she eventually married a kind, tenderhearted man named Larry Jenkins and made a life with him in Georgia, she never forgot her family and the best friend she had left behind. As the years advanced, though she and Larry settled into a lovely life on the East Coast, she often chastised herself for her actions. She didn't just lose Savannah Mae and Jack; she'd lost everyone she loved. Year after year, and decade after decade, although she'd built a full life, her inability to call, write, or visit the people she loved in Texas severed the relationships, one painful connection at a time. After a while, she lacked the courage and determination to reach out to anyone, figuring it had been so long that no one cared about her anymore and would likely hang up on her if she tried to call. And so she didn't, regretting her behavior of long ago, and regretting that she couldn't make amends now. After Larry died, she felt more alone than she ever had in her life.

When Savannah Mae and Emma's sister, Ruth, found Emma in Georgia, she was dumbfounded. They wanted to take her home. *Home*, that magical word, so full of hope and promise. That place where, as a child, all was well with the world, where she was happy and her soul blossomed. It sounded so comforting, yet she wondered whether it was really possible to go home. Thirty years had passed. Everything would be different now—or would it? It took some cajoling, but eventually she agreed. On the flight to Dallas, she wondered how she would be received, whether she would be accepted. Maybe this was a big mistake. *Too late now,* she told herself, expecting the worst.

At the airport and at the Clayburne family home in Waxahachie, her reception was far more than she anticipated: Everyone was overjoyed to see her. No one reprimanded her or questioned why she had stayed away. They seemed genuinely glad to see her. Even so, her remorse made her unnaturally shy, and that compelled her to turn inward. How could they be so forgiving when she couldn't forgive herself? Returning home, she realized, was not as easy as getting on a plane.

As the months passed, her self-confidence continued to be a problem. She never felt like she could simply call up family members or friends to get together. Even though they said otherwise, what if they were actually angry with her and didn't want to see her? She knew that would break her. She couldn't take the rejection, so, like she did in Georgia, she didn't call or see anyone. Except for

Savannah Mae's cat, Sophie, she felt like she didn't have a friend in the world. She was grateful that Savannah Mae had left Sophie in her care when she married Travis Sheridan and moved to his ranch. Then one day, Stella, her childhood best friend, called and asked to come see her.

"Really, you want to see me?"

"Of course I want to see you, Emma. That's why I'm calling. You've been back for a while, so it's time you and I pick up where we left off."

"You mean my leaving and abandoning you and everyone else?"

"Emma, don't be so hard on yourself. What's done is done. Don't beat yourself up over it."

"Stella, what I did was terrible. Can you ever forgive me?"

"I forgave you long ago, Emma."

"You did?"

"Yes, I knew what Jack and that baby meant to you. If it had happened to me, I couldn't have stayed either. I understood. I just hoped that you'd return some day. Now, can I come see you this afternoon?"

Emma felt a tear meandering down her cheek. "Yes—that is, if you really want to."

"Oh, Emma, what happened to you in Georgia? You never lacked faith in yourself before. Of course I want to!"

Emma nodded, unable to say much more on the subject. She could feel her spirit breaking—or perhaps, she wondered, was it mending? Either way, it hurt.

"What time do you want to stop by?"

"How about two o'clock?"

"Okay, see you then."

Emma wiped away the tear and went upstairs. She sat at the vanity, brushed her hair and pinned it up into a chignon, applied some makeup, and put on her favorite teal and pink floral dress with her teal flats. Even though she didn't feel pretty or self-assured, she thought that if she dressed the part, maybe it would rub off on her self-doubt and improve her demeanor.

She went back downstairs and decided she would bake something for Stella's visit. Baking always cheered her up, and she remembered that when they were growing up, Stella was an insatiable chocoholic before anyone ever used the term. She combed through her box of cookie recipes and found one for old-fashioned soft chocolate cookies.

"Perfect," she murmured aloud. As she went through the pantry, gathering the ingredients, she found a package of chocolate chips. *Hmm, too much?* she asked herself, knowing that the recipe didn't call for the chips. She shook her head and smiled. "There's no such thing as too much decadence when it comes to chocolate."

She quickly mixed the ingredients, formed the dough into balls, and laid them out in rows on cookie sheets her mother and grandmother had used for baking. In short order, the cookies finished baking. After they cooled, she placed them on a pretty three-tier china cake stand, perfect for displaying all the cookies. Next, she brewed a pot of coffee, and just as it finished brewing, the doorbell rang. She walked into the foyer and opened the front door. Stella stepped inside and wrapped her arms around Emma, holding on to her for a long time. Suddenly, Stella stepped back and sniffed.

"Do I smell chocolate?" she asked, a wide grin showing off her impeccably white teeth.

"Maybe," Emma replied, smiling demurely.

"You remembered how much I adore chocolate?"

"Of course. I've never known anyone who could eat as much chocolate as you and still stay skinny."

"Then let's indulge. I haven't had any chocolate all week."

"It's only Monday, Stella." Emma took her hand and led her toward the kitchen. "Come on, let's get you some cookies before you faint."

They each put several cookies on their china plates and poured themselves coffee, stirring in a dollop of cream just as they had done when they were younger. Stella noticed Emma adding the cream to her cup.

"Some things don't change," Stella noted.

"It's the only way I drink coffee," Emma said. "And I see you still do as well."

"As you said, it's the only way."

They sat down at the kitchen table and began nibbling at their cookies.

"This is your grandma's recipe, isn't it?" Stella asked, holding up a cookie.

"You remember it?" Emma cocked her head to the side.

"Of course I remember it. I remember every bit of chocolate I've ever eaten."

"Seriously?" Emma chuckled.

"Yes, seriously, and if that's what it's gonna take to see that radiant smile of yours, I'll spend the rest of the afternoon telling you lies."

A broad grin spread across Emma's face. "Oh, Stella, I've missed you so."

"Probably not as much as I've missed you. I'm so glad you're home."

"I'm sorry I never called or wrote or came home to visit," Emma began.

"Bygones," Stella said. "You really need to put that out of your mind because you're starting a new chapter of your life. And I am not going to allow you to sit around doing nothing and feeling sorry about something that happened long ago."

Emma felt her heart expand with tenderness and joy. Stella reached over and took Emma's hand in hers.

"Promise me that you'll stop feeling morose over leaving."

"And staying away?" Emma added.

"Yes, and staying away. You're home now, you're with people who dearly love you. Celebrate that, just as all of us celebrate you and thank God you're back."

Emma nodded.

"Promise that there will be no more sulking and feeling melancholy."

Emma stared at her.

"Do you promise?" Stella asked again.

Emma took a deep breath. "I promise to try."

"Not good enough, my friend. I know that the old Emma is inside there," she said, pointing to Emma's chest. "You can do this, and if you can't, I'll march you into the psychiatrist's office in the clinic where I work and sic him on you."

"You wouldn't!"

"Don't test me, Emma, because I will. Now, snap out of it."

Emma shot Stella a small grin. "Yes, ma'am."

After Stella left and throughout the evening, Emma felt remarkably cheerful. She knew she wasn't back to her old self, who had felt assured, confident, and brave enough to tackle most anything. But she did feel different: She felt hopeful and calm and a bit more certain of herself. She knew that she was on her way to mending her spirit and her self-confidence. She also knew that it wouldn't happen overnight, just as she knew that it would happen eventually because Stella wasn't going to cut her any slack.

A week after Stella's visit, Emma was still feeling upbeat and positive about the future. One afternoon, she busied herself in the kitchen, glancing up at the wall clock every few minutes. She didn't know why she was so anxious about the time. Her daughter, Savannah Mae, and her new husband, Travis Sheridan, were due home from their honeymoon any minute. She was baking them a batch of her divine lemon bars, a family favorite. As soon as the filling hit the tongue, it melted down the throat like a lemony cream river.

She loved to bake in the family's vintage enamel range. It was considered a family treasure, and baking in its double ovens felt like taking a walk back through time. Her great-grandfather had bought her great-grandmother the state-of-the-art range as a wedding gift back when such appliances were an extravagant purchase. Emma and her siblings grew up eating their mother's and grandmother's special dishes made in the ovens from recipes that had been passed down from generation to generation.

She reminisced about how Savannah Mae had loved the lemon bars the first time Emma baked them for her. Of course, Savannah Mae was a grown woman by then. Now reunited, Emma was doing everything she could to make up for precious lost time. And baking was just one way she was trying to fill what felt like a gulf of memories that never happened, missing remembrances.

She took the pan of lemon bars out of the vintage oven that, despite its century-old age, still worked as well as the day Great-great-grandfather James had it moved into the Victorian house and presented it to his dear new wife, Lillian. Emma dusted the bars with confectioner's sugar just as she heard Savannah Mae and Travis coming in the front door and calling for her.

"I'm in the kitchen!" She quickly rinsed her hands of the confectioner's sugar sticking to her fingers and wiped her hands on an embroidered tea towel.

When Savannah Mae and Travis entered the kitchen, Savannah Mae ran to her mother and wrapped her arms around her. "I've missed you so much, Mama!"

Emma pulled back to get a good look at her daughter. "And I've missed you. And you too, my good-looking son-in-law," she added, gazing directly at Travis, who tried not to blush.

"How are you, Emma?" he asked. "Did you create a bunch of hully gully while we were gone?"

Emma smiled. "Now, that's an expression I haven't heard in years. You know, Travis, I tried to stay out of trouble, honestly I did. Wasn't easy."

"As if you could get into trouble, Mama," Savannah Mae exclaimed. She looked at Travis and back at her mother. "Hully gully?"

Travis smiled endearingly at his wife. "It's slang for *chaos*," he said.

Emma looked at the two of them. "It's also a line dance that, if not organized properly, can turn into chaos." Emma saw the blank look on her daughter's face, as though Emma were speaking a foreign language. "Have you ever danced the Electric Slide or the Macarena?"

"No."

"Savannah Mae, honey, you need to get out more. The Electric Slide and the Macarena are easy line dances that don't take much time to learn. The Hully Gully is another line dance. It's fun to watch and even more fun to dance."

"Did you and Aunt Ruth dance the Hully Gully in your younger years?"

"Sure did! There used to be a club here in town we went to. Your dad often went with us. Bet you didn't know that they're both excellent dancers."

"Uh, no, I didn't." Savannah Mae turned to Travis. "We should go dancing some time and learn the Hully Gully."

Travis poked his hands into the front pockets of his jeans, shook his head, glanced at the floor, and back up at Savannah Mae. "Have you forgotten what a lousy dancer I am? How I messed up our first and only dance at the wedding?"

"Oh, yeah." She grinned and scanned his face, seeing genuine contrition. "Travis, that's silly. It was no big deal. You just need to learn. Would you be up for taking dance lessons? It would be fun."

Travis cracked a small smile. "Sorry, sweetheart, I'd rather muck out the horse stalls."

Savannah Mae shrugged her shoulders. "Oh, well, I tried." She turned back to Emma. "Did you spend time with Aunt Ruth and Thelma, Uncle Keith, or visit the McDonalds while we were away?"

"Not much. Bonnie Ada and I had lunch together once. I think we're going to be good friends. I like her. It's easy to see why Jack married her."

The corners of Savannah Mae's lips lifted as she smiled and looked over at Travis and back at her mother. "It's not surprising, Mama. Surely you married Dad for the same reasons. I imagine that you and Bonnie Ada have a lot in common."

"Oh, and Stella came over once. I baked her soft chocolate cookies that my grandmother used to bake for us when we were children. They brought back a lot of good memories."

Savannah Mae watched her mother's face and noticed that the anxiety that had frequently shown on Emma's face when Savannah Mae first found her and brought her home from Georgia was still there, though to a slightly lesser degree. She wondered how long it would be before Emma settled in.

"Enough about me. Tell me about the honeymoon!"

"Do you have any coffee?" Travis asked, staring at the lemon bars.

"I just brewed a pot. I take it you want a cup of coffee with a lemon bar?"

"Two, please."

"Two cups of coffee?" Emma asked, struggling to keep a straight face. She had grown fond of teasing Travis because, she said, it was so easy.

Travis let out one of his now-famous gut-belly laughs. "Two lemon bars, please. We haven't eaten since breakfast."

Emma looked at Savannah Mae.

"Me too, Mama. I'm starved!"

"Coming right up," Emma said as she began cutting the squares and sliding them onto plates while Savannah Mae took down mugs and poured the coffee. They all carried their mugs and plates to the kitchen table, where they settled in to tell Emma about their Mississippi riverboat cruise.

Two hours later, not a morsel of a lemon bar remained in the baking pan. The three retired to the parlor and collapsed in the upholstered wingback chairs.

"I think I overdid it," Savannah Mae murmured, patting her belly. "They were so good, I couldn't help myself."

"Me too," Travis said. "I'm as full as a tick on a hound dog."

"That is quite the compliment, but it's a bit more than that," Emma said, pointing to the empty baking pan. "What you just ate is love, pure love."

Suddenly, they heard an insistent screech coming from the stairs.

"Uh-oh, you're in trouble," Emma joked. "I told Sophie you were coming home today, and you've completely ignored her."

"Sophie? My sweet girl? How could I forget about her?" Savannah Mae got up and jogged toward the stairs. She saw the long-haired white cat sitting on the top step, staring at her. She walked up the stairs and settled onto the top step, where she lifted her into her lap and began petting her and massaging her behind the ears. Sophie began a slow, deep purr, eventually progressing into a loud rumble, like an overloaded construction truck sounds ambling down the street. She looked up at Savannah Mae, giving her the slow blink. She stretched up and affectionately licked the tip of her nose, jumped down and strutted into Emma's room. Emma and Travis stood at the bottom of the stairs. Savannah Mae walked back downstairs to join them.

"Mama, how did she do while we were gone?"

"She was fine, honey. It wasn't like we were newly acquainted. Sophie and I hit it off when I moved into the house months ago."

"Of course, I was just concerned she might have become withdrawn. I've never been away from her this long."

"Not to worry, we've been inseparable. She follows me everywhere, all over the house. And she slept on my bed every night."

"That's good news because I have something to ask you."

Emma nodded, urging her to continue.

Savannah Mae looked at Travis and back at Emma. "First, I know you said you would be okay living here on your own while we were gone. Were you all right in this big house all by yourself?"

Emma pulled back and looked quizzically at her daughter. She didn't want her to pick up on her lack of confidence. "Of course I was, sweetie. Why wouldn't I be? I grew up here, and I know all the nooks and crannies of every inch of every room. I even know Keith's ghosts."

"You do?" Savannah Mae blinked repeatedly.

"Of course I do. He thinks he's the only one who can see them."

"That's what he told me when I first moved in."

Emma shook her head. "Not so. Thelma, Ruth, and I saw them too. We just didn't make as big a fuss over them as he did."

Savannah Mae looked down and back up. "You know, Mama, I can too."

"Can you, now? They're quite nice, aren't they?"

Savannah Mae nodded. "Yeah, they are. I found their presence comforting."

A mysterious smile crossed Emma's face, as though she were about to reveal a secret, an expression Savannah Mae had gotten used to seeing her mother make.

"You know they're family, don't you?" Emma asked.

Savannah Mae shrugged. "I figured as much. Uncle Keith confirmed it when we had the 'ghost' talk. He thought I might have been frightened of them. I asked him, why would I be? They aren't scary. They're calming and were nice to have around when I was alone. Did they keep you company while I was gone?"

"Oh, yes. We're old friends. Really, honey, you don't need to worry about me. Living here, even alone, is quite cozy. Kind of like being wrapped in a quilt all day long. This is home."

"That answers my first question. I was worried about abandoning you, and now I can see that I'm not."

"Of course you're not. Was there something else on your mind, honey?"

"I've been thinking about how Sophie is going to adjust to living on a ranch. She's such a city cat. I'm concerned about her getting out and being chased by a big fox or getting stepped on by one of the horses. She's not ranch-savvy."

"Plus, you have a horse to take care of now," Travis interjected. "She's a lot of work. Your kitty may not like being replaced by Annie Oakley."

"I wouldn't be replacing her, Travis."

"Would she understand that?"

Savannah Mae gazed at him, sincerely questioning him. "Travis, are you sure I should leave her here with Mama?"

Travis ran his arms around Savannah Mae. He could feel her distress. "I think you should consider it. Living on the ranch might be too big a change for her, and obviously, she likes living with Emma. It's not like you'd be giving her away to a stranger or you wouldn't see her again. You're over here every week, if not twice a week."

Emma stood watching the interchange between Savannah Mae and Travis, feeling a twinge of guilt. After all, Sophie and Savannah Mae had been together since Savannah Mae adopted her as a kitten. Even so, Emma couldn't imagine living in the big house without her. Sophie had become her constant companion.

Savannah Mae slowly nodded her head. "Okay, let's give it a try. I can't think of anyone I'd rather have take care of her." She turned toward Travis. "Hon, I still have some clothes in my closet that need to go to the ranch. Help me put them in the truck?"

"More clothes?" he feigned shock, trying to lighten the mood. Savannah Mae snickered and shot him a look of tender annoyance.

"Sure 'nuff," he said, eager to quell her unease over leaving Sophie behind. He headed for Savannah Mae's bedroom as Sophie jumped on top of Emma's bed. She stretched out and began purring again, like a tractor humming in a field of cotton.

Chapter Two

Emma woke early a few days later to a thin fog cascading through the massive pecan trees that dotted the property. The scene of the mist draping itself over the rose bushes, grass, and trees created what she used to imagine was a window to the past. She threw on her robe, stepped into her slippers, and scurried down to the yard to stand among the trees, fancying herself back to when the trees had been lovingly planted. Wouldn't whoever planted them revel in how grand they had become, still standing as windbreaks to powerful squalls blowing across the prairie.

As a child, Emma believed that if she walked through the mist at just the right moment, she would be transported to an earlier time. She smiled at the innocent childhood memory, at the many times she had tried fruitlessly to time-travel back to when the house was built. Back then, she truly thought that the impossible was possible if she believed and wished and wanted enough. She closed her eyes and wished once more, then waited a few moments. She opened her eyes. Nothing, as she knew it would be. Unlike the disappointment she felt during childhood, now, the sweet memory was sufficient. Over the years, while living on the other side of the country, the memory had become an allegory for her life, one she often thought about when she missed home. As she struggled with her stubborn decision to leave Texas and abandon her family and friends, she embarked on a lifelong search to figure out who she was because she no longer knew.

She stood among the trees, deeply breathing in the moist air, realizing that now there was no question who she was: She was a daughter of Texas. She always had been and always would be. Slowly, she ambled up the stairs and back into the house. She looked around the kitchen, trying to recall something important she was going to do today. What was it? Suddenly, she remembered. How could she have forgotten? She'd been toying with the idea for weeks.

Although Emma wanted to give Savannah Mae some time to get over leaving Sophie behind, she needed to talk to her daughter about another matter. She had waited a few days for Savannah Mae to settle into her new home. Today felt like the time was right to broach the subject. She dialed her number.

"Hi, sweetheart, how are you settling in at the ranch?"

"Hi, Mama, pretty good actually. I'm out riding Annie Oakley right now." Savannah Mae looked up at the brilliant blue sky, smudged with threadlike clouds. "I've spent so much time here that it doesn't feel all that different. And I'm getting pretty good at the finer points of picking dirt, debris, rocks, and all sorts of stuff out of Annie Oakley's hooves. You remember Tyler, the ranch hand? Anyway, he tells me it's sorta like giving a horse a pedicure. Can you imagine? He says that it feels good to have all that hard gunk out of there. Tyler swears that she's relieved to have her hooves cleaned out. Mama, do you know that all the horses here get their hooves picked out every day?"

Emma chuckled. "Really? Do you give pedicures to the other horses too?"

"Good lord, no. Just Annie. I don't have time to do any horses other than her. When Travis gave her to me as a wedding present, he said it was on the condition that I learn how to care for her. At the time that I agreed, I didn't think it would be very time-consuming, and now I'm finding that cleaning her hooves and brushing her daily and bathing or showering her every couple of weeks is quite a bit of work. She seems to attract dirt like a dog that rolls around in mud for the fun of it."

"I'm impressed. Travis was right, it does sound like a lot of work. Can't Tyler do it?"

"Of course he can. But I promised Travis I would care for her now that she's my responsibility. Mama, it's so sweet. She knows me and trusts me. And she senses or smells me when I enter the barn. She starts stamping her hooves 'cuz she's excited to see me. I've never been loved by a horse before. It's pretty cool."

"It sounds like it is. What about your other love? Do you have any time for making quilts?"

Savannah Mae heaved a sigh. "Not as much as I'd like, and that's my own fault. I love spending time with Annie and riding her around the ranch. I just need to organize my time better."

"Speaking of time, can you get away for lunch today?"

"Tomorrow would be better. I have to get back to the barn and clean her up. She splashed through a muddy creek, spewing sludge all over the two of us. What's up?"

"I've got an idea I want to discuss with you, and I thought we could talk about it over lunch. I want to run it by Ruth and Thelma too, if they're available. I was thinking that the four of us could try that new Thai restaurant in Midlothian."

"It opened?"

"Yes, while you were away. I haven't been there yet. Bonnie Ada and Jack have, as well as Stella and her sister. They say it's very good. You game?"

"Absolutely! I haven't had Thai food in I don't know how long. Maybe since California. Do you know if they serve pad thai?"

"I can't imagine that they wouldn't. That's the gold standard dish of all Thai restaurants, isn't it?"

"Good point. Meet you and the aunties there tomorrow at noon?"

"See you then, honey."

When Savannah Mae entered the restaurant, she spied her mother, Aunt Ruth, and Aunt Thelma sitting in the back corner, sipping on Thai boba tea drinks. Aunt Thelma had already finished hers and was ordering two more, one for herself and one for Savannah Mae.

"Oh, you're here," Aunt Thelma remarked when she saw Savannah Mae, who bent down to kiss both her aunts' and her mother's cheeks. "Mind if I order lunch for us?" Thelma asked. "I've got some favorites." She ordered pad thai, the noodle dish with shrimp and vegetables; green papaya salad; tom kha gai, a slightly sour coconut soup with chicken; as well as poh pia tod, the Thai equivalent of spring rolls, deep-fried and filled with thin glass noodles and slivered vegetables.

"That's a lot of food, Aunt Thelma. I didn't know that you knew so much about Thai food, much less liked it," Savannah Mae remarked.

Thelma pouted. "I'm more worldly than I appear, you know. I took a break after graduating from college to spend a year in Thailand. It's where I met Bodin. He taught me everything I know about Thai culture and food."

"Wait a minute." Savannah Mae shook her head, as though clearing cobwebs in her brain. "I had no idea you spent a year in Thailand! That seems like something Uncle Keith would do, but not, not ..."

"Not me?" Thelma snapped, shooting her a chagrined look. "Keith did come visit me for a couple of weeks before he had to go home to get back to school. You may be surprised to hear that back then, I was the adventurous one in the family, until life took over and I had to settle down. Just ask Ruth and your mother," she said, gesturing to her sisters.

Savannah Mae looked at Emma and Ruth, who nodded.

Intrigued by this new revelation about her normally sourpuss aunt, Savannah Mae pressed for more details. "You've always struck me as the staid one of the family. How did life take over, Aunt Thelma?"

Aunt Ruth and Emma exchanged looks of concern, looks with the kind of uneasiness that signals extreme distress.

"Maybe we should have this conversation another time," Aunt Ruth piped up.

"Why?" Savannah Mae turned to Ruth. "This is really interesting. I didn't know any of this about Aunt Thelma." She turned back to Thelma just as the boba tea and food arrived. They each took a portion of pad thai, salad, soup, and a poh pia tod. "Please, go on, Aunt Thelma. Who was Bodin?"

"My husband," Thelma answered quietly. "I brought him home with me. I was pregnant with our child, and Mother wasn't too happy about it."

Savannah Mae shook her head, looked at her mother, who nodded, and back at Aunt Thelma. "Did Grandma like anyone's choice of a husband?"

Aunt Ruth interjected feebly. "She liked your Uncle Lyle."

Savannah Mae looked back at Aunt Thelma. "I've never heard about Bodin or your child. Where are they?"

Thelma reached up and quickly wiped away a tear escaping down her cheek, despite her fighting it back. She lifted her chin and looked straight at Savannah Mae, rolling her lips inward before speaking.

"We named our son Panit, which in Thai means 'beloved boy.' He was a stillborn who died three weeks before my due date. Bodin fell into a deep depression. He couldn't get over our loss. It was difficult for him because he hadn't adjusted to life in America or Texas. It was so foreign to him. He thought that having a son would help him adjust. When Panit died, he lost it, emotionally. One day, he told me that he was returning home, where he wouldn't be faced with constant reminders of the place that took his son. I tried to change his mind, to get him to see reason; he wouldn't listen. We divorced, and he went back to Thailand. I stayed in touch with his sister, who told me he remarried a few years later and had a large family with his new wife. She told me that their whole family blamed me for the loss of our son. That hit me hard."

"Why?" Savannah Mae asked. "You didn't do anything wrong."

"They blamed me because I was carrying our child, and it was my responsibility to carry our baby to full term. In their minds, because I didn't—or rather, couldn't—made me responsible for his death."

Savannah Mae hardly knew what to say because she knew that anything she said was sure to sound trivial. She had never seen this side of Aunt Thelma, the heartbroken side. She reached over and took her aunt's hand and murmured, "I'm so sorry."

"Thank you. At first I thought there was something wrong with me. Turned out, there wasn't. Bodin and I had both developed malaria after being bitten by mosquitos on a wilderness hike. I was young, and I thought I had a bad case of the flu. That's when I became pregnant, and ultimately the malaria caused the stillbirth." Thelma stopped for a few moments to take a breath and gather her thoughts.

"And just in case you are going to ask, no, I never remarried nor tried to have another child. He wasn't the only one who was devastated. Long ago, I made up my mind to never put myself through that again. Ever. So, now you know why I sometimes come off as bitter. I have reason to be. After going through a period where I could barely get up in the morning, I decided either I would die of sadness or I could pick myself up and do something with my life. That's when I enrolled in law school."

"You're a lawyer?" Savannah Mae remarked, louder than she intended. "How didn't I know that? Where do you practice?"

"At first, I went to work handling contracts for our family textile and cotton mills. I got a lot of experience doing that, but eventually I opened my own business law practice."

"She graduated summa cum laude," Ruth added. "Besides giving her a career, the grueling work of law school helped her get on with her life. We were all very proud of Thelma. I wish you'd been here to see the graduation party we threw for her."

Savannah Mae, Emma, Ruth, and Thelma sat there, looking at their now-cold food. Slowly, they began to pick at their lunches, none of them particularly hungry.

Savannah Mae felt terrible that she had drawn a black curtain over their lunch. She should have listened to Aunt Ruth and her mother when they suggested they talk about Aunt Thelma's affairs another time. She was so eager to learn about her often-reclusive and disagreeable Aunt Thelma, but she realized that she shouldn't have pushed the subject. Right now, though, Savannah Mae knew she had to right the sinking ship. She turned to Emma.

"Mama, what was it you wanted to discuss today?"

A reserved smile formed on Emma's lips. She realized her daughter was attempting to rescue their lunch, which she appreciated, even though she wasn't sure it was possible.

"As you know, I am perfectly happy living alone in the house," Emma began, hoping she sounded confident, even though she was anything but. "That doesn't mean that I wouldn't appreciate some company once in a while."

"Okay. What are you thinking? Parties? Family get-togethers? A book club?"

Emma glanced at her sisters and back at Savannah Mae. "I was thinking of turning the house into a part-time quilting retreat center."

Savannah Mae sat back in her chair, crossed her arms over her chest, and stared at her half-eaten lunch while she pondered the idea, feeling her mother and her aunts scrutinizing her. Finally, she nodded.

"I think it's brilliant!"

Emma felt her anxiety wane, clearly relieved to hear Savannah Mae's reaction.

"There's only one hitch," Emma said. "Although I plan to teach classes, and Stella wants to as well, we can't do it alone. Will you be one of the instructors?"

Savannah Mae scrunched her face, pursing her lips. "Hmmm. Maybe. Can I pick my schedule and, perhaps once in a while, choose what we'll teach?"

"Of course!"

"Okay," Savannah Mae said. "I guess we need to do some research on how to put together a quilting retreat center and figure out what changes will need to be made to the house to accommodate students."

"Whoa! Hold your horses," Thelma injected. "You need to start with a business plan. At square one."

"Doesn't a business plan need ideas on how to start and run a retreat center?" Emma asked Thelma.

"Of course it does, Emma. But you don't just throw it out there willy-nilly. You have to be methodical about it. All the pieces have to fit together. If they don't, the whole thing could come tumbling down like a house of cards. Plus, if you're planning to finance it through a bank, you have to submit a solid business plan."

"Oh, I never thought of that," Emma said in a demoralized voice. "Well, it doesn't matter, it was just a thought," she backtracked, thinking she didn't know the first thing about business plans or how to run a business. What little confidence she had mustered was going downhill fast. What had she been thinking?

"Now, Emma, don't get discouraged," Thelma said. "It's not a bad idea—it's a good one, actually—but for it to be successful, you have to do it right."

"No, no, it's okay." Emma waved her hand and attempted to back out again. "I don't know how to write a business plan, and what do I know anyway about running a business? Just forget I mentioned it."

"No!" Thelma said. "No one knows how to run a business until they do it and have the right tools. You just happen to have the right tool sitting right in front of you."

Emma looked around, not understanding what Thelma meant.

Ruth piped up. "Emma, Thelma specializes in business law. That's what she does. I'll bet she knows how to write a business plan."

They all looked at Thelma, who said, "I could probably write one in my sleep. I've seen so many of them that I can make sure that your business plan is legally sound and properly aligns with the goals of your business."

"And you'd help me?" Emma asked Thelma.

Thelma threw her head back. "Of course I would. You're my sister. I'd do anything to help you."

"Thank you," Emma whispered, feeling a sudden lump developing in her throat.

"Come to my office the day after tomorrow, and I'll show you a scad of business plans so you understand the options. Do you have any ideas written down on what you're envisioning for the retreat?"

"Actually, I do," Emma responded weakly. "I've been thinking about this for a while now and have put together a binder of ideas."

"Perfect, bring it with you," Thelma said.

Savannah Mae reached over and squeezed her mother's hand and looked at Thelma. "If it's okay, I'd like to come too. Maybe I can help."

"If you plan to be involved in it, then absolutely you should come," Thelma said. "Especially if y'all are going to apply for a business loan. You'll both have to sign for it."

Emma looked at Ruth. "What about you?"

"I love the idea. If you need me to do anything, just ask. Otherwise, I'll stay out of your way."

"And what about Uncle Keith?" Savannah Mae asked.

"We could give him a job, one only he can do better than the rest of us," Ruth said.

"What's that?" Savannah Mae asked.

"We'll ask him to talk to the ghosts and request that they not bother the students. He can suggest that they either stay in the attic or basement while students are in the house."

"Will they do that?" Savannah Mae asked. "Wouldn't they be offended and refuse to cooperate?"

All three sisters shook their heads. Thelma said, "When we were growing up and your grandparents would hold parties and special events in the house, Keith would talk to the ghosts ahead of time about not annoying the guests. Because our ghosts are family, they always agreed to keep a low profile."

"Whaddaya know?" Savannah Mae turned to Emma. "Well, Mama, Aunt Thelma, we have a big job ahead of us." She beamed at her aunts and mother. "Mama, have you thought of a name for the retreat?"

"Not really," Emma admitted. "Everything I've thought of sounds hokey."

"Aunt Thelma and Aunt Ruth, will you help us come up with a name?"

The two sisters looked at one another and nodded. Thelma glanced at Ruth, Emma, and Savannah Mae. "How about keeping it simple? You know, calling it something like 'The Yellow House.' That's what everyone in town already calls it. I mean, it beats calling it 'The Ghost House,' doesn't it?"

Savannah Mae chuckled. "Love it!"

Emma and Savannah Mae met at Thelma's office a couple of days later to discuss the business plan and to look through the binder of ideas Emma had put together. Upon entering Thelma's office, they marveled at the wall of awards Thelma had won for her pro bono work.

"You did all this?" Savannah Mae asked. She leaned forward and saw that the awards went back many years.

Thelma nodded. "It's been my way of doing some good. When I am focused on the needs of others, I don't think about the sadness of my early life."

"You mean by helping children and their families?" Savannah Mae asked, looking at the case names on the awards.

"Exactly. You can either wallow in self-pity or direct your energies to improving the lives of others. It's worked for me. But enough about that, please step into my office so we can get started on bringing the Yellow House Quilting Retreat to life. Emma, did you bring your ideas?"

Emma nodded, pulled the binder out of her tote bag, and handed it to her.

Over the course of the next two hours, Emma showed Thelma and Savannah Mae her ideas, and Thelma spread out several business plans that had resulted in helping clients start and run successful entrepreneurial businesses.

Emma could feel her heart start to race. She felt overwhelmed and doubted her ability to take even the smallest first step. Thelma saw the fear on her face.

"Emma, this isn't brain surgery."

"It sure does feel like it," Emma's insecurity answered.

"It's not. Let me explain. A business plan takes into account nearly every aspect of a company and how each decision might affect those aspects. Let's think about the most essential elements before we draft your business plan. Are you both with me?"

Savannah Mae nodded enthusiastically, and Emma slightly nodded, still not sure she could do this.

"Here are the key elements: business description and mission statement, competitor analysis, executive summary, financial plan, marketing strategy, operations overview, details of products and services, financial projections and assumptions, request for funding, exhibits and appendices, and SWOT."

"What's SWOT?" Savannah Mae asked.

"Strengths, Weaknesses, Opportunities, Threats."

Emma sat in her chair, taking deep breaths to alleviate her growing panic. She was sure glad Savannah Mae was there to express the enthusiasm she could not.

"Next, let's look at some business plans to give you an idea of what they look like."

Thelma pointed to the business plans she'd laid out earlier. She first showed them the most complicated plan, which ran more than 100 pages. She couldn't help noticing the alarm on Emma's face.

"Emma, I'm not suggesting we do one like this, I'm just laying it out here so you can see how complicated a plan can be, and why."

Thelma showed them five more plans, each one simpler, until she came to the last one, the simplest of all.

"Which one do you suggest we use?" Emma asked, trying to allay the fear rising in her throat.

"Probably something in the middle. Would you mind if I hold on to your binder for a bit and use the ideas to start the business plan?"

"You're going to write the plan?" Emma asked, a flood of relief coursing through her veins.

"Of course I am," Thelma smiled at her sister. "That's what I offered to do."

"Oh, I thought you were just going to show us plans, and I would be writing it."

"Well, you can, if you want to," Thelma offered. "Do you want to do it?"

Emma felt the weight of the question on her shoulders. She seriously doubted she was capable of even starting the plan, but she didn't want her sister or Savannah Mae to realize what a bad idea the retreat center was turning out to be. Nervous paralysis momentarily took away her voice, and Thelma and Savannah Mae noticed it.

"Tell ya what, Emma," Thelma said. "I think I have a pretty good idea of what you want in the retreat center. Let me work up a business plan draft, then the three of us can get together and go over it to revise or expand it. How's that sound?"

Emma felt the anxiety and paralysis dissipate immediately.

"I-I-I think that would be a good start," Emma responded.

"Okay, I'm working on a big case right now that must take precedence. As soon as I'm done with it, I'll start drafting your plan. I should be able to get started on your plan in a couple of weeks, then have it ready to show you a couple of weeks after that. All together, we can meet up in about a month. Sound good?"

Emma and Savannah Mae nodded and thanked Thelma. As they walked to the car, Savannah Mae stopped and turned to her mother.

"Mama, this whole business plan seems to have freaked you out. Are you okay?"

"I never used to let things like this bother me, and I'm not sure why it does now. I am working on tamping down my insecurities about being able to put together a quilting retreat. When I was imagining it, I thought it would be a good idea, and easy to do."

"Well, it was your idea."

"I know, and now I have you and Thelma involved, and I don't want to take advantage or disappoint you."

"What is it that scares you?"

"I'm not sure. Maybe it's my lack of confidence. I may be my own worst enemy."

"I don't believe that for a minute, Mama. You're not doing this alone. I'm here, and Aunt Thelma is here, and together we can do this. I just know it. Your idea is spot-on. Waxahachie needs a quilting retreat center. Please don't let your fear or whatever is driving this destroy your dream before we even have a chance to launch it."

Emma nodded, looking down and then back up at Savannah Mae. "You're absolutely right. I'm being silly."

"Mama, do you remember when Travis asked me to marry him, and I had a meltdown?"

Emma nodded. "How could I forget?"

"Right, and I'll never forget what you told me. Now, I'm going pass it back to you: You told me to grow a backbone or I'd lose Travis."

Emma looked at Savannah Mae as the whole scene came rushing back as vividly as the day it happened. "What are you saying, Savannah Mae?"

"I'm telling you to grow a backbone and snap out of your insecurity or lack of confidence or fear of success or whatever it is because if you don't, you're going to lose this dream. And I don't think you want that."

Emma took Savannah Mae's hands into her own. "You're absolutely right; I don't want to lose the dream. I want this retreat center."

"Then start growing that backbone, Mama, and let's make it happen."

As she waited to hear from Thelma to go over the business plan, Emma started thinking about the logistics of turning the house into a retreat center. She knew there were enough extra bedrooms to house ten students in five rooms, two to a room. The only problem was that they would need to switch out the double and queen beds in those rooms for new twin-size beds. The larger beds could be stored in the attic. With the smaller-size beds, she'd also have to purchase twin-size bedding. Quilts, she had. In addition to the bedding, she'd have to purchase lots of new towels. Fortunately, the house had three full bathrooms, one of which was on the ground floor. For ten students plus Emma and Savannah Mae, for when she and Travis stayed over, it was not ideal, but it would have to suffice.

Second, she needed to determine which room would serve as the schoolroom. It had to be large enough for ten sewing machine tables, one for each student, as well as a large fabric-cutting table, a bookcase, shelving for fabric and notions, cubbies for students' belongings, plus a dozen chairs for the sewing machine tables and a couple of comfy chairs for when students wanted to take a break and relax. She walked all over the house, trying to figure out which room would be large enough to accommodate their needs.

She called Savannah Mae and asked her to drop by and help her figure out which space would work best for the schoolroom. Savannah Mae agreed to stop by the next day because she knew her mother was doubting herself and her decision to open a retreat. She figured that whatever she could do to support her mother, she would, and hopefully Emma's lack of conviction would pass.

When Savannah Mae arrived, Emma showed her all the largest spaces: the dining room, the living room and parlor, and the back porch. Finally, it became obvious that only one space was big enough.

"Mama, of all the spaces we've looked at, the porch is the only one big enough. It could be expanded and enclosed."

"Yes, I know," Emma responded unenthusiastically, "but we'd lose our charming porch. We all love to sit out there and take in the magic of the garden."

Savannah Mae nodded. "True, I love the porch the way it is."

They sat down on the porch and pondered a while longer. "I don't think we can figure this out by ourselves, Mama."

"Who do you suggest we ask?"

"We already know that we're going to need a contractor to expand the downstairs bath; let's work on finding a contractor and asking him or her."

"Are there any lady contractors in Waxahachie?" Emma raised her brows. "It would be great if there were because a woman would certainly understand the needs of a houseful of women."

"True," Savannah Mae agreed with a nod.

"And who knows?" Emma added. "Maybe she will be a quilter and would really get what we need in the schoolroom."

Savannah Mae looked over at her mother. "Mama, with all due respect, what are the chances of that?"

"A girl can dream, can't she?" A childlike expression crossed Emma's face. "Even though Thelma hasn't finished the business plan yet, I'm going to call her and ask if it would be okay to get some construction estimates because surely that will need to be in the business plan."

"As well as in a business loan application to fund the construction."

Savannah Mae wasn't fifteen feet out of the driveway before Emma dialed Thelma's phone number.

"Hello, Emma, what's up?"

"First, I'm not calling to check up on the progress of the business plan. I know you have another project to finish first."

"Yes, I do, and I'm not done with it yet. I hope to get started on your plan next week."

"That's fine. I have a different reason for calling you. Savannah Mae and I did a walk-through of the house, trying to figure out which space would be large enough for the schoolroom. The only feasible solution seems to be the back porch."

"You'd lose that lovely porch. You'd do that?"

"I don't want to, but it's the only space big enough. Because we're planning to apply for a business loan that would cover the cost of construction, furniture, marketing, and whatnot, would it be alright for Savannah Mae and me to start getting construction estimates from contractors? We thought it would be good to get started on the costs to plug into the business plan and eventually the loan application. What do you think?"

"Well, I think it's quite forward-thinking. You'll need those figures eventually. However, starting a new business, especially one that's going to require construction, new furniture, supplies, and a full-blown marketing plan, which will take some expenditure, isn't going to happen overnight. Emma, I know you're excited about this new venture, and I don't want to burst your bubble, but this could take most of a year."

"A year?!" Emma yelped into the phone.

"Yes, a year."

"Why so long?"

"Once I finish up the business plan and show it to you, I think you'll understand the whole picture. There are permits you'll need and applications to file. There's a lot of paperwork involved, and that is often what causes the delays. Not to mention the inspections that will be required after every phase of the construction."

"So, you're saying I shouldn't do anything yet?"

"No, I'm not saying that at all. I'm simply giving you a realistic picture of how long this could take, and not to get your hopes up that you'll be opening your doors in a couple of months."

Thelma could feel Emma's disappointment bleeding through the phone. She quickly changed course.

"Oh, heck, Emma, go ahead and start getting some construction estimates—just warn the contractors that you're nowhere near ready to begin construction. As long as you're at it, get estimates on making the downstairs bedroom and bathroom ADA-compliant. That's an absolute must. And if you want, price out whatever furniture and items you'll need in the classroom. That should keep you busy for a while."

"Thelma?"

"Yes?"

"How does anyone ever have the patience to start a new business? It sounds overwhelming."

"Dreams, Emma. People will go to any length to make their dreams come true. Gotta go, my other line is ringing. We'll talk as soon as I've got your plan ready."

Emma slumped onto the couch and leaned her head back. She felt a tiny trepidation stirring in her chest, a trepidation that she knew could fester into a roller coaster of self-doubt. Instead, she bolted upright. "No, no!" she announced to the room. "I'm not going to crater just because this is going to be a lot more complicated than I originally thought. I'm going to do whatever it takes because this is my dream, and nothing is going to stop me!"

She got up and marched into the kitchen to make herself a pot of mint tea and bake a batch of peanut butter cookies. After she loaded the cookie sheets into the ovens, she called Savannah Mae and told her they had the green light from Thelma to start getting construction estimates, even though the project could take most of a year.

"When I told Travis about the quilting retreat, he said the same thing. Mama, as long as we're all patient, it will all come together. I know it will. Meanwhile, I'm going to ask Travis and Dad for contractor recommendations. When I get some names, we can split up the list to call and invite them to come to the house, where we'll interview them together. How does that sound?"

"Great. Don't forget to ask them for the names of lady contractors in the area too."

"You're right. I would love to have a female contractor if we can find someone who has the experience to bring our vision to life. But as much as I'd love to give the opportunity to a woman, I think that the priority should be finding someone with the best reputation, whose work is exceptional."

"That goes without saying, sweetheart," Emma said. "I know this is going to sound really premature, but I can't wait for our first retreat!"

"Me too, Mama, me too."

Chapter Three

Later that day, Emma poured herself a glass of lemonade and moseyed onto the back porch, where she sat in a big wicker chair with overstuffed rose-patterned cushions and put her feet up on a matching ottoman. She had no sooner reached for her lemonade on the side table than Sophie jumped up and settled into her lap, purring before Emma could take her first sip.

Suddenly, Emma's phone rang. It was Stella. She had barely answered when Stella blurted, "Can I come over? I'm so excited! I want to talk to you about the retreat center because I have several ideas."

"Sure, Stella, come around back. I'm on the porch."

"What're you doing back there?"

"Relaxing. Thinking about everything that needs to be done to start a business is exhausting. I'll tell you about it when you get here."

When Stella arrived and saw Emma drinking lemonade, just as she had done in her younger years, she walked down the hall into the kitchen, got a glass, and poured herself a hearty serving. Before going back to the porch, she took a small sip and smiled. "World's best lemonade," she said aloud, licking her lips.

She returned to the porch and sat down on a wicker rocking chair. "You do know that you make the best lemonade in Texas, don't you?"

Emma smiled. "Lemonade is lemonade."

"No, yours is special."

"Well, I use honey that comes out of East Texas, maybe that's it."

"Come on, Emma, there's something else in here."

Emma grinned a bit devilishly. "It wouldn't be the rum, would it?"

"Bingo! I knew it!" Stella laughed. "Well, I should have another glass, just to make sure it's as good as my first."

Emma put her hand over the top of Stella's glass. "Maybe you shouldn't."

Stella's lips turned downward. "Why?"

"I need your help in putting together a list of what I'll need for the retreat center. If you're half woozy, who knows what that list will look like."

Stella blinked. "Honestly, Emma? You've been away for many years, maybe you don't know me as well as you think. I'm still the same person inside that I was when you left 30 years ago. I didn't over-imbibe back then, and I certainly don't now."

Emma blushed and felt a little embarrassed. "I'm sorry," she said, looking down at her lap. "You're right, that was rude of me."

"Never you mind. Let's get started with your list, and I won't get any more lemonade until I'm dying of thirst."

"Oh, Stella, stop it." Emma gently patted her hand. "Go get your lemonade now before we start."

Stella looked at Emma's glass. "Yours is empty too. You want a refill?"

"Does a cat turn down a bowl of fresh milk?" Emma held up her glass, trying not to smirk.

Throughout the afternoon, the two women went over every possible item that the retreat center would need to accommodate students.

Finally, Stella sat back in her chair and let out a long breath. "Whew! That's a lot of stuff, Emma. Are you sure you'll need all of it?"

Emma looked over at her friend. "I think so. You're a quilter. Don't you have all these things in your sewing room? Wouldn't you want them on a retreat?"

Stella ran a hand over her pitch-black hair, strands of gray beginning to sprout along her temples.

"I suppose so. I was thinking, wouldn't it be good to have things like board games for people to play when they want a diversion for a little while?"

"What a smart idea! Yes. You mean like Monopoly?"

Stella grinned. "Sort of. You know how that company makes all kinds of themed Monopoly games now?"

"Yeah. I've seen them themed as specific cities, and even a chocolate one."

"Really? That would be fun. I have a better idea. There's a quilt-themed one."

Emma's jaw dropped. "No!"

"Yes!" A laugh rolled out of Stella. "It's called Quilt-opoly. And there's also a quilt bingo and, of course, lots of quilt jigsaw puzzles."

"Stella, you're so smart!"

Stella smiled shyly and batted her lashes. "I know."

"Well, my humble friend, I have a couple of thoughts myself. What do you think about asking the students to bring a fat quarter for a fabric swap?"

"I like it!"

"I was also thinking about asking each student to bring a completed twelve-inch block of their choosing, and you and I can sew the blocks into a quilt during the retreat to donate to a local charity at the end of the week."

"I love that!"

"I have one more idea."

"Keep going, Emma, you're on a roll."

"Entertainment. A couple of evenings, we could host a musician for a mini-concert."

Stella nodded. "What musicians did you have in mind?"

"I was thinking of students who are looking for a place to perform to get practice playing in front of audiences. There's an art and music academy on Ferris Avenue. They teach piano, guitar, and voice."

Stella sat up straight. "Have you called the school to see if they would be interested in having their students perform? At least the singers and guitar players. You didn't plan on buying a piano, did you?"

Emma laughed. "No, of course not. And no, I haven't called the school yet. I wanted to first find out what you thought of it. I could also check with the high school. They have a band and a choir, so maybe we could get a small ensemble, like a jazz group if they have one, to play for us, you know, to give them more exposure and practice."

"Emma, if we can make all of this happen, this is going to be the best quilting retreat in the state!"

"You really think so, Stella? It's not too much?"

"No, not at all. I love everything. What's next?"

"Well, I'm waiting on suggestions for caterers and contractor recommendations from Jack and my son-in-law. Savannah Mae and I will be interviewing potential contractors here at the house."

"Oh, oh! That reminds me, I made a list of restaurateurs and private individuals who cater." She reached into her purse and handed Emma a list of ten names.

Emma read all the names. "I recognize only the ones with restaurants. Do you have favorites on this list?"

Stella pointed to the numbers on the side. "I listed them from my highest recommendation to my lowest, but honestly, even the lowest isn't bad. It just isn't as spectacular as the first one."

"The family and some friends at the quilt guild are going to give me some recommendations too. Once I get them, I'll figure out which ones to make appointments with. You do know that you're going to have to help me with this part too, don't you?"

"Oh, you mean sampling the dishes? I don't know, Em. That's a really tough job. If I apply myself, I might be able to do it," she laughed.

"Tell ya what—you free for dinner? It's getting late, and I'm getting hungry. How about we go to the first one on the list?"

Stella put her glass down on the side table and stood up quickly. "All this talk about food has me ready to devour a whole side of beef."

Emma rose out of her chair. "Tiny little you, eat a whole side of beef? Okay then, let's skip the first one on the list and head for the barbecue restaurant. I could use some hearty food myself. You order the brisket. I'm gonna have their baby backs with the side of coleslaw, and we'll share, okay? I don't think anyone makes it better."

"Agreed," Stella said as she picked up their glasses and carried them to the kitchen.

Chapter Four

A few days later, Jack, Emma's first husband, called with a recommendation for a contracting company he'd used a few times. He explained that it wasn't just one person but a woman and her son, who had been in business for several years. Emma called Savannah Mae, told her about Jack's contractor, and asked when she would be available to interview them at the house.

"Anytime, Mama. Just let me know the date and time, and I'll be there."

Emma called the mother-son team and arranged for them to stop by the next day. They arrived at two o'clock and seemed quite as professional and pleasant as Jack had said they would be. First, Savannah Mae and Emma explained that they planned to create a retreat center, and the work that would need to be done, from enlarging and enhancing the first-floor bedroom and bathroom to be ADA-compliant to turning one of the first-floor spaces into a schoolroom. Emma did say that while turning the back porch into an enclosed space and enlarging it was an option, it was not her first choice. The contractors agreed that it would be a shame to take away the porch, as it was original to the Victorian home, adding that such a change would slightly decrease the value of the house. After an hour of walking all over the first floor, the duo concluded that the only other spaces large enough to convert into the schoolroom for the project would be the dining room or parlor. They asked whether Emma and Savannah Mae wanted them to develop a proposal with pricing and a timeline on converting one of those spaces. Emma and Savannah Mae glanced at one another and back at the contractors. They thanked them for their time and told them they would get back to them if they wanted to pursue converting one of those spaces. After the contractors left, Emma and Savannah Mae plopped down in the parlor's wingback chairs.

"Mama, I really liked them, but to be honest I can't see converting either the parlor or dining room into the schoolroom. I do love the idea of creating a retreat center here, though not at the expense of losing the charm of this wonderful old house. I think that would be a mistake."

"No argument here," Emma agreed.

"I was hoping that they would come up with something more creative than using the dining room or parlor." Savannah Mae groaned. "I know that the only other option is the back porch ..."

"No, honey," Emma interrupted, casting her daughter a straightforward glance that spelled her determination. "That isn't an option. The porch stays as is. We'll keep looking for contractors. Somebody is bound to have a better solution."

Savannah Mae nodded, relieved they were in agreement.

Over the next week, they received more contractor names and invited them to the house to tour the first floor and make suggestions on how to create a schoolroom without jeopardizing the charm of the house. Some also said the parlor and dining room were the only options if they didn't want to convert the porch. One told them to get over their attachment to the porch because it was the best space for the project. They didn't like him at all. Finally, they had one last person to interview, an old friend of Travis's who was stopping by the next morning.

Savannah Mae kissed her mother on the cheek. "I'll be back in the morning. Let's hope Travis's buddy has a better idea than the last bunch we've interviewed."

"Me too."

The next morning, Emma's phone rang early. It was Savannah Mae.

"Mama, would you be okay meeting with the contractor without me? Something's come up."

'Sure, sweetheart. What's going on?"

"There's something wrong with Annie Oakley, and the vet is on the way to check her."

"What seems to be the problem?"

"We're not sure. She's lethargic, not eating, and when I examined her all over, she has a tender spot in the belly area."

"That sounds serious."

"Let's hope it isn't. I'm in the barn with her now. The vet should be here in the next hour or so."

"Don't worry, honey, take care of your horse. I can handle a contractor. I know he's a friend of Travis's. Other than that, is there anything else I should know about him?"

"I don't really know much, other than Travis says he's known him for years. He says that he's honest and trustworthy and does excellent work."

"Considering how picky Travis is, that's a good endorsement. Call me when the vet is done and let me know what she says."

"Will do. Thanks, Mama."

Exactly at ten o'clock, the doorbell rang. Emma hurried from the back of the house, waves of copper red hair escaping her half-made chignon. She opened the door to a tall, long-legged man with a striking physique; he was lean, muscled, and rugged, with Mediterranean blue eyes that tilted at the corners, twinkling and gleaming at her. A sudden, gentle breeze wafted across the front porch, tossing his dark blond hair. He leaned forward, extending a hand. Emma reached out, forgetting about the teacup she was holding. It fell to the hardwood floor, shattering into a dozen pieces, tea going everywhere. They both stared down at the floor.

"Sorry about that," the man said. "I hope that wasn't a family heirloom." He carefully bent down to pick up the pieces.

"It's okay, I was being clumsy, not you," Emma responded, thinking she had made an awful first impression. "We have enough teacups to start a tea shop."

He gathered the broken pieces and handed them to her. "Let me begin again. I'm Jesse Rieger. I have an appointment to look at some possible construction projects?" She noticed that he spoke with a soft voice that belied his imposing stature. He looked like the kind of man whose voice would bellow.

Emma liked him right away because he used the term *possible.* All the other contractors used terminology that assumed they would be getting the job. He exuded an air of confidence and intelligence without the accompanying ego. This contractor was different; she instantly liked that.

She opened the door wide. "Yes, please come in. I'm Emma Clayburne Jenkins."

He smiled again, stepped inside, and watched her gaze follow his leg: He limped. "War injury," he stated simply.

"I apologize for staring," she said remorsefully.

He nodded. "You must be Travis's mother-in-law."

"I am. Luckiest mother-in-law in the world. He's a good man."

"You got that right. I was out of town when he married your daughter and couldn't get back for it. He texted me photos. Thought it was pretty gutsy that they got married on their horses in all their wedding finery."

"Gutsy? Why?" she cocked her head sideways, trying to understand what he meant.

"I talked to Trav that morning, and he said it was threatening to rain and he was hoping there wouldn't be a downpour during the ceremony."

Emma chuckled. "You're right, I'd forgotten about that. Luckily, the clouds parted right before the ceremony started. Then, the sun came out. It was truly a beautiful day."

"Well, I don't want to take up too much of your time. Can you show me what you need done?"

Emma nodded and steered him to the first-floor bathroom, after detouring to the kitchen to throw the broken teacup in the trash. They stepped into the bathroom and she explained what they wanted to do, and that the first-floor bathroom would need to be enlarged and made ADA-compliant.

"I take it that the room next to it will be the ADA-compliant bedroom?"

Emma nodded.

"Mind if I take a look at it?"

"No, go on in. It's being used for storage right now. We'll figure out furniture later."

Jesse stepped inside and took out a digital measuring tape to take all the dimensions. When he finished, he turned to her. "This'll be big enough to maneuver a wheelchair in here." He proceeded to measure the width of the door opening. "Fortunately, this door opening is not standard. Conventional wheelchairs run 28 inches wide, and this door opening is 32 inches, which is plenty of room to accommodate a wheelchair."

He stepped into the bathroom and found that its doorway was also 32 inches wide. "The door width is okay, but the bathroom isn't ADA-compliant. It'll need to be expanded and upgraded."

Emma recalled that most of the other contractors had barely addressed the guest room or bathroom, being more interested in the schoolroom project. Jesse was impressing her more and more by the minute.

"I'd advise replacing this old bathtub. It's hard for a disabled person to use. It should be replaced with a roll-in shower that has a folding seat." He pointed to the walls. "Grab bars will be required on two walls in the shower."

"Not all three walls?" Emma asked.

"No. When there's a folding seat, a bar isn't necessary on that wall, because it can hinder the person's ability to sit comfortably. It's kind of dark in here, don't you think?" he asked, looking around.

"I never use this bathroom. Never really thought about it."

He pointed to a wall a couple of feet above where the folding seat would be. "We could bring in some natural light by making a hole up here and installing glass blocks. The kind that let in light, but no one on the outside can actually see through them. I put a lot of them in. There's room for four, six, or eight blocks."

He swept his hand indicating the side wall. "The controls, faucet, and shower spray unit would be located on the side wall, here. And of course, there will be a new floor, tiling on all the walls, and a threshold that will still allow access to wheelchairs."

"You really know a lot about ADA regulations," Emma remarked.

"When I was in the VA hospital after my injury, I got to witness firsthand the importance of making rooms, and especially bathrooms, accessible for people in wheelchairs. I know how important it is."

"Sounds like it was a tough way to learn about the regulations."

"It was. I used my time at the VA to learn everything I could, and I'm a better contractor because of it. I don't know of any other contractors in the area who have the personal experience that I do. Now, what about the schoolroom you want? What will it be used for?"

Emma beckoned him to follow her, explaining that she wanted to turn part of the house into a quilting retreat center. He looked at her quizzically, as though she were speaking a foreign language. "Ma'am, I am not familiar with what a quilting retreat center is."

Emma pursed her lips. "Jesse, I'll tell you only if you don't call me 'ma'am.' I think you and I are pretty close in age. I'm not old enough to be a ma'am."

He dipped his head. "My apologies, I was being respectful."

"I get that, no harm done. Let's just do this informally, shall we?" She smiled sweetly at him as she attempted to pin the hair that had fallen out of her chignon back where it belonged.

He nodded. "And now will you tell me what a quilting retreat center is?"

"Of course." She explained that the purpose of the center was to teach students how to make various types of quilts and how there were hundreds of retreat centers all over the country, including more than 50 that she knew of in Texas.

"I've never heard of such a thing. Tell me what you'll need in the schoolroom."

She proceeded to paint a visual picture of the tables for each student's sewing machine; rolling carts of sewing supplies next to each sewing machine table; other larger tables for cutting fabric; ironing boards with plugged-in irons; design walls for laying out quilt blocks; a mini-shop of fabrics, notions, tools, and patterns; lots of good overhead lighting; and multiple electrical outlets to accommodate extension cords and surge protectors.

"And where are you thinking of putting this schoolroom?"

She waved him toward the back porch and admitted that it was probably the largest space on the property, but she was hesitant to put it there because she didn't want to lose the porch. "I really love this porch."

"I can see why." He shook his head. "This wouldn't work anyway. What else have you got?"

She looked up and silently thanked God. Emma walked him up to the front of the house and told him how the other contractors had suggested that she give up the parlor or dining room. Jesse glanced around each room, keenly appraising the two spaces. He folded his arms over his chest.

"Would you want to do that?" he asked.

"No, but what other choice do I have?"

"Then, it's not an option. You said you plan to continue living here, correct?"

She nodded.

"Now, I realize that I don't know you, but somehow I get the feeling you wouldn't want to be living in a schoolhouse."

"No, I wouldn't. But like I said, I think my choices are limited."

He looked straight at her. "Would you show me the backyard?"

"Uh, sure," she said, silently wondering why. She walked him out the side kitchen door into the side yard and back to the one-acre space that was big enough for another house.

He took out his digital tape measure and began noting the dimensions. He walked over to the shed. "Do you use this shed much?"

"Not really, I keep a few gardening tools in there."

"Do you have room in your basement for them?"

"Yes," she said slowly, curious as to why he was asking.

He walked the whole backyard several times, stopped, and nodded his head. "This'll work," he mumbled to himself.

"What will work?" Emma asked, following close behind.

He looked over at her. He clearly had barely remembered she was there.

"There is absolutely no reason for you to give up space in your home when you have more than enough room out here to build a freestanding structure to serve as a schoolhouse."

Emma double-blinked. "What kind of freestanding structure?"

"Any kind you like. It could be a simple metal building that looks like a barn, or it could be an architectural replica of your home, pitched roof, gingerbread details, yellow paint, and all. Whichever you prefer."

She stood there, staring at him. "What about electricity, and waterlines, and, and ... everything?"

"We'd put them in. I take it you've never had any remodeling or construction done in a home?"

"No."

"So, this is a foreign concept to you?"

She nodded. He walked over and stood in front of her.

"Emma, this isn't heart transplant surgery. I do this kind of thing all the time, though I admit that I've never built a quilting schoolhouse. But it really wouldn't be any different from other structures I've done."

She looked hard at him, assessing his intent, his honesty. "What about wheelchair access going from the house to the schoolhouse out here?"

He stepped away from her and pointed to the side of the house. "Piece of cake. I'd build a ramp, could even give it Victorian ironwork flair to match the house."

Emma looked stunned. "I can't believe this."

Jesse turned around. "Can't believe what?"

"You are the eighth contractor to come out here, and you are the first who actually understands my vision and needs and who used his noggin to come up with a creative alternative outside the porch, parlor, or dining room."

He grinned. "You like my ideas?"

"I don't like them, Jesse, I love them. You're a genius!"

He cracked a small smile. "Whoa, hold on," he said, putting his hands in front of him as though blocking a lineman coming at him. "I wouldn't go that far. I've never been accused of being a genius before."

"How long will it take you to work up an estimate for everything we've talked about today?"

"Probably a week, depending on whether you want the metal building or the little yellow house. If you choose the little yellow house, I'd need to know if you want it built of metal or fire-resistant wood."

"The yellow house, and definitely wood," she stated matter-of-factly.

"That'll take a little more time. Maybe ten days, is that okay?"

"More than okay. Now, come in the house, I have something for you."

He followed her inside and into the kitchen. When they'd passed through before, he hadn't noticed the plate of cookies on the counter or the smaller plates and glasses next to it. He felt his mouth water. She took a pitcher out of the fridge and poured milk into the glasses.

"Help yourself to as many cookies as you want."

He rubbed his jaw and leaned on the kitchen counter. "You didn't have to go to all this trouble."

"It wasn't any trouble. I bake all the time."

He gingerly placed two cookies on a plate, picked up a glass of milk, and motioned to the kitchen table. "Alright to sit here?"

"Yep." She took a cookie and a glass of milk and joined him. She watched as he bit into a cookie. A crumb fell out of his mouth. He scooped it up, put it back into his mouth, and sighed.

"You're as good as any bakery in town."

Emma smiled demurely.

"I'm serious. How did you learn to bake like this?" he asked, pointing to the cookies.

Emma tossed her head side to side. "It's not me. It's the ovens."

"Whaddaya mean?"

Emma pointed to the antique enameled range standing against the far wall. "It's been in our family for generations."

"How old is it?"

"There's a card in one of the kitchen drawers that says it's a double oven that was manufactured by the Wedgewood Company in 1923. "

"And it still works?"

"What do you think? You just tasted what it can do."

"I'd say there's no reason to buy a new one."

"It's been said that you can bake something in this oven, and bake the exact same recipe in someone else's oven, and it won't be near as good."

"And why is that? You realize that doesn't make sense."

Emma nodded. "Oh, I know, but it's true. When I was growing up, my mother and grandmother won every baking competition at the county fair. And I mean every year, they won. After a while, the judges suspected they were cheating somehow, so one of the judges came to our house and supervised whatever they were making to enter into the fair."

"And?"

"The supervising judge observed every step plus all the ingredients and then signed an affidavit that nothing out of the ordinary occurred in our kitchen. Grandma's and Mama's entries always won."

Jesse's eyebrows shot up.

"I'm telling you, it's the oven," Emma pressed.

"This has got to be the strangest story I've ever heard."

"Granted, it is odd. The family has a theory about it, and my brother, Keith, has his own."

Jesse nodded, urging her to continue.

"Somebody way back proposed that the oven, or maybe the kitchen, has an angel who oversees what's being made and ensures it comes out as close to perfect as possible. Sort of heavenly intervention."

"You're kidding, right?" Jesse reached up and scratched the back of his neck.

Emma shook her head.

"You said your brother has a theory too?"

"Yeah, he thinks there's a ghost in the kitchen who helps whoever is cooking or baking."

"A ghost?"

Emma nodded. "Actually, ghosts have inhabited the house for decades, so it's not that far-fetched."

"You're joking."

"Nope."

"Well, whether you had celestial or paranormal intervention, it doesn't matter to me. What are these?" He pointed to the plate.

"Moravian spice cookies."

"Never heard of 'em," he said, taking another bite, and another, devouring both cookies.

"Moravia is part of the Czech Republic, so technically, they're Czech cookies."

"And how do you know how to make them? Where'd you get the recipe?"

"I'm sure you know that there's a huge Czech population all over Texas."

He nodded, taking a big gulp of milk.

"There's a bunch of towns with Czech communities, like Ennis, and farther south in West, La Grange, Schulenburg, Praha, and Hallettsville. I really like Czech food and Czech baked goods, so when I found a Czech cookbook in one of the towns with a whole bunch of recipes, I bought it. These cookies are one of my favorites."

"I think they're now one of my favorites too. I haven't had cookies this good since my mom used to bake for me when I was a kid. I could eat that whole plate of 'em," he said, gesturing to the plate piled high on the counter.

"Excellent!" Emma got up, gently placed most of the cookies in a large plastic container, put on the lid, turned around, and handed it to him.

"What's this for?" He hesitantly took the container.

"Oh, it's very simple. I baked them earlier and decided that if I liked you and liked your ideas, I'd give them to you. Of course, I first had to see if I liked your ideas, which I do, and if you liked the cookies, which obviously you do."

"And did you bake cookies for all the contractors you interviewed?"

She shook her head. "No, just you."

"Why only me?" He creased his brows together.

"I had a feeling you were going to be the right person for the work, and I was right."

He beamed as he held up the container. "Well, thank you. I don't mean to eat and run, but I have to start working up the numbers so I can get the estimates to you by the end of the week."

"I thought you said it would take ten days."

He winked at her. "That was before you baked me cookies." He got up and walked toward the front door, Emma behind him. He turned back to her before exiting. "Be sure to tell your ghost or angel how much I liked your cookies."

Emma grinned. "I'm sure they already know."

Chapter Five

A few days later, Jesse called and told her that he had the estimate ready plus architectural sketches of how the bathroom and the schoolhouse would look. He asked whether he could stop by the next morning with his brother.

"I'd love to meet your brother, but what is his interest in coming with you?" Emma asked.

"Ah, I should have told you when I suggested the idea of the freestanding schoolhouse in the yard: He's an architect. Though he's not exactly a partner in my construction business, he often draws up plans for my projects. I think you'll like what he's come up with. Okay for us to drop by at 11:00 a.m.?"

"I think so. I want my daughter to be here too. I'll call her and find out if she can make it. She actually owns the house and needs to weigh in on this."

"Sure, sure. Why wasn't she there when I stopped in a few days ago? Seems she probably should have been, if she gets the deciding vote."

"She was supposed to be. Early that morning, she called to tell me that her horse was ill and the vet was on the way."

"Hope her horse is okay. That's not something you mess around with."

"No, it's not. Turns out she has a gastric ulcer."

"Huh!" he remarked. "How does the vet treat it?"

"Have you ever taken omeprazole?"

"As a matter of fact, I have."

"That's what the vet gave her, in larger doses than humans take. Even though it's been only a few days, she's back to her old self, stomping around her stall and whining for Savannah Mae to take her on a ride. Anyway, I'll call her and find out if she can join us. If she can't, I'll text you to find another day and time. And if she can, I won't text you, and you'll know that we're good."

"Sounds fine. Hope to see you in the morning."

As punctual as at his first visit, Jesse rang the doorbell exactly at 11:00 a.m. Savannah Mae opened the door and introduced herself. In turn, Jesse introduced himself and his brother, Tom. She led them into the kitchen, where Emma was placing freshly baked pecan tassies on a plate. She carried them to the dining room table, where she'd laid cups, a carafe of hot coffee, a creamer, spoons, and a sugar bowl.

"We'll sit in here," she called to them. "More room to spread out."

Everyone filed into the dining room, and Jesse introduced Emma to Tom, who shook her hand and immediately began to unroll the plans for the bathroom and little yellow Victorian schoolhouse. He proceeded to point out dimensions and details, which would allow ample room for all the items Emma had told

Jesse the schoolhouse needed to hold. Then, he unrolled a second plan for the schoolhouse, this one with a small half-bath in the back corner, near the storage closet. Like the bathroom by the first-floor bedroom in the big house, it would be big enough for a wheelchair, which he said would be more convenient for any students who didn't want to go up to the house when they needed to use the facilities.

Emma and Savannah Mae looked at each other and back at the men. "Never occurred to me," Emma said, "though I sure don't know why. Of course we need a bathroom in the schoolhouse building."

Savannah Mae looked at Tom. "Thank you for this detail. I sure didn't think of it, either. So, let's go with the plan that includes the bathroom." She flipped back to the front page that illustrated the exterior front. "This," she said, pointing to the illustration. "I love it! When Mama told me your idea, Jesse, to emulate the architecture of the big house, I thought it was brilliant."

Jesse nodded, followed by a broad grin. "I'm glad you approve."

Emma tried to quell her growing excitement over the plans, to be professional about it, but it was proving to be a useless effort. She had been pretty sure that Savannah Mae would like it, though she hadn't expected her to love it the way she did. But it wasn't surprising; even though she hadn't raised Savannah Mae, after all, she was her daughter. Their shared DNA made them similar in countless ways.

The group turned to the coffee and pecan tassies. The men tried unsuccessfully to eat just one. They weren't very large, and before anyone noticed, they'd each eaten four.

Tom apologized, saying he'd never seen, much less eaten, miniature pecan pies before. "Do you think it would be possible to pay us in these pecan things?"

"Hey, watch it, Tom, that's my livelihood," Jesse cautioned him, trying to suppress a laugh. "They are good. You should have had the spice cookies she made the first time I was here."

Savannah Mae turned to her mother. "Did you bake the Moravian spice cookies for him?"

Emma nodded, and Savannah Mae looked at Jesse. "You are one lucky man. She doesn't bake those very often, and only for special occasions."

Emma blushed and quickly steered the conversation in a different direction.

"Jesse, can we see your estimate of what all this is going to cost?"

"In dollars, or cookies?" Jesse asked, his face as serious as a lawyer arguing a complicated court case.

Emma leaned her head sideways, keeping a straight face. "What do you think? Show us the figures, gentlemen."

Over the next half hour, the two men went over every expense, even offering alternatives to the most costly items. The women stared numbly at the cost sheets. They hadn't known what to expect, and when they realized that the schoolhouse was exactly what they wanted even before they knew what they wanted, they accepted the expense proposal, seeing no reason to make changes.

Emma looked at both men. "Tom, as I explained to Jesse a few days ago, we are in the very beginning stages of creating this business. We're in the process of working with a lawyer on our business plan, and then our financing. What I'm saying is that we love your plans and would like to include them in both the business plan and the business loan application, if you can be patient with us."

The two men exchanged glances and nodded.

"Sounds good to us," Jesse said. "Call us when you're ready or even slightly before so we can start filing construction permits."

Thelma finally called Emma and asked when she and Savannah Mae could come to the office to review the business plan. Emma said they'd come the next morning.

That day, the three women sat down around a conference table. At each place was a printout of the business plan. Thelma turned to both of them.

"Emma, I want to thank you for doing so much legwork in finding an honest contractor who provided you with a comprehensive estimate for building the schoolhouse and remodeling the downstairs bathroom and bedroom. I checked him out: He has one of the highest ratings of any contractors in the county, and in the state of Texas. The man hasn't incurred a single infraction, which is almost unheard of in the construction business. May I ask where you found him?"

Emma pointed to Savannah Mae.

"Actually, he's a friend of Travis's," Savannah Mae said. "He's known him for years and highly recommended him."

"His estimate and plans made my job much easier. I don't usually get such comprehensive estimates and plans on projects involving construction. Emma, the rest of the costs you provided on furniture, supplies, and materials pertaining to the retreat center were excellent. Let's take a look at the business plan."

Over the course of the next hour, Thelma detailed every aspect of the plan, including a troubleshooting section, which she explained was something she included to discuss worst-case scenarios.

"What kind of worst-case scenarios?" Savannah Mae asked.

"Primarily natural disasters, emergencies, accidents at the place of business, that kind of thing. As you'll see on the list of costs in the first addendum, I included a line item for insurance, which you absolutely must have. If you'll turn to page 35, you'll see a basic marketing plan I put together for you. This is where you'll need to work with a marketing company to put together a website, social media sites, and a full-blown plan to make sure every quilter, quilt shop, and quilt guild in Texas, Oklahoma, New Mexico, Louisiana, and Arkansas knows about your retreat center. I've listed a few marketing firms that I recommend, ones who have done an excellent job for other clients. While these firms are not cheap, their expenses can be rolled into your business loan."

"Thelma, is the business plan complete enough that we can take it to a bank for the business loan?" Emma asked.

"Yes. And because I assumed that neither of you has ever applied for a business loan before, I took the liberty of filling out a mock application for you to look over." Thelma gave each of them a copy. "If you want me to fill out a real application for you, I'll need you to fill out some personal and financial information and decide on which bank you want to use." She pushed another piece of paper toward each of them. "This is a list of Ellis County banks and their current business loan rates. For comparison, on the second page is a list of Dallas banks with their rates. As you'll see, going local is more affordable than going to the Big D. Local banks do try to reward local customers for borrowing locally."

"Wow, this is incredible, Aunt Thelma!" Savannah Mae said as she stared at all the paperwork.

"I'm speechless, Thelma," Emma added. "I never expected this level of work. Six months ago, I didn't even know you did business law. To say 'thank you' simply isn't enough; you have gone far beyond my greatest expectations."

"I do it for clients all the time. I was more than happy to do it for my own family. And you know why?"

Emma and Savannah Mae shook their heads.

"Because I want to see the Yellow House Quilting Retreat succeed. Next, you'll need to talk to a couple of the marketing firms and decide which one you want to use. Get a proposal from the one you like, and let me know who it is, the cost, etc. I'll plug it into your loan application. Once it's ready, it's just a matter of walking it into the bank."

When they stood up to leave, Emma stepped over and embraced Thelma. "Thank you," she whispered before she stepped back. She and Savannah Mae left the office and got in their car, parked in front of the building. Instead of heading home, Emma drove to a nearby flower shop.

"What are we doing here?" Savannah Mae asked.

Emma waved her into the shop. As soon as they entered, the woman behind the counter asked whether she could help them.

"You sure can. I want the biggest, most beautiful arrangement of flowers that you can make delivered to the law office of Thelma Clayburne on Rogers Street."

"How big?" the woman asked.

"Big," Emma answered. "Show me what you can do."

Fifteen minutes later, Emma paid the woman, and both she and Savannah Mae signed a card to be placed in the arrangement. By the time they left, the flower shop woman was dashing all over, gathering star lilies, roses, fragrant stock, and sweet peas in various shades of pink, Thelma's favorite color. They got back in the car and smiled all the way back home. When Emma pulled up at the house, next to Savannah Mae's pickup truck, she asked whether she wanted to review the bank options for the loan or look into the marketing companies Thelma suggested.

"I think I'll take the banks. That way, Travis can give me some input on any banks he's dealt with. I can make calls and find out if their loan rates have changed and who the bank officer is who handles business loans."

"Didn't Thelma put names by some of the bank loan officers she's dealt with?" Emma asked.

Savannah Mae looked down at the list. "Yeah, she did."

"Maybe you start there? Say your aunt recommended them? Maybe it'll open the door for us to meet with them."

"Good idea, Mama. So, you'll tackle the list of marketing companies?"

"Yeah, that sounds a little more interesting. I'll check their websites first and see if they've done any campaigns even remotely similar to a quilting retreat. And I'll contact any that look like possibilities."

"When you narrow the list and decide which ones to approach, I'd like to know which ones you like and, of course, be at meetings to interview them on what they can do for us."

"Absolutely. And I'd like to be at the loan officer meeting."

"Of course, Mama, looks like we got it covered. Oh, one other thing ..."

"Yes?"

"You seem a lot more confident and focused. I'm not picking up on any self-doubt. What's changed?"

Emma smiled, reached over, and took her daughter's hand. "A few things, actually. It started with Stella telling me that if I didn't snap out of it, she was going to sic the psychiatrist at her health clinic on me. Then, you had that 'Come to Jesus' talk with me and told me to grow a backbone. When Thelma told me that it could take a year to get this done, I started to falter, but with everyone's support, something happened. It was like someone was hoisting me up, and I had my own revelation that I really could do this. And ever since then, I've been okay."

Savannah Mae squeezed Emma's hand. "This is a huge relief, Mama. I was getting really worried about you."

"I know you were, honey. Don't worry anymore. The old me is back. And I'm raring to see this quilt retreat through."

Savannah Mae kissed her mother on the cheek, hopped out of the car, got into her truck, and headed toward the ranch to tell Travis about the progress they were making on the retreat.

That very afternoon, Emma began researching the marketing companies online. They all had stellar websites, including a couple that were so slick that she wondered whether they would be able to design something simpler, something sort of homey that would appeal to quilters. Most of the marketing companies provided links to websites and marketing campaigns they'd done for their clients. As she scrolled through them, she saw that her initial hunch was right: The websites were smooth and highly polished, which she figured was what the clients had wanted. And although they were skillfully designed, and streamlined, which she appreciated, they were so corporate-looking that she doubted quilters would go past the home page if her website were designed like that.

Finally, she looked at the last company on Thelma's list: M&M Marketing. On their website, they listed several companies whose campaigns they had conducted and links to their websites. One caught her eye. It was for a local craft woodworker who hand-carved tables, chairs, hutches, doors, armoires, bookcases, cabinets, beds, cutting boards, even dough bowls for breadmaking. She was so intrigued by the home page that she scrolled through all the product pages, each one displaying wood products more enticing than the last. She stumbled upon a new but vintage-style wooden sewing box with sewing-inspired carvings on the top. Although their approach for marketing a wood-carving operation was different from what a quilting retreat center would need, she recognized that the marketing company understood the passion and warmth behind a crafting operation. She looked up where the woodworker was located. He was in Ennis, the next town over, and his store was open. In an inspired moment, she got her keys and drove over to the man's woodworking shop.

As soon as she stepped inside the shop, her senses were blanketed with the aroma of freshly cut wood, as though she were standing in a forest after a spring rain. She looked around and spied the wooden sewing box she'd seen on his website. It was even more lovely in person. A man in his thirties was working on a saw when he noticed Emma. He stopped, walked over, and asked how he could help her.

"Are you Will Anderson, the owner?"

"I am."

"I was referred to the marketing company you used and looked over the website they created for you. I am really impressed; however, I do have a couple of questions I hope you won't mind answering."

"Uh, sure," Will responded.

"Thanks. First, I was wondering how easy M&M was to work with."

"I'm a craftsperson, so things like websites, marketing, social media, and running a business don't come easily to me. I gotta say, M&M Marketing was great. They understood that my market was unique and developed the marketing plan, social media, and the website accordingly, All the other companies I looked into were so slick, I knew they wouldn't work for my market."

"Did they increase your sales and custom orders?"

Will nodded his head wildly. "Like you wouldn't believe. Within the first month, I ran out of almost everything I had in stock. I had to bring in an apprentice to help me replenish the items that sold the best. I'm still trying to catch up, and that was six months ago. And I've got a backorder list that will take most of the year to fulfill."

"I'm surprised you still have that lovely sewing box over there," she said, pointing to it.

"I was surprised by that too. I worked really hard on it. I researched vintage sewing boxes and modeled mine after classic nineteenth-century models. I don't know why it hasn't sold."

"I'm a quilter, and we quilters love handmade items. In fact, that box over there is calling to me."

"Even though it's my only one, I'll sell it to you. But first, I gotta ask: What kind of business are you opening that you need a marketing firm?"

"A quilting retreat center in Waxahachie. Do you know what that is?"

"Sure do, my wife is a quilter and is always running off to a retreat somewhere. Did you say you're going to open one in Waxahachie?"

"I did."

"Susie will be your first student. Do you have a card or flyer I can show her?"

Emma shook her head. "Not yet. We are still in the beginning stages. We probably won't be open for the better part of a year."

"I get that, starting a new business takes much longer than you think. Just curious, will you be selling patterns, fabric, and notions at your center?"

"Yes, that's the plan."

"I have an idea. I need to create a market for the sewing box. If I give you that one, will you display it in your center with a stack of my cards?"

"Seriously, you're going to give it to me?"

"Yeah," Will grinned. "We can help each other out here."

Emma thrust her hand out to Will. "Deal! Just remember that I won't be displaying it for a good while."

"It's fine with me. When you're up and running, give me a call. I'd like to see it. I could bring over a few more sewing boxes—that is, if you have room, you could put it in the shopping area of your classroom. And I'll bring Susie with me. She'll be real excited when I tell her about this. She sleeps, dreams, and lives quilts." He turned and wrapped up the box in thick brown paper, put it in a sturdy cardboard box, and added a stack of his cards. "Let me carry this out to your car."

"I can't thank you enough. You made my day."

"And you made mine." Will followed her and placed the box on the front passenger seat. "Now, you be careful driving home so this beauty arrives safely."

Emma reached over and shook his hand. "I will. It just became a family heirloom."

On the way home, she called Savannah Mae and told her about the marketing firms, finding Will's website, and her impromptu decision to pay him a visit. Telling her about the vintage-style sewing box almost made her miss the turn into her driveway.

"Wait till you see it, Savannah Mae. It's precious. He wants us to carry some in the shop part of the schoolhouse."

"Oh, Mama. That sounds like the stars were aligned! Send me his website. Did he say how much he paid for all of it?"

"No, I didn't ask. All the other websites that marketing firms created were too slick and corporate-looking. This was the only one I saw that came even close to the feel of our cozy retreat center."

Chapter Six

A few days later, Emma and Savannah Mae met with the folks at M&M Marketing, a firm that turned out to be owned by two women, Mandy and Marguerite. Their logo featured M&M-looking candies. "Clever!" Savannah Mae remarked when they saw it on the wall of the company waiting room.

During their meeting with the owners, Emma and Savannah Mae outlined their plans for their new quilting retreat center, including the custom-built schoolhouse, the main yellow Victorian house where the students would stay, catered meals, how the students would learn a different quilt at each retreat, and the warm environment of the center and their home.

"Do you have a business plan we can see?" Marguerite asked.

"It's nearly finished. The final numbers to plug in are the marketing expenses."

"How did you find us?" Mandy asked.

"Thelma Clayburne, the lawyer putting together the business plan, recommended you," Emma responded. "I looked over websites for the clients of several marketing firms, and it wasn't until I saw Will Anderson's website that I felt I'd found the right firm. I think you understand the needs of a crafting business better than any other firm I researched."

Mandy and Marguerite looked at one another and back at Emma and Savannah Mae. "We're glad you appreciate the effort we put into Will's marketing. It was certainly challenging, but it seems to be working for him," Mandy said.

"I visited him at his workshop," Emma confessed. "I'd say it's more than working for him: He has backorders up the wazoo."

"We haven't talked to Will in a while," Marguerite responded. "That's good to know."

"Let's get down to specifics, shall we?" Mandy suggested. She pulled out some price lists and several examples of marketing plans. "We believe in being up front on costs from the very beginning so you know what you're getting into and there are no misunderstandings."

She and Marguerite outlined the various plans and what would be included. Emma and Savannah Mae didn't think that they needed television or radio advertising but said that advertising in national quilting magazines, through occasional local newspaper ads, and on various social media channels would be important to include.

"Are either of you savvy at posting on social media?" Marguerite asked.

Savannah Mae said, "I'm probably the more savvy one of the two of us; however, my time is more limited." She turned to Emma. "Mama, you have more time than I, do you think you could take it on?"

"Sure." Emma looked at Mandy and Marguerite. "I've done a little posting, and with a little one-on-one training about the finer points, I see no reason why I couldn't do it."

"Well, we have an excellent social media specialist who would be happy to come to your home, set up the accounts and pages on your computer, and train you."

"Oh? That's great." Emma looked around and didn't see or hear anyone else in the office. "Does the person work here?"

"She mostly works from home," Mandy said. "It's my daughter, Madeleine. Having grown up around marketing and social media, she knows it better than anyone. We use her because we could hire an older, more experienced social media guru, but we've found that those gurus overcharge and aren't nearly as good or as fast as Madeleine. Plus, she's more interested in building her portfolio than in the money. We do pay her, but it's minimal."

"Does Madeleine also build your websites?" Savannah Mae asked.

"No, my son, Matt, does that," Marguerite answered. "He majored in website design in college. He's very good at it."

"Did he design Will Anderson's website?" Emma asked.

Marguerite nodded.

"That is one of the nicest craft websites I've seen. It seems like your marketing firm is a family business. Are the two of you related?"

Marguerite and Mandy glanced at one another and said together, "Sisters."

Savannah Mae and Emma chuckled. "Obviously, we are family too, and our lawyer, Thelma Clayburne, is my sister," Emma said.

"Then we all understand each other well," Marguerite said. "I think we have enough to get started. We'll circle back with you in a couple of weeks and present you with our plan and a rough mock-up of the website's home page. How does that sound?"

"Perfect," Emma agreed.

As promised, Marguerite contacted them a few weeks later to go over the marketing plan. Emma and Savannah Mae met with them in their office and were ecstatic over the plan, which included the help of Madeleine and Matt. The proposal looked reasonable to both of them and in line with the original pricing they'd been shown. Emma promised to get back to them as soon as the business loan came through. She told them that although that meant they could begin construction, it would be months before they would be ready to open the retreat center. As they'd discussed earlier, three months before the retreat's opening date, the firm would begin running preliminary ads about the new quilting retreat center and launch the website and social media campaign.

After leaving Mandy and Marguerite, Emma and Savannah Mae drove over to Thelma's office and, seeing she wasn't with a client, walked into her office. Emma placed a copy of the Yellow House Quilting Retreat marketing plan on her desk. Thelma smiled as soon as she saw it.

"Thanks! I take it this has all the costs included?" Emma and Savannah Mae nodded. "Okay. I'll plug the figures into the business plan, and I'll calculate a total on how much y'all will need to borrow from the bank. You decided on which bank to use, didn't you?"

"Yep, we're going with the Cotton Farmers Bank, like you suggested. They had the best rate, and we liked that we're connected to them through the family business," Savannah Mae said.

"I should have the business plan finished as well as the loan application done by next week. I'll confirm when it's ready for your signatures. When that's done, I'll make an appointment with Trevor Aguilar, the senior loan officer, and go with you to meet with him. I've worked with him for years. I know that if he sees that I created the business plan and that we are all Clayburnes, which links us to the bank through our cotton and textile mills, that it'll grease the wheels to getting the loan approved."

"Thelma, how do we thank you?" Emma squealed with excitement.

"A simple 'thank you' is enough. Now, don't you go spending another small fortune on flowers."

Emma's smile dropped. "Didn't you like them?"

"Of course I liked them, Emma. I loved them. You just don't need to be spending money on me. It's meant a lot to me to be able to help you, and when the retreat is up and running, I'll take special pride in knowing I was able to help make your dream come true."

"Love you, Thelma," Emma said as she and Savannah Mae left Thelma's office. They were out of earshot when Thelma whispered, "Love you more, Emma."

As Thelma predicted, her making an appointment with Trevor Aguilar at the bank and escorting Emma and Savannah Mae to meet with him and deliver the loan application and business plan went miles in expediting the loan application process. The moment that Trevor was introduced to Emma and Savannah Mae as not just members of the Clayburne family but Thelma's sister and niece, the man made it his primary duty to move the loan application to the top of the list.

Two months later, Trevor called Thelma to say that the project had been approved for a $70,000 Small Business Administration loan. He asked Thelma to bring Emma and Savannah Mae into the bank to sign papers.

Thelma called Emma and shared the good news.

"I was beginning to think they weren't going to fund the loan," Emma said.

"Why would you say that?"

"You said that Trevor was prioritizing the loan application. I just figured it fell down some rabbit hole or was being denied. Otherwise, wouldn't we have heard sooner?"

"Emma, they're funding you for a Small Business Administration loan, which has some of the lowest rates in the financial world. The catch is that it takes longer to review and approve the applications. They usually take 90 days; yours took only 60."

"I guess I have a lot to learn about loans and finances."

"Yes, you do. I'll buy you a copy of *The Complete Guide to Small Business Loans and Banking*. As a business owner, you're going to need it."

Emma smiled into the phone. Rather than doubting her ability to understand finances and loans, she raised her head and said, "That would be wonderful, Thelma. Thank you. I'll get started reading it as soon as I have it in my eager hands."

"Good, I'll order you a copy today. If you and Savannah Mae are available, let's meet at the bank on Thursday at ten thirty. I'll let Trevor know to have the paperwork ready for signing."

After Thelma's call, Emma phoned Savannah Mae to tell her the news.

"Oh, Mama! That's fantastic. This is really happening!"

"It sure is, baby. You sure you're ready for this?"

"Absolutely!"

"Then, see you at the bank on Thursday morning."

As much as Emma and Savannah Mae were excited and slightly nervous about signing the loan documents, it turned out to be the least difficult part of the process to date. All Emma and Savannah

Mae had to do was sign the documents and set up a business checking account to access their funds as they needed them. When they were done, Emma and Savannah Mae told Thelma they wanted to show their appreciation by taking her to lunch at the Dove's Nest, a family favorite. Thelma checked her calendar on her phone and determined she had enough time for lunch before her two o'clock appointment.

"Sure, why not?" Thelma remarked. "Let's celebrate!"

When she got home, Emma called Mandy and Marguerite to tell them they could begin working on the marketing plan and asked them how much of a deposit they needed to get started. They told her they would drop a contract by her house on Friday, pick up the check, and bring Madeleine to meet Emma so the two of them could set up a schedule to begin working on the social media campaign. When Matt got back into town, he would stop by to meet her too and start going over what she wanted to see on the website.

Next, she called Jesse and got his voicemail.

"Jesse, this is Emma. Our business loan got funded this morning, and we are ready to rock and roll on the quilt retreat schoolhouse. Please give me a call at your convenience or text me when you want to get started. Bye!"

She set her phone down and poured herself a big glass of lemonade. She was heading toward the back porch with Sophie in tow when her phone rang. She answered right away when she saw it was Jesse's number.

"Congratulations!" he blurted before she could even say hello.

"Thank you, Jesse. It's taken a while, but we're finally on our way."

"These things do take time. As soon as we get the building permits, you're going to want to start wearing earphones to block out the noise we're going to make."

"Ha!" she laughed into the phone. "It'll be happy noise."

"How do you figure that?"

"It'll be the sounds of dreams coming true."

"Hey, I just finished work. I think this calls for a little celebration. Tom and I are meeting at the Cork House Winery on East Main. Can you join us?"

"Uh, I don't want to intrude."

"You wouldn't be intruding. I'm inviting you. Tom and I can get to know you a little better. I'm sure there's more to you than baking the best cookies in Waxahachie. And you can get to know me, even though I'm sure you're gonna get real tired of seeing my mug every day."

"I doubt that. Well, okay. I can be there in twenty minutes or so."

"Great, we'll grab a table and see you then."

When Emma entered the Cork House Winery, she looked around and saw Jesse and Tom at a back table, waving their arms. Upon reaching the table, Jesse pulled out a chair for her. She sat down and saw a bucket of champagne chilling and three champagne glasses.

"You didn't have to order champagne," she chided them.

"We weren't going to order milk. This calls for a real celebration," Tom remarked.

Emma let out a guffaw. "I doubt they have milk in this place."

"You're probably right." Jesse picked up the bottle and carefully filled their glasses. He raised his glass, as did Tom.

"To Emma and the Yellow House Quilting Retreat, the next best quilters' Shangri-la in the Lonestar State!"

Emma could feel her cheeks blushing as she clicked glasses with the brothers and took a sip of her champagne. She had no sooner put her glass down than a waitress brought a charcuterie board. Emma raised her brows.

"Dinner too?"

"Nothing but the best for our new employer," Jesse declared.

Although Emma hadn't planned to stay more than a half hour, she ended up staying much longer, getting to know the brothers. She found them smart, funny, and full of entertaining stories. They asked her lots of questions about her life, which she kept brushing off because she didn't want to get into her past.

Finally, she let out a long sigh. "I really don't have much to tell you because I'm not nearly as interesting as the two of you. I used to be married and was living in Georgia. A few years after my husband died, I moved back home to Texas. I like to quilt, work in the garden, bake, read, and play with our house cat, Sophie. As you know, I have a daughter as well as two sisters and a brother. Plus a niece. Like I said, not a very interesting life."

"Are you happy?" Jesse asked, which took her by surprise.

"Jesse," Tom interjected, raising his eyebrows, "isn't that kind of personal?"

"I'm curious," Jesse answered, looking straight at Emma.

She smiled before responding. "I suppose so. I've never really thought about it. I'm probably as happy as most people."

Unknowingly, she'd opened a Pandora's Box discussion on the definition of happiness and whether anyone other than a child is ever truly happy. Around nine o'clock, she began stifling a yawn and apologized. "I'm sorry. With all the excitement of today, I guess I'm a bit tired. I should be getting home." She stood up to leave. "Thank you so much for the celebration. This was fun."

"Where are you parked?" Jesse asked.

"Not far, just in the next block."

"Hold up, we'll walk you to your car."

"That's not necessary."

"Yes, it is. It's what gentlemen do."

Emma stared at them, her mouth hanging slightly open. *How chivalrous of them,* she thought. And sweet.

"Well then, gentlemen, let's go."

Chapter Seven

"Hey, Keith," Emma said when her brother answered his phone.

"Hi, Emma, what can I do ya?"

"Did you hear that the quilting retreat business loan came through?"

"Yeah, I did. Congratulations!"

"The workmen are coming in a couple of days, and I need to move everything out of the shed because the first thing they're going to do is tear it down."

"They're going to tear down that ancient, decrepit shed that should have fallen down on its own decades ago? It's practically a historical landmark."

"Ha! You're right, but it's gotta go 'cuz that's where the new schoolhouse will be built."

"A much better use of that patch of dirt. I approve," he said.

"I was wondering if you have any free time today to stop by and help me move all the tools in the shed into the basement. There's a lawnmower in there too, that I can't lift."

"Happy to help. I've got a meeting with the board of directors of the textile mill at one o'clock. I could stop by after, say, midafternoon?"

"Perfect. Thanks, Keith."

By the time Keith arrived, Emma had pulled out all the gardening tools and leaned them against the side of the shed.

When Keith saw the tools, he whistled. "I didn't realize there were so many tools in there. Some of these are honest-to-goodness antique relics. Do you still use them?"

Emma nodded. "Yeah, I do. I figure if they're not broke, keep 'em."

"Ya know, if you clean 'em up, you could probably get a small fortune for them on eBay."

"And then turn around and spend a small fortune to buy new ones?"

"Good point," Keith grinned.

Emma unlocked the outside access door to the basement and turned on the inside light. Keith first moved the lawnmower, a string trimmer, and a leaf blower into the basement, then he began moving the heavier tools. When he finished, Emma carried in the smaller hand tools and laid them on shelving someone had built long ago. She found a broom and took it out to the shed, where she began sweeping out the accumulated dirt.

"Emma, why are you sweeping out a shed that's about to be demolished?" Keith asked, looking at her like she was missing a couple of cerebral marbles.

"I know it's being torn down, brother. I just don't want the workmen to think I keep a messy house or, rather, shed. It would reflect poorly on me, and they may get the impression that they can do a half-way messy job and I won't notice."

"Isn't there a contractor who will be supervising their work and inspectors who will be signing off on each aspect of the project as it's finished?"

"Well, yes."

"Then don't worry about it. That's the contractor's and inspector's jobs to make sure each step is done to the highest standard. You really don't need to sweep out the shed. There's probably a century of dirt embedded in the floor."

"Okay, then I'll leave it be." She returned the broom to the basement and locked the door. "Thanks, Keith. Can I offer you a glass of lemonade before you leave?"

"Is it your 'special' lemonade?"

"Do I make any other kind?" she grinned at him.

"Then yes, I'll take a glass. Do you have any of your cookies to go along with it?"

"Have you ever come to this house and not found cookies in Grandma's big ol' cookie jar?"

"You know you should open a cookie bakery, don't you?"

"I'm focused on opening a quilting retreat, Keith. Maybe when it's a huge success, I'll think about a cookie bakery."

Jesse and a demolition crew showed up at 7:00 a.m. two days later. By 7:15, they had started tearing down the shed and hacking away at the downstairs bathroom. It took three strong burly men with biceps the size of Emma's thighs to carry out the bathtub. Even though they were strong, they were covered in sweat, glistening like they'd rubbed oil over themselves. Two men returned to the bathroom to remove and carry out the old toilet, sink, and cabinets. Emma came out and watched them set everything on the front curb.

She turned to Jesse standing next to her. "What's going to happen to all of that?" she asked, pointing to the pile on the curb.

Without missing a beat or looking at her, he said, "I thought I'd leave the tub and toilet here for you to plant flowers in."

"What?!"

Jesse burst out laughing, turned, and looked at her. "Are you always so gullible?"

Emma frowned. "Maybe. I assume that people aren't trying to pull one over on me."

"Emma, I was joshing you. It's all still in good condition, so I thought I'd donate it to the Habitat for Humanity ReStore. They'll pick it up this afternoon—that is, unless you *do* want to plant flowers in the tub and toilet."

Emma smirked. "No, I don't want to plant anything in it. If the ReStore can sell all this stuff and make a profit to fund their homes, all the better. That was a good call."

"It's something I do on all the remodeling jobs. If there's something salvageable, I always contact them. Not only does it go to a good cause; it saves me from having to take the stuff to the dump."

Over the next two days, the crew completely demolished the shed and the bathroom. Emma watched with interest; she'd never seen a demo of this scale before. Jesse sidled up to her.

"The crew is wondering if you're going to be supervising every step."

"No, is that a problem?"

"Naw. We've had some homeowners stop the workers at each step to make them explain what they're doing and why. That adds on a lot of unanticipated time to the job. Other homeowners want to help with the demo, which we don't allow because my insurance only covers my guys. Your standing and watching without getting in the way is fine."

"I was thinking it looks like fun to smash everything."

"It is. You ever watch any of those home remodeling shows on TV?"

"Of course! It's like living vicariously."

"That reminds me, I brought a bunch of tile samples to show you for both the floor and the shower walls. Plus some brochures on the new lights, cabinets, sink, and toilet. You got a minute to follow me to my truck?"

Emma nodded and followed him outside. First, he took out the tile samples and lined them up on the tailgate. Below the tiles, he laid out the brochures. Emma bent over and picked up the tile samples to get a closer look. She set one aside, then began examining the brochures.

"I love this tile," she said, picking up the one she had set aside, "so that was easy. Picking out everything else isn't so simple. How do you do it with so many choices?"

"Think about the style of the house, which in your case is nineteenth-century Victorian. You wouldn't want to detract from that. Pick out vintage styles that will complement what's already here."

"You mean, mid-century modern isn't going to cut it?" she said, trying hard to keep from laughing.

"Uh, no."

For fifteen minutes, they looked over the brochures, and with Jesse's help, she picked out the rest of what would be needed in the bathroom. Fortunately, Jesse had provided several vintage-looking options in each category, which made choosing a lot easier. She laughed when she saw Tahitian tiki lights and ultramodern steel fixtures that looked better suited to the International Space Station. She decided to have a little fun with him.

"I think I've changed my mind. I'm leaning toward these—what do you think?" she said, keeping a straight face while pointing to the tiki lights and modern steel fixtures.

"I'm thinking I won't let you do it."

"Then why did you include these brochures?" she asked innocently, blinking repeatedly.

"Okay, you got me," he said, grinning.

She laughed and asked, "Can you imagine someone remodeling a bathroom with these fixtures?"

"You'd be surprised. I've actually installed these on a job. That's why I had the brochures."

"Did the tiki lights go in a Polynesian-style home?"

Jesse shook his head. "Actually, they went in an outside bathroom next to the backyard pool."

"And the horrible modern steel fixtures? Who would want those in their home?"

"Actually, no one. I installed them in the employee bathrooms in a factory."

Emma nodded. "Makes sense. Ya know, all this decision-making has made me thirsty. You up for some iced tea? I made it this morning."

"Is it sweet tea?"

"Is there any other way to drink iced tea?"

"Lead the way," he said, extending his hand forward.

After lunch, while the crew was outside removing the wood and foundation they had torn down from the shed, the doorbell rang. Emma opened the door to Madeleine, Mandy's social media managing daughter. Short and extremely thin, Madeleine sported shoulder-length purple hair, black-painted nails, and rose vine tattoos running up her arms.

"Hi, Madeleine. Glad you're here. I can't wait to get started."

"Hi, Mrs. Jenkins. What's all the noise?"

"It's a demo day. The work crew is demolishing the backyard shed where the schoolhouse will be built, as well as the first-floor bathroom that will be remodeled."

"Is there anywhere in the house that's quiet so we don't have to yell at each other to be heard?"

"The best place is probably the third-floor front bedroom. It's as far as we can get from the demo work."

"Does that bedroom have an Internet connection or Wi-Fi?"

"Yep, and a very large desk where we can spread out. My laptop is all set up and ready to go."

"I'll set up mine next to yours. We'll build your social media pages together, but we won't launch them until the advertising campaign begins. My mom told me it'll begin about three months before the grand opening. Is that right?"

"Yep."

Madeleine showed Emma the various types of social media pages, from commercial to personal, in addition to the types of posts that would get a lot of hits.

"See how many followers this quilter has?" she asked, pointing to the follower count.

"Is that number right?" Emma asked. "Does Penelope the Patchwork Quilter really have 8,000 followers?"

Madeleine nodded. "And here's why." She scrolled through her Facebook page, pointing to all the photos and videos it displayed. "This lady has built up an audience by posting photos and videos that her followers find helpful. It used to be that posting copy was enough, but not anymore. Quilters in particular want to see photos and want to be educated. It's not worth their time to scroll through posts that don't offer them something worthwhile."

"Madeleine, are you a quilter?"

"No, Mrs. Jenkins."

"Then how do you know what quilters want, and how did you find Penelope's successful Facebook page?"

She grinned proudly. "When Mom told me about your new quilting retreat center and that social media was included in the marketing plan—which is really smart, by the way—I knew I needed to educate myself real fast."

"You are one bright and industrious young woman, Madeleine! Thanks for doing the legwork. That's less I have to teach you, unless you actually want to learn to quilt."

"Maybe I'll take you up on that someday. Right now, I have enough going on. Okay, let's go look at other social media platforms so you get the gist of what's out there."

"Do I need to use all of them?"

"No, some quilters do just one, others do two, even three. Everyone has different preferences. The most popular ones are Facebook, Instagram, Pinterest, TikTok, and YouTube. Over time, that may change. New ones will emerge, and others not frequented right now may become more popular in the future."

"How will I know when trends change? How will I keep up with it all?"

"It's not as hard as you'd think. There're a lot of blogs and websites with newsletters you can subscribe to on what's new and what's changing. When you're done learning the ropes on setting up your pages, I'll send you a list of the best sites worth subscribing to, okay?"

"Got it. And thank you, Madeleine."

"Oh, and one more thing to consider is starting a blog, which can be hosted on the website my cousin Matt will create for you."

"Is a blog necessary?" Emma was starting to feel a little overwhelmed and wondering where she would find the time to do it all.

"In my mind, yes. You don't have to do it, but it's a tool that can help you grow your business. It would be a shame to miss those opportunities."

They worked together until late afternoon, when Madeleine looked at Emma and recognized social media overload.

"You're getting tired, aren't you?" she asked.

"It's okay, we can keep going," Emma responded.

"Actually, it's not. Learning all this can be daunting. When you get to the point of saturation, it does no good to keep going 'cuz your brain is at capacity and won't take in any more information."

"Really? I thought you could teach me everything today."

"Nice thought, Mrs. Jenkins, but no. Let's get back together in two or three days. That'll give you a few days to digest what you've learned so far as well as give you time to research quilting and other retreat websites you like. When we get together next time, you'll be fresh and ready to learn how to put a social media campaign together."

Emma acquiesced because she could feel she had reached her max for the day. She was so tired, she wasn't sure how much she would remember the next day. Plus, it was plainly obvious that Madeleine knew what she was talking about. Why ignore her suggestions when it was part of what she was paying M&M for?

After Madeleine left, Emma went downstairs, poured herself a large glass of lemonade, and headed for the porch. Jesse and one of his workers were hauling off the last boards from the demolished shed when he saw her sitting on the back porch. After Jesse and his workers loaded the boards into the back of his pickup truck, Jesse waved the workers goodbye and walked back around to the porch.

"Whatcha drinkin'?"

"Lemonade."

"You got any more? I'm parched."

Emma giggled. "You're 'parched'? That sounds like something a refined Southern lady would say."

"Okay, I'm *thirsty*. Can I have a glass of lemonade? Please?"

"Coming right up. You just sit your behind on this porch."

He did as told, and in moments Emma returned with a big glass of lemonade with ice. He barely waited for her to sit before he gulped down a third of the glass.

"Wow, you really were thirsty. Don't you bring water to the jobsite?"

"Yeah. I ran out an hour ago."

"You could have filled up at the kitchen sink."

"I know, but I didn't want to stop what I was doing. By the way, what's in this lemonade?"

"What do you mean?"

"There's something different in here," he said, looking down into the glass.

She shrugged her shoulders. "It's just lemonade," she managed to say without giving up her secret.

He gulped down the rest of the glass and laid his head back. "I think you're fibbin', but I don't care 'cuz that's the best lemonade I've ever had."

"You look like you're about to fall asleep."

"Today and yesterday were hard. Demo is always physically demanding, but the worst is over now. Tomorrow, we pour the foundation, and when it's thoroughly dry, we start framing the schoolhouse."

Jesse barely finished his sentence before he closed his eyes and quickly fell asleep as fast as a newborn. Emma didn't know whether to be amused or sorry he had worked so hard that he had fallen asleep on her porch. When he began softly snoring, she got up and went into the house, and unbeknownst to her, Sophie slipped out onto the porch. Sophie looked up at the stranger sleeping in her favorite chair. She tried rubbing herself on his legs to wake him up; he didn't stir. Then, she reached up and pawed his knees. No response. Finally, she jumped up and kneaded his belly like a batch of dough, and when that didn't work, she curled up in his lap, soon softly snoring herself.

Two hours later, Jesse woke up, Sophie still on his lap with darkness quickly approaching. He stood up and carried Sophie into the house, following an aroma he figured was probably coming from the kitchen. He found Emma stirring a pot of something. He ran a hand through his disheveled hair.

"Emma, I am so sorry."

She looked up. "For what?"

"I don't usually make a habit of falling asleep on my clients' porches."

"No biggie," she said, flipping her hand like she was shooing away a fly. "Obviously, you were really tired. You hungry?"

"Yeah, but I need to get home and clean up and prep for tomorrow."

"You have to eat, don't you?"

"I'll pick up a burger on the way."

"You'd rather eat a burger that's been sitting under a warming light in a fast-food restaurant than have a bowl of my gumbo?"

"No, no. I've been enough of a bother."

"Why? Because you and my cat napped together on the porch? You two were really cute, by the way." She couldn't suppress a grin.

"I should go."

"No, you should sit. Here." She handed him a bowl of gumbo she ladled out of the pot and pushed a plate of cornbread toward him. "Take a serving of cornbread and sit. Please."

He was too tired to argue. He sat down at the kitchen table and waited for her to join him. As soon as she did, he dove into the gumbo. "Where did you learn to make gumbo like this? I haven't had gumbo this good since my last trip to New Orleans."

"That's quite a compliment. It's an old family recipe. The story that has been passed down is that a housekeeper sometime in the nineteenth century used to make it for the Clayburne family. She lived to an old age, 90-something, I think. When she was no longer physically able to work, she made it one last time, allowing one of the women in the family to write down the ingredients, quantities, and instructions while she watched the housekeeper make it. That was the only time the family got one of her recipes because the woman couldn't read or write, so none of them were written down. All her recipes were in her head. Anyway, she was so elderly and so tired, that apparently she died in her sleep that very night. As the story goes, the family felt that once she'd given them her pride and joy recipe, she could finally pass on, knowing the family would forever be well fed."

"True story?"

"True as I'm standing here."

"Do you know the housekeeper's name?"

"I think it was Neelie ... no, it was Nellie. Why do you ask?"

"Because I'm going to call it 'Nellie's Gumbo.' Seems fitting."

"I agree. I think she would like that."

Early the next morning, Emma heard the workers in the backyard. She put on her robe and slippers and peered out the back window of the sitting room that overlooked it. Jesse was standing there, talking with someone who appeared to be the concrete subcontractor. A crew was sectioning off the area where the concrete would be poured for the foundation. She could see they were laying boards framing a wood box. She was fascinated; she'd never seen a concrete operation before. She decided to take a shower and get dressed, as it looked like nothing much would be happening for a while.

When she returned to the sitting room, she saw they'd brought in a revolving drum mixer churning the concrete. Several men were standing around the wood box frame with what looked like rakes. All of a sudden, it was go time. The subcontractor pushed the drum mixer mouth toward the frame, and tilted it causing the concrete to flow into the box. The men with the rakes quickly smoothed it out. The subcontractor was using a laser level, and he directed the men to smooth and further level certain areas that weren't perfect. Finally, everyone stepped back, apparently satisfied that the foundation was done. Emma flew down the stairs and out the porch to the backyard.

"Hey, Emma," Jesse said. "You missed seeing the concrete being poured. There's no going back now."

"I didn't miss anything, Jesse. I watched the whole process from the sitting-room window," she said, pointing upstairs.

"You could have come down here and had a front-row seat."

"I didn't want to get in anyone's way," she said. "I had a great view from up there."

"What did you think?"

"Riding a roller coaster is a bit more exhilarating. However, knowing this is the first step to building the quilting retreat, it was thrilling. How long does it have to set until you can start framing the building?"

"Kinda depends on the weather. If it doesn't rain, and it doesn't get over 80°—neither of which is forecast to happen—it should be as dry as a piece of petrified wood and able to support the weight of construction in a week. Just to be on the safe side, we applied acrylic concrete cure and seal to help it dry faster. Right now, everything is going according to plan, and we should be able to start framing in seven days. The subcontractor will come out then and check it. If he deems it dry enough for framing, we'll get started, and by next week, you should be able to see the schoolhouse skeleton."

"Oh, Jesse, this really is exciting! I'm going to bake cookies for your whole crew."

"What kind?"

"Does it matter?"

"Good point. Nope."

Chapter Eight

Over the following weeks and months, Emma watched the Yellow House Quilting Retreat come to life. Feeling like she was treading water while waiting for the schoolhouse to be completed, she decided that it probably wasn't too early to decide which quilts would be taught, who would teach them, and tentative dates for posting on social media and the website.

She needed to hunker down with Savannah Mae and Stella to discuss options. They couldn't waste any more time making those decisions.

She invited Stella and Savannah Mae to come for cookies and coffee for the planning session. The three women sat down at the table in Emma's kitchen to figure it out.

"I do have a few ideas," Emma began. "Here's what I'm thinking: For the first retreat, I'm kinda torn between several different patterns. Let's shelve it for now. For the second retreat, they could learn the Double Wedding Ring quilt, like the one you made from my wedding dress," she said, pointing to Savannah Mae. "Ever since you won Best of Show at the International Quilt Festival in Houston, people have been asking me how you made it.

Students can bring their own wedding dress or buy a used one at a thrift shop."

"That's not a bad idea," Savannah Mae remarked. "They'd need to take the dresses apart before the retreat because that step is quite time-consuming. If they do that before the retreat, the learning will go much faster."

Emma looked at Stella and back at Savannah Mae. "For the third retreat, I'd like to suggest that Stella teach the Spiral Lone Star pattern by Jan Krentz."

"Y'all liked my quilt?" Stella asked.

"It's spectacular," Savannah Mae said. "And I can't think of anyone better to teach it.

With those decisions made that would be executed when they were ready to launch their online presence, Emma felt a little more relaxed. Sometimes, she sat on the porch, keenly watching every step of the construction, while other times, she observed from the upstairs sitting room. Occasionally, she stood in the hallway next to the downstairs bath, watching it slowly being transformed into an ADA-compliant bath. She was careful not to bother the men working in the bathroom and didn't ask questions unless Jesse was around to answer them. The workmen became used to her and would always nod to acknowledge her presence. She appreciated that. Emma just happened to be watching when a plumber began sawing into a wall. All of a sudden, he cut right through a waterline. Water gushed everywhere, flooding not only the bathroom but also the hallway, and moving quickly toward the front of the house. Emma yelped and dialed Jesse immediately.

"Hey, Emma, what's up?"

"Are you in the schoolhouse?"

"Yep. What's up?"

"Can you come up to the bathroom right away? We've got a flood on our hands, and it's bad."

Jesse hung up and began limping as fast as he could to the first floor, where he saw water everywhere. He looked at the plumber. "What the hell happened?"

"I'm sorry, boss. I used a reciprocating saw instead of a handsaw to cut into the wall, looking for the waterline. Dumb mistake."

"No kidding, that's an apprentice mistake. What a mess!"

"I'll get it cleaned up."

Emma stepped forward, holding her temper as best she could. "I urge you to get it done as soon as possible. These wood floors are 150 years old, and if they get damaged, they're irreplaceable."

The plumber looked at Jesse, who said, "You heard the lady. Get crackin'!"

Jesse escorted Emma away from the flooding. He could see she was upset. "Emma, I'm so sorry."

"Not as sorry as I am. I really don't want to have to sue the pants off him, but I will if he ruins these floors!"

"Technically, you'd have to sue me."

"I'm not going to sue you, Jesse. But what kind of plumber makes the dumb mistake of using a power saw instead of a handsaw to cut into a wall that you know has a waterline? Even I know that, and I'm not a plumber!"

"Can you go upstairs and work on your social media stuff or something? I'll take the guys off the outside build, and we'll get this cleaned up. Oh, and you might pour yourself a big glass of that rum-spiked lemonade to help settle you down."

"You knew?"

"Of course I knew it wasn't regular lemonade. You're not a very good fibber."

Feeling a bit chagrined at being found out, she headed toward the kitchen and poured lemonade into the biggest glass she could find. Meanwhile, Jesse called the crew at the schoolhouse and told them to come inside and help clean up the plumber's mess. Emma retreated upstairs to calm down and stay out of their way. At first, she stewed for a bit, then decided that looking over the plans for the social media launch would be a good way to get her mind off the downstairs. The plans looked tight and ready to launch, so she looked at the full mock-up of the website that Matt had designed. It, too, was in perfect shape. She especially liked the page Matt had created where people could register and prepay for the retreats. Initially, she'd thought she'd have to do everything by phone, but after Matt showed her how easy it would be to do it on the website and how the prepayment would go directly through to the retreat's bank account, she decided he was the smartest 25-year-old she'd ever met.

Not having much else to do, Emma headed up to the attic. She'd seen what she thought was a quilt in a large box and wanted to get a closer look at it. She was right, it was a quilt—and an old one. She brought it downstairs and spread it out on a large table in the quilting room. It was a Grandmother's Fan quilt. She texted Savannah Mae, asking her if she could stop by the next day to see something she'd found. Just as she hit "send," she heard a knock on the doorjamb and looked up to see Jesse standing there.

"It's all cleaned up."

"That was fast."

"We have an industrial vacuum made especially for cleaning up messes like that. We also have a fan dryer that dries the floor. Do you want to come see the floor?"

She nodded and followed him downstairs. He was right, it was thoroughly cleaned up; only the fan dryer remained, which Jesse said he would leave running overnight to continue drying whatever moisture was left in the wood floors.

"Again, I'm really sorry about all this."

Emma glanced at him and back at the floor. He knew she was upset, and she figured there was nothing more to say.

"Emma, this is the first problem I've had with him. He's very experienced. It was just a stupid mistake, and he feels terrible about it, especially after you told him that these floors are 150 years old and irreplaceable."

"I wasn't making that up. They are irreplaceable."

"Emma, we all make mistakes from time to time, especially in this business. Can you let it go?"

"I can if you'll supervise him more closely."

"Deal. To set things right with you, let me take you to dinner."

"Why?"

"Why not? I need to get back on your good side."

"You're not on my bad side, Jesse. The plumber is."

"Yeah, but I hired him, so I'm partly to blame. Dinner?"

"Okay. Where are you taking me?"

"It's a surprise."

"That's ridiculous. Why a surprise?"

"Grab your purse. You'll see."

After a short drive, they arrived at an old building, the former County Bank building. As they stepped inside Prime 115, an upscale steakhouse, her face lit up like sunrays on a snowbank. "I thought you'd be taking me out for a burger or chicken-fried steak, not one of the best restaurants in town."

"After today's debacle, you deserve a whole lot better than chicken-fried steak."

Emma looked at the menu and felt her mouth start to water. As she was reading, a waiter set down a plate of bruschetta, grilled sourdough slices topped with marinated tomatoes, capers, and balsamic vinegar. "Compliments of the house," he said. "May I get you a glass of wine?"

"Emma, do you like Cabernet Sauvignon?"

"I do."

Jesse turned to the waiter. "We'll have a bottle of your best California Cab."

"Very good, sir. I'll bring that right away."

After he left, Emma couldn't get over the menu. "So many great choices. I can't decide."

"Would you mind if I order? We could share a steak."

"Sure."

When the waiter returned, he opened the bottle of Cab and poured their glasses. Jesse ordered the Delmonico rib eye steak and a side of asparagus.

"Did you just order the eighteen-ounce steak?" she asked after the waiter left. "I hope you're really, really hungry 'cuz there's no way I can eat half that steak."

"If you can't, you can take the rest home and put it in your next batch of cookies," he said without cracking a smile.

"Blech!" she said, laughing. "That's pretty gross."

"Haven't you ever had steak cookies?"

She was still laughing when she answered. "No, and I don't plan to anytime soon. I'll put it in a salad or shepherd's pie or enchiladas or something, just not cookies."

"You are certainly an enigma, Emma."

"I could say the same about you."

"Me? I'm pretty transparent."

"Not really, Jesse. Other than your business and Tom, I don't know much about you."

"What do you want to know?"

"Are you from Texas?"

"Born and raised. I'm a fourth-generation Texan."

"Where?"

"Waco."

"Is that where you went to college?"

"Yep, Baylor."

"How long have you lived in Waxahachie?"

"After I completed my military service, I wanted a change of venue. I knew that Travis lived in the area, so thought I'd give it a try."

"How did you injure your leg?"

"I told you, war injury."

"I got that. How?"

"Tonight's not the time to talk about it because you gotta trust me when I say it would spoil our evening."

"Will you tell me another time?"

"Why do you want to know?

Emma looked down and bit her lower lip before speaking. "Because wouldn't you agree that you and I are becoming pretty good friends, over and above our working relationship?"

"Yeah. It's been great. Hopefully, we can stay friends after the job is done. I'd like that."

Emma nodded. "I would too. The reason that I want to know what happened to you in Afghanistan is not because I'm nosy; it's because good friends share stuff like this. It helps create a reciprocal relationship, not in a romantic way, but in the way that friends know a lot about the people they are close to. So they can support and be there for one another. Am I making sense?"

"Of course you are, and I agree with you, except, as I said, now is not the time to have that discussion."

"Okay," she agreed, hoping he wouldn't forget. She sensed that whatever had happened to him during the war had affected him in ways she couldn't imagine. It didn't matter that she didn't know him before the war. She knew him now. War had a way of doing that. No one who ever went to war ever stayed the same, and she figured it was the same with Jesse. Without knowing what happened to him, she felt there was a chasm between them, and unless it was bridged, she could never really know him.

"One last question?" she asked.

Jesse nodded, cautiously.

"If at all possible, can you tell when the construction will be done?"

"Not so easy."

"I'm asking because the marketing group I'm working with plans to launch the website, social media campaign, and advertising three months before we open."

"I'd say call them right away. We're probably two months out from completion."

The next day, Emma called M&M Marketing and shared the good news that the construction would be finished in two months, and with all the prep work they'd need to do after that, they would be able to open in about three months. Emma made appointments with Madeleine and Matt to come to the house in a couple of days to help her launch the retreat's online presence and set up a schedule for social media posts that would launch automatically.

Later that day, Savannah Mae dropped by, first stopping in the backyard to see the progress on the schoolhouse. Jesse walked up to her.

"Whaddaya think?"

"Amazing, Jesse, absolutely amazing," she said, scanning the construction site. "The retreat students will think they went up in a hot-air balloon and were dropped in Oz."

Jesse suppressed a smile. "Do you want to go inside the building and meet the craftsmen who are working on the interior?"

Savannah Mae nodded. "In a bit. I need to talk to my mother first. Have you seen her?"

"I think she's in the house. She might be watching from the sitting room or in her office working on social media stuff."

"Thanks, I'll find her."

Savannah Mae found Emma in the sewing room, the vintage Grandmother's Fan quilt laid out on the table.

"Wow! This is the quilt you found in the attic?" Savannah Mae asked, fingering the fabric. "It's in amazing condition." She turned it over and discovered small brown spots embedded in the fabric. "I wonder what all these brown spots are."

"Hard to say. Other than the spots, it's in great condition," Emma agreed. "I think it's pretty old. Funny thing is, I found it in the attic in a box with a lot of very old medical supplies. I brought it downstairs," she said, turning to lift an old wooden box onto another table.

Savannah Mae opened it and began gently removing various items, including an 1882 newspaper with a front-page article about a massive fire that had occurred in Waxahachie. She read the article out loud, and they discovered that there had been not one but two fires in May that year. It described buildings that had burned, listed the names of some of the firefighters, and included a sketch featuring a man sitting in a rocking chair at a home serving as an aid station, a quilt laid over him. Under the newspaper, they found a loose photo of the same man in the rocking chair with the quilt. Emma stared at it.

"Savannah Mae, look at the quilt design and the chair the man is sitting in. I think that's the rocking chair in the parlor. *Our* parlor. And that quilt is this quilt right here," she said, pointing to the Grandmother's Fan quilt on the table.

Savannah Mae took a closer look, glancing back and forth from the photo to the newspaper sketch to the quilt on the table. "I think you're right." She tried to read the man's name under the newspaper sketch, but it was smudged.

"Savannah Mae, let's take this newspaper over to Sandy at the museum. Maybe they have copies of the old newspapers that could tell us who this man is. While I know the pattern is called 'Grandmother's Fan,' I think we should rename it 'the mercy quilt.'"

"Why?"

Emma pointed to the photo. "This quilt obviously served as a healing quilt during those devastating fires. It brought comfort to people who were injured, most notably the man in the photo." She pointed to the quilt lying on the table. "I'm pretty sure this quilt is part of our family history."

"Who's Sandy?" Savannah Mae asked.

"I met her awhile back at the museum. She knows everything about the history of Waxahachie. Before we leave, let me show you the Spiral Lone Star that Stella made."

Emma went to a shelf and took down a large quilt that she spread out over the table. Savannah Mae bent down and looked closely at the flawless piecing and extraordinarily tiny quilting stitches.

"I have seen plenty of Lone Star quilts because they're so popular here in Texas. But I've never seen one like this, Mama. This quilt is amazing. The spiral adds an intriguing element."

"I thought so too. And it's going to be a challenge for anyone who isn't an advanced or at least an intermediate quilter."

"All the more reason for us to offer it in a retreat. If the students are willing to pay what we're going to charge them, they should be offered the chance to make something extraordinary, a project they might not undertake on their own. I mean, we are a Texas quilting retreat, are we not?"

After they folded and put the mercy quilt into a large plastic bag, the two women drove over to the museum to show it and the newspaper to Sandy. She directed them to the microfiche, where they found a copy of the newspaper and the page with the sketch of the man and the quilt covering him. Underneath the sketch was printed "James Clayburne receiving aid for burns sustained during the fire on May 18, 1882."

Emma and Savannah Mae exchanged glances.

"That's my great-great-grandfather, Savannah Mae. Your great-great-great-grandfather!" Emma exclaimed. "He was married to Lillian."

"The woman on the wall of old photos? The source of our brilliant red hair?"

Emma nodded. "That's the one!"

"Wow! Ya know, there's one more thing we need to find out." She turned the quilt over to look at the brown spots. "I'm thinking that these spots could be 140-year-old dried blood. He was burned, right?"

Emma nodded. "Makes sense. Wish we could find out for sure."

"Maybe we can. I'm gonna look around for a quilt appraiser. Someone who regularly evaluates vintage quilts might be able to advise us if it's blood or something else."

"And the appraiser might be able to determine the year it was made," Emma added. "Obviously, the quilt was sewn before the fire. I wonder if Lillian made it. I've got a hunch that she did."

"And I've got a hunch that you're right," Savannah Mae agreed.

"Sweetheart, if you can find an appraiser, I'll take it to be done. Hmm, I have an idea. Remember that we tabled deciding on which pattern to teach for the first quilt retreat?"

Savannah Mae nodded and looked down at the quilt. "Let me guess—the mercy quilt?"

"Yep, and just think how we'll be able to tell the students about our family's connection to this particular quilt."

"I'm lovin' this, Mama!"

As the construction dragged on, it felt like an eternity had passed. Emma wondered whether something was holding up the completion of the schoolhouse. She wanted to ask, but she didn't dare. She was diligently practicing patience, or at least trying to. She also remembered Jesse telling her that each major phase of the construction had to be signed off by an inspector. He told her that sometimes they took their fine time getting to the worksite. *That had to be it,* she told herself. The inspections were holding up everything. She wondered whom she could call to get the inspector to move it along. Then, she reminded herself that she was trying to practice patience and she needed to back off.

A couple of weeks later, Jesse sought her out to let her know that they'd be finished by week's end. It had been ten months since the loan was funded and the construction began. She could barely contain herself. She felt as giddy as a little girl ready to open her birthday presents. She gave Jesse a bear hug. "Let's go, show me everything."

"No can do," he said, his arms crossed over his chest.

Emma furrowed her brow. "I don't understand. Why not?"

"Because that'll spoil the surprise."

"What surprise?"

"Now it wouldn't be a surprise if I told you, would it?"

"No, but that's not fair. I didn't know there was going to be a surprise."

"Well, you know now. Do you promise not to go in there until we're completely finished and I give you a proper tour?"

She pursed her lips. "I suppose."

"You suppose?"

"I really want to see it."

"Tell ya what, you can see the bathroom by the first-floor bedroom. It's finished."

"Including the hole in the wall? After that fiasco, I'm not sure I ever want to look at that bathroom again."

"It's fully repaired. You can't tell what happened in there. And it came out really nice. You liked the plans, you even picked out the tile."

"Yeah, but it's a bathroom with a bad memory. I've been chomping at the bit to see the inside of the schoolhouse."

"Like I said, you can't go in there right now."

Three days later, the crew packed up and left the premises. Jesse walked through the house, calling for Emma. He found her in the sewing room, bent over her sewing machine, working on a quilt.

"Can you take a break? We're done, and I want to give you your long-awaited tour."

She didn't look up, only shot up her index finger. "Give me one minute to finish this, and I'll be right with you."

Now, he was utterly confused. A few days before, she had been dying to see the schoolhouse, and now she had to finish sewing something before she would go see it? She finished the last stitch, rolled the piece up, stood, and held it behind her back.

"Close your eyes and put out your hands, palms up."

Jesse let out an annoyed puff of air and did as instructed. She placed the piece in his hands.

"You can open your eyes now. Sorry, I didn't have time to wrap it."

He opened his eyes and unrolled a long, quilted wall hanging that featured appliquéd construction tools. Below them, she had embroidered "Jesse: The World's Best Contractor." He turned away, feeling a lump forming in his throat.

She leaned toward him. "Are you okay? Don't you like it?"

Having quickly blinked away the moisture pooling in his eyes, he turned back. "Of course I do. You didn't have to make this. You didn't have to do anything. You're already paying me a lot."

"That's beside the point. I wanted to do something to show my appreciation for all you've done. I think I've baked you every cookie in my recipe box, so I figured I would give you something more permanent, something you could keep. It's a wall hanging. Here, look on the back. Run a dowel or drapery rod through the sleeve and hang it on a wall."

"You didn't need to, Emma."

"Yeah, I did."

"Let's go see your schoolhouse," he replied, his voice soft and restrained. He took her hand, guided her downstairs, and ferried her out to the backyard.

First, they stood in front of the building. She had watched the outside under construction, so although it wasn't a surprise, seeing it complete gave her a feeling of immense satisfaction. She could see her dream coming to fruition. It was an unmistakable Queen Anne–style replica of the big house, right down to the same yellow paint color, same gingerbread trim, bay windows, and a steeply pitched roof below an octagonal tower topped with a round, pointed roof. Emma placed her hands over her heart. "It's perfect," she whispered.

Again, Jesse took one of her hands and led her inside. Her face lit up with unabashed joy, the way a young mother looks the first time her baby smiles at her.

She gasped as she looked around. Wallpaper featuring tiny Singer Featherweight sewing machines covered the walls, and where the walls met the ceiling was crown molding exactly like the basketweave crown molding in the big house's parlor. Along one wall were a dozen large wooden cubbyholes with filigree carved doors for the students to store supplies and personal belongings. She looked straight up and saw a tin ceiling, each square showcasing a floral motif, each painted off-white. The brightness of the ceiling reflected the light coming in through the bay windows, illuminating the entire room. Three crystal chandeliers hung from the ceiling down the middle of the room for when they needed light late in the day or evening. Jesse pointed to the floor that was constructed of blond red oak laid out in a hexagon pattern.

"This floor was custom-made by flooring royalty."

"What do you mean?" she asked, taking a closer look at it, recognizing the popular quilting hexie pattern.

"It was laid down piece by piece by an 85-year-old legendary artisan named Henry Walter Raven. He learned the trade as a teenager and eventually took over his father's shop. People seek him out from all over the country, but at his age, he only takes on local jobs."

"Where's his shop?"

"Out in West Texas in Ranger, a small town near Abilene."

"That's hardly local."

Jesse laughed. "He considers anything within Texas's borders to be local. Henry won't be around much longer. When he passes, the world will be a lesser place, and there won't be anyone to replace him."

"Surely there are others who lay wooden floors, aren't there?"

Jesse shook his head. "Not like him, not his quality or designs or dedication to the craft. He's one of a kind."

"Doesn't he have a family who would take it over?"

"Nope," he replied, shaking his head. "He never married and never had kids, or as he likes to say, any that he knows about." He shot her an amused glance.

"It's extraordinary," Emma remarked, walking around and staring at the floor. "It's a piece of art. He should have signed it."

"He did," Jesse said, pointing to a back corner.

Emma walked over to where he was pointing and saw a small inscription etched into the wood with the name Henry Walter Raven and the date.

"This is all too much. I gotta sit down before I faint."

"Why?" Jesse pinched together his brows.

"This is way, way more than I anticipated." She looked over at him. "I know you went over budget. This is all so much nicer than what was in the original plans."

"Well, maybe I went a little over budget. Don't you like it?"

She swung around toward him. "'Like' isn't the right word. I love it, every inch of it. In fact, I think I'll move my bedroom down here. You outdid yourself!"

"Don't worry about the little touches that went over budget. Consider it my and Tom's gift. We wanted it to be extra special so that your retreat center would be as much of an attraction as the classes."

Suddenly, she felt emotions come rushing out, as though she'd run a race and barely had a breath left in her lungs. "Y'all definitely nailed it. Seriously, I need to sit down and take it all in. Wish there was a chair in here." She glanced around the room, looking for a place to sit, even though she knew there wasn't yet any furniture in the room.

"Coming right up," Jesse announced, walking to the large storage closet. He opened the door and pulled out something heavy covered in a large sheet. He beckoned Emma toward him. She reached down and started to lift up the edge of the sheet. "Not yet," he said, holding up an index finger. "Stand back a foot or so. And turn around."

"Let me guess, another surprise?" she asked.

As soon as she turned her back toward him, he lifted the sheet and tossed it aside. "Okay, you can turn around."

Emma's mouth dropped open when she saw a wingback chair upholstered with a Hunter's Star quilt block pattern in her favorite combination of colors: blues, greens, and teals, studded with white accents. She started to speak; nothing came out. Jesse walked over and led her to the chair. He pointed to a small label sewn on the top of the back. It was embroidered with Emma's name. She looked at Jesse; he asked her to sit. She melted into the seat as tears began to slip down her face faster than she could wipe them away.

"Jesse, this is way more than I envisioned. First, you created a room greater than I ever could have imagined, and now this lovely chair? How did you know that I've wanted one of these quilt-upholstered chairs for years?"

"A little cardinal told me," he said, looking away, his hands in his pockets.

"Where did you get it?"

"I didn't exactly 'get' it."

"Oh, come on! Tell me."

He rubbed the back of his neck, stalling for time. Finally, he said, "I told Savannah Mae that I wanted to give you something extra special as a thank-you gift, and I asked her what you might like. She said that you'd been wanting a chair like this. At first, I had no idea what she was talking about until she pulled up some photos online. I visited some antiques stores and found the quilt in one shop and the chair in another. Savannah Mae tracked down an upholsterer who could get it done quickly." He ran his hand through his hair. "I sure am learning a lot about quilts since I met you and your daughter."

She gently stroked the arm, noticing that it was padded. "I won't say 'you shouldn't have' because I love it more than you know," she said, wiping a tear escaping down her cheek.

"Savannah Mae and I thought that since you're going to be spending so much time here, you'll need a comfortable chair."

"I'm just a little bit speechless, Jesse." She stood up and threw her arms around him in a bear hug, not letting go until Jesse removed her hands and slid out of her embrace.

Chapter Nine

Over the next few days, Stella and Savannah Mae joined Emma to shop for the tables, chairs, rolling carts, and everything else the schoolhouse would need, as well as the twin beds, bedding, and towels for the students' rooms. On the third day, they finished their purchases and made arrangements for everything to be delivered.

Now, they had to think about catering. They'd gathered a list of recommendations from family members and friends. Each day, they visited one of the restaurants on the list of potential chefs and caterers who could prepare and serve the meals. The decision was proving to be enormously difficult, as all three of them agreed that there were more fine chefs in Waxahachie than they had anticipated. There was one in particular that all three felt had not only the skills but also the drive to succeed. He sounded like someone who would bring in a "wow" factor with his innovative recipes. He was young and talented beyond his years, being a fairly recent culinary school graduate. He'd also won a number of competitions on television cooking shows. They couldn't wait to meet him.

They sat down with Tony Sherman and were charmed by him right away. They particularly liked his breakfast ideas, such as an avocado-toast station, and lunch and dinner offerings, such as a farm-to-table buffet and a Mediterranean mezze platter. Mouthwatering as all these offerings were, it was his desserts that really sold the women. The young man was a god with pastry. His desserts ranged from strawberry custard brioche to parfaits to choux pastry puffs filled with hazelnut Chantilly cream. Tony seemed as excited as his new employers, and ready to get started on opening day.

As they were leaving the restaurant, Stella asked, "Do you think you can get him to make the Sacher torte, chocolate-filled croissants, and chocolate éclairs on the first day?"

"Told you Stella is a chocoholic," Emma said to Savannah Mae with a smirk.

"If we're gonna ask him to make special desserts for us, then I put dibs on his Italian cream cake and raspberry cheesecake. What about you, Mama?"

"Well, you both know that I'm a traditional kind of girl, so I'd want peach cobbler and key lime pie too."

"Mama, I gotta tell ya, I'm over the moon with how all this is coming together. The food that Tony is going to serve is going to be the proverbial icing on the cake. After the students see the schoolhouse, we could serve hot dogs and they wouldn't mind. They're going to drop their jaws when they see the little yellow schoolhouse. Mama, you do know that you have the most beautiful quilt retreat schoolhouse in the whole state. I have one question though."

"What?"

"When I'm teaching a class, can I sit in the quilt chair Jesse gave you?"

Emma grinned like the Cheshire Cat and winked at Savannah Mae. "Well, you did help him with it, so yes, you get special privileges."

"You do realize he's a keeper, don't you?"

"Savannah Mae, we're just friends, very good friends, and yes, he's a keeper in that way."

Emma walked down the restaurant's steps. "Well, ladies, I think we have our work cut out for us. That first retreat is going to be here before you know it. I need to get home. I have more uploading to do on the website and social media posts to get out."

Savannah Mae and Stella looked at one another and grinned. Emma glanced from one to the other.

"What?" she asked.

"Emma, you're becoming a social media guru," Stella said.

"And a webmistress extraordinaire," Savannah Mae added.

"Okay, you two, I have to go. I seriously have updating to do. Plus, I gotta upload a post on my blog."

"Blog? What blog?" Stella asked.

"My social media mentor told me that a blog would help increase business, and she's right. I've posted it on all the social media sites we're using, and so far it's driven around five hundred people to the website."

"Mama, tell me you don't have 500 people already signed up for classes!"

"Oh, no! I have 500 people signed up to be notified when we open enrollments for the classes, which is going to happen soon."

Savannah Mae and Stella looked at each other and back at Emma. "Does the blog have a name?" Stella asked.

"Of course it does. I named it *A Stitch in Time.* I was going to call it *The Yellow House Blog*, but that seemed kinda boring."

"I can't believe you've done all this and didn't tell us," Savannah Mae exclaimed.

Emma grinned. "Surprise, surprise! Okay, you two, I seriously need to do some work. Gotta go."

Savannah Mae and Stella got the hint and headed to their vehicles. As soon as they got out of earshot of Emma, they stopped and looked at each other.

"Can you believe she's been doing all this by herself?" Savannah Mae remarked.

"I'm not surprised," Stella said. "I knew she had it in her, I just didn't know to what extent. I'm real proud of her."

"Me too, me too," Savannah Mae.

After she got home, Emma logged onto the new website that had been hinting about the opening of the Yellow House Quilting Retreat. She had already posted photos and videos for the past several weeks. She updated the home page with the dates of the first three retreats and which quilts would be taught. Each retreat entry was accompanied by a photo illustrating the quilt pattern. Her copy encouraged visitors to jump to the registration page to register, as the number of students would be limited to ten. Next, she went to the registration page and updated it to reflect the retreat dates, quilt patterns, deadlines, and student limit. In addition, she added the waiting list Matt had created for each retreat.

When she finished all the updating, she sat back and slowly placed her finger on the button to activate the pages to go live. She closed her eyes and pressed. She opened her eyes a sliver and burst out in a grin: It was live. She sucked in a big breath of air and let it out. Now, she just needed to wait and watch the registrations and the waiting lists. She figured that nothing there would happen for a while, so using what she learned from Madeleine, she launched the social media campaign with the retreat dates and what would be taught on Facebook, Instagram, Pinterest, TikTok, and YouTube. All the posts linked back to the website. She watched the videos and was so proud of how they had come out. She was eternally grateful to Madeleine for showing her how to create the videos, something she had had no idea she could do.

She pulled up a file she'd created on topics she would be posting to get people excited about the retreats. She planned to post photos of the students' completed quilts, a few behind-the-scenes videos she would take of students making quilts and dining together, and several photos of Tony's spectacular food. She'd be working to create helpful tutorial videos on how to overcome common problems, such as bobbin nesting, perfecting points, identifying types of batting and their best uses, and overcoming being color-challenged. Just as she thought that was enough, she remembered an idea that could be helpful: free-motion quilting challenges. They seemed to be every beginning quilter's pet peeve. Each time she looked at the list, she added one or two more ideas. They were endless. She was getting tired and was about to turn off the computer when her curiosity got to her. She pulled up the registration page for the first retreat. It was already half full with paid registrations. Then, she went to the pages for the second and third retreats and found they, too, had several paid registrations. Before logging out, she checked the waiting lists: Each retreat had a dozen names on it.

"Well, I'll be," she said aloud.

Two weeks out from the first retreat, Emma was excited and nervous about finally opening the doors to students. Stella assured her that she would be there to help, and Savannah Mae would be too. She felt a little better, knowing she wasn't doing this all alone; still, she had a queasy feeling in her stomach. The doorbell rang, which she hoped might be a diversion. It was. She opened the door to find Jesse standing on the porch, holding a bouquet of vibrant yellow roses.

Emma blinked hard. "What's this?" she asked, pointing to the fragrant flowers wafting their intoxicating scent into the house.

"They're called roses," he kidded, trying to keep a straight face.

"Silly man! Thank you, that's very sweet. Now, get in here before they wilt."

Jesse followed her to the kitchen, where she began rifling through cabinets. "Aha! Here it is." She took out a pretty white china vase decorated with yellow roses. She took the rose bouquet from Jesse, ran water into the vase, gently placed the roses right in the center, and used her fingers to spread them apart.

"What are the chances that you would have a vase that matches the roses? That's quite a coincidence," Jesse remarked.

"I was thinking, what are the chances that you would bring me roses that matched the vase? Coincidence? I think not."

Jesse shook his head. "I'm not going to argue with that. So, how are things shaping up for the first retreat?"

"Other than trying to ignore the butterflies in my stomach, pretty well. Everything's ready to go."

"Then why the butterflies?"

"I don't know. I've just got the heebie-jeebies, like I've forgotten some important detail, or no one shows up, or something goes wrong." Her worries were like free-floating clouds, coming and going, gathering like a storm, then instantly dissipating when lanced by a ray of sunshine.

"Emma, you don't have anything to worry about. If anything, you've overplanned and overthought every detail," he assured her. "It's time to relax." He put his hands on her shoulders. "Geez, you really are keyed up. You got any of that famous lemonade of yours in the fridge?"

Emma nodded.

"You sit, I'll get it. On second thought, go sit on the porch. I'll bring the lemonade."

As soon as Emma departed, he took down the two largest glasses he could find, as well as the bottle of rum she used to spike the lemonade and the pitcher of lemonade from the fridge. Figuring she could use a little more to take the edge off, he poured a shot of rum into the pitcher. He stirred it with a spoon he found in a drawer, poured some into a glass, and tasted it. He smiled. Now, it was perfect. He went through the pantry till he found her stash of homemade cookies. He took what looked like vanilla pinwheels out of the canister and nibbled a bite. He decided they would go well with the lemonade. He shoved the rest of the cookie into his mouth, placed the canister and the two full glasses of lemonade onto a tray, and carried it all out to the back porch.

Emma looked up and smiled at him as he stepped onto the porch. He set everything down on an iron filigree table between the chairs. She picked up her glass and took a sip. "Oh my! Did you add more rum?"

Jesse placed his hands on his chest. "Who, me? Would I do that?"

"As a matter of fact, I do think you would, and I thank you for it. I have been a little on edge over the retreat."

Jesse blinked. "Ya think? I hadn't noticed."

Emma scrutinized him and lifted her glass. "Thanks for this. It may be just what I need today."

"That's what I thought. Drink up, 'cuz I'm having an awful pizza craving. Though you know I love your cookies, they aren't gonna cut it for supper tonight."

"You mean, go out for pizza?"

"Of course, how else are we gonna get a pizza?"

Emma giggled. "Really, Jesse? Frozen pizzas aren't as good as mine. And neither are the ones in restaurants."

Jesse tossed his head to the side. "Seriously? You know how to make pizza?"

Emma nodded.

"From scratch?"

"How else would I make it? Of course from scratch. Last I looked, pizza doesn't grow on trees," she laughed and stood up. "Tell you what—tonight, you are going to learn the fine art of pizza making. From scratch."

"Well, okay, if you want to. I was going to take you out for pizza."

"After you eat my pizza, I promise, you'll never want to order it out ever again."

"Okay, if you say so," he said, raising his brows, startled that she knew how to make a real pizza. He picked up the tray with their drinks and the cookie canister and followed her inside.

First, she grabbed a couple of aprons, making sure to tie the girliest one around Jesse's waist. He looked down. "Uh, don't you have a more manly apron?"

She shook her head. "Nope, no manly aprons. That'll have to do."

"You're not expecting anyone else this evening, are you?"

She shook her head. "No, why?"

"I feel a little ridiculous," he said, pointing at the ruffles.

Emma burst out laughing. "I think you look adorable."

"Can I make one request?"

"I guess so."

"If you're gonna keep teaching me how to cook, could you make me a manly apron? One I won't be embarrassed to be seen in should anyone stop in?"

Emma burst out laughing. "Are you saying you don't want someone like Travis to see you wearing one of my ruffled aprons?"

"That's exactly what I'm saying."

"Okay, I'll see what I can drum up for you. For now, let's get on with making our pizza. You have a lot to learn."

"'Learn'? I thought I was just going to help you," he said, grabbing his glass of lemonade and finishing it off.

"Hardly, you're not getting off that easy," she smiled coyly at him.

She walked to the pantry and pulled out bread flour, cornmeal, yeast, sugar, salt, and olive oil. She pointed to a large mixer on a shelf. "Would you please carry this out and place it on the counter by an electrical outlet?"

"Your sous chef is at your service," he said, trying not to snicker as he removed the mixer and carried it over to the counter, where he plugged it in.

Emma took out a small bowl, added a package of yeast, a spoonful of sugar, and a cup of warm water. Jesse watched as she whisked it together. He peered into the bowl.

"Now what?" he asked.

"We let it proof while we get everything else together."

She got out two measuring cups, handed them to Jesse, and pointed to the bread flour.

"Please measure out two and a half cups of bread flour straight into the mixer."

"Does it have to be exact?"

"Not really. Close is good enough." She watched as Jesse carefully measured the flour into the mixer. "Now, mix in a half teaspoon of salt," she instructed, "and one teaspoon of sugar." He looked up at her after adding the ingredients. "Okay, now add two tablespoons of olive oil."

He did as instructed and stared down at the ragged mess. "How's this going to come together?"

"Magic," she responded, twirling her hand through the air as though she were using a magic wand. "See that dough hook over there?"

Jesse looked all around, "What's a dough hook?"

Emma pointed to a pigtail-shaped accessory lying on the counter that she'd taken out of the mixer's bowl. "Here, it fits up inside the beater shaft, like this," she said, demonstrating. "Here, feel it," she said, taking his hand to feel where it fit. "Press it up there as far as it will go, then turn it to make sure it's secured."

He followed her instructions and let go. "That wasn't so hard. What's next?"

"Look inside that bowl where the yeast is proofing with the water." Jesse leaned over and looked.

"It's kinda bubbly."

"Just as it should be. Bring it over here and grab a whisk and a spatula from that container."

He laid everything in front of her.

"Grab the whisk and blend the yeast mixture together."

"You want me to do it?"

"Of course, you're the sous chef."

"Okay." When he finished, she told him to pour it into the large mixing bowl and use the spatula to remove every bit of the yeast, water, and sugar.

"When does the magic start?" he asked.

"Now. Turn this dial, first on slow, then gradually up to medium."

"For how long?"

She shrugged her shoulders. "As long as it takes."

He shook his head. "Whatever you say." He turned it to the slowest speed and watched the dough hook start to incorporate the mixture. Then, he turned up the speed to medium. In no time at all, the mixture started to resemble a large ball.

"So, it's done?"

Emma shook her head. "Keep the speed on medium so the dough hook will knead it."

"How long does that take?"

"It varies. From five to ten minutes."

"How do you know when it's done?"

"By feel. This is where experience comes in. Concentrate on the dough's texture and how it feels. When it's been properly kneaded, it will be smooth, a little tacky, and a bit elastic."

They watched the dough hook knead the dough over and over. After several minutes, Emma stopped the machine and pressed her finger into the dough, watching it spring back. "Here, you try it." She took one of his index fingers and pressed it into the dough. "How does it feel?"

"Kind of spongy. It definitely springs back."

"Congratulations! You just made your first batch of pizza dough. Let's turn the oven on to 450°."

"And now you're going to throw it in the air and toss it around until it flattens out like they do in Italian restaurants?" Jesse asked, a deadpan look on his face.

"And risk dropping it on the floor?" She shook her head. "I've got an easier method." She sprinkled an ample amount of flour on the counter, placed the dough in the middle of it, flipped it, and grabbed her rolling pin. Using just enough pressure, she rolled the dough into a circle. "Want to give it a try?"

"You're doing just fine on your own. I'll watch."

"Could you reach under that counter? There's a large wooden pizza peel in there."

"A what?"

"Pizza peel. Just look under there," she said, pointing to the narrow cabinet door.

He opened the door, found what he figured must be the pizza peel because it was the only thing in the narrow cabinet, and handed it to her. She sprinkled a couple of tablespoons of cornmeal on the peel and spread it around. Then, she placed the rolled-out dough onto the pizza peel, using her fingers to spread it all the way to the edges.

"We're almost done. What do you like on your pizza?"

"Chinese kung pao chicken, if you have it," he said with as straight a face as he could muster.

"Darn, I am smack out of kung pao chicken. How about pepperoni, Italian sausage, ham, sun-dried tomatoes, roasted red peppers, sauteed onions and mushrooms, anchovies, some feta cheese, and lots and lots of mozzarella and parmesan cheese?"

He tilted his head. "You had me until the anchovies."

"Not a fan, huh?"

He shook his head.

Next, she sliced up a sweet onion and several mushrooms and tossed them into a pan with olive oil. She sautéed them until they wilted, turned off the heat, and set the pan aside. She stepped over to the fridge and took out the remaining ingredients.

"Okay, let's build this pizza." She opened a jar of her homemade tomato sauce and spread a light coating over the dough. "Now, it's your turn."

"In what order?"

"However you want to build it. This is your pizza. Just make sure that the cheese is on top."

Jesse first spooned the sauteed onions and mushrooms over the dough, followed by roasted red pepper slivers, bits of sun-dried tomatoes, and all the meats. He looked up at her. "How am I doing?"

"Splendid. Now, it's time for the glue that will hold it all together."

"I'm hoping you mean the cheese."

"Of course," she said with a grin. "Household glue is really nasty on pizza." She handed him a bowl of cubed feta and another of shredded mozzarella and Parmesan cheese. He carefully sprinkled the cheeses over the top, covering every inch, just as the timer went off to signal that the oven had reached 450°.

"It's ready to go in?"

"As ready as it will ever be, chef."

Emma opened the oven door and pointed to a pizza stone on a rack. "Using a gentle jerk of your hand, dislodge the pizza from the peel and slide it onto the stone."

"What is that thing?"

"I'll explain in a second. For now, slide the pizza onto the stone before too much heat escapes."

Jesse didn't look convinced. He did as she instructed, and to his surprise, the pizza slid off the peel and onto the stone. "Huh! I didn't think that was going to work."

"Why not?"

"I thought it would stick."

She set the timer for fifteen minutes and turned back to him. "It doesn't stick because the cornmeal prevents it from sticking, provided there's enough on the peel."

"And what's with the thing in the oven? Why not use a round metal pan instead?"

"More magic," she said, raising her eyebrows. "It's a ceramic pizza stone that can tolerate very high temperatures. By leaving it in the oven while it heats, it acts like a professional brick oven that restaurants use."

"And that's important why?"

"The bottom of the pizza crust should be crispy, not soggy, right?"

Jesse nodded.

"If we baked our pizza on a metal pan, it wouldn't be crispy on the bottom because the metal pan doesn't get hot enough to crisp it. Plus, the pizza stone bakes it faster than a metal pan. It just tastes better."

"What do we do now?"

"Dump all the dirty dishes in the sink and find a really good red wine to drink with supper."

"I'll do the dishes, then there won't be a mess to clean up after."

Emma shook her head. "Nope. My house, my rules. No cleaning up until after supper."

"We've got time, why not let me wash the dishes?"

She gave him a stern look. "You're sweet to offer, but no."

"Okay, okay, I get it—your house, your rules."

She grinned sweetly. "Come on, let's pick out a good bottle of wine. I'm thinking of a Chianti or a zinfandel."

He followed her, slightly shaking his head. Emma had more layers to her persona than he had imagined, even though it seemed like they'd been getting to know one another pretty well. And now he found out she knew how to make pizza from scratch and the proper wine to drink with it.

Emma was right. When the pizza was done and they sat down to eat on the back porch, Jesse had to admit it was the best pizza he'd ever tasted. Life was feeling pretty good to Jesse.

"What a perfect evening," Emma quipped. "Even the fireflies are happy."

Jesse looked up and around, suddenly noticing an army of shimmering fireflies dancing around the backyard. "Do fireflies always put on a nightly dance in your yard?"

Emma nodded. "Yep, pretty much. I love how they light up the night sky. It's mystical, don't you think?"

Jesse glanced all around. "I don't think that I've ever thought of them as 'mystical.' You're right. They definitely add an otherworldly aspect to the night sky. Speaking of all things magical, do you mind if I get another slice of your incredible pizza?"

Emma shook her head. "I don't mind at all, especially since you did most of the work." She winked at him and handed him her plate. "I'll take another slice too. You really did a magnificent job. Now that you're done building my quilting retreat center, you should think about opening a pizzeria."

Jesse chuckled. "Think I'll stick to building things and let you be the pizza maker."

"Deal!" Emma smiled at him and took another sip of her wine as Jesse carried their plates into the house to serve up the last two slices of pizza.

Chapter Ten

Opening day finally came. Emma unlocked the front door at 8:00 a.m., an hour before she had told the students to arrive. She heard a noise outside, and when she looked through the sidelight window, she saw a line of women standing on the porch with rolling suitcases, big bags, and rolling sewing-machine cases. She opened the door, and before she could even greet the women, they walked into the foyer and stood in line again.

"Where do we sign in?" one woman with a long gray ponytail asked.

"Follow me." Emma waved at her and the others to follow her to the parlor, where she had her laptop set up on a desk.

First, she pointed to a corner of the room and asked the students to leave their sewing-machine cases there along with any supply bags they had brought, explaining that they would take everything to the schoolhouse shortly. She checked all the women in online and led them to their rooms, with some of them meeting their roommates for the first time. She handed each one a key and told them to take their time getting settled and to return to the first floor in 30 minutes to go to the schoolhouse.

"You mean, the classes are not in the house?" a woman with short hair colored with streaks of blue and purple asked.

Emma took a big breath. "You'll see shortly, and I'll bet all my cat's nine lives that you're going to love it."

"You have a cat? Where? I didn't see a cat," a woman sporting a short pageboy haircut said.

"Sophie will make an appearance when she's ready," Emma assured them. "She's very friendly."

Thirty minutes later, the women returned to the parlor. Emma instructed them to grab their rolling sewing-machine cases and supply bags and follow her out the kitchen door and down the ramp. They were right behind her as she turned around the back corner of the house and headed toward the Victorian yellow schoolhouse. Immediately, she heard loud chatter behind her.

"Look at that! It's a smaller version of the big house."

"It's even the same color."

"Check out the gingerbread. It matches the big house exactly."

"That's the cutest thing I've ever seen!"

"It's like a dollhouse, only bigger."

Emma stopped at the door, turned around, and said, "Welcome to the Yellow House Quilting Retreat. Please step inside and find a table to set up your machines. You'll have a rolling cart next to each table for your supplies. Anything you don't have room for, you can stash in one of the cubbies along the far wall."

She opened the door and the women followed her inside. Silence ensued. The women walked around, looking up and down at everything. Considering how chatty they had been moments before, their silence made Emma nervous. Slowly, they began claiming tables for their sewing machines. Suddenly, the women all started talking excitedly. Emma realized it was a good thing that Jesse had hung a lot of quilts on the walls to absorb the noise. Otherwise, the chitter-chatter might have been deafening. She waited by her quilt chair for the women to get settled. The ponytailed woman walked up to her.

"This is the most amazing quilt retreat schoolhouse I've ever seen, and I've seen a lot. I go to two to three retreats a year."

"Thank you, I appreciate that," Emma said, smiling at her.

"You had this built, didn't you?" Ponytail continued.

"Yes," Emma started, "the contractor did a phenomenal job, don't you think?"

"He or she must be a quilter," an elderly woman with spiked white hair said. "That, or you gave your contractor explicit instructions on what you wanted, right down to the Featherweight wallpaper, the hexie wood floor, and those beautiful chandeliers," she added, pointing upward.

Emma chuckled. "No, he isn't a quilter, though he told me that he learned a lot about quilting while working on this project. He didn't even know what a quilting retreat was when we started. And no, I did not give him explicit instructions, just the basics. He and his architect brother came up with all the clever additions."

"That must have been a pricey surprise when you got the bill!" a large woman snapped. "Maybe you should have found a more trustworthy contractor."

Taken aback, Emma sucked in a breath of air to calm herself, turned to the woman, and said, "He's a kindhearted friend of the family and wanted to make sure this schoolhouse would be the perfect environment for learning and making quilts. I think he nailed it. And just for your information, he didn't charge for any of the additions."

Savannah Mae had quietly entered the schoolhouse and observed the exchange. She stepped up next to Emma to redirect the conversation.

"Hello. I'm Savannah Mae Sheridan. I'll be coteaching the Grandmother's Fan quilt with my mother, Emma. We're so glad y'all like the schoolhouse, but now let's get started, shall we? First, did all of you bring a block as we requested when we confirmed your reservation?"

All the ladies nodded.

"What are the blocks for?" a woman in the back asked.

Savannah Mae smiled. "We decided that at each retreat, we would gather blocks from each student. One of us"—she pointed to Emma and herself—"will sew the blocks into a quilt top that will be quilted by Stella Rogers, one of our instructors. Then, it will be bound and donated to a local shelter."

"Which shelter will receive the quilt?" another woman asked.

"The Anchor Home. It houses women who are currently or are at risk of being homeless."

"How will the shelter decide who receives the quilt?" the woman pressed.

"That will be up to the shelter," Savannah Mae said. "We will not interfere or tell the administrators how they should gift the quilt. Now, if you will, please put the block you made in this basket that we will pass around the room."

All the women took their blocks out of their supply bags and placed them neatly in the basket. When they had all placed a block in the basket, the last woman walked the basket up to the front of the room and handed it to Savannah Mae. "This was a great idea," she said. "It's nice to be able to give back while learning something new."

Everyone settled down and gave Savannah Mae their attention. She and Emma held up the Grandmother's Fan quilt, the one Emma had found in the attic. It had since been carefully cleaned and didn't look nearly as worn and tired as when Emma had first found it.

Emma explained the history of the quilt and the integral role it had played in helping James Clayburne at the aid station in the big house during the fires of 1882. She held up the photo they had found showing James Clayburne sitting in a chair under the quilt.

Savannah Mae piped up. "While the pattern is distinctly Grandmother's Fan, we have renamed it 'the mercy quilt,' due to the role it played in helping my great-great-great-grandfather James Clayburne heal from his wounds sustained while fighting the fire. When you're back up in the big house, look in the parlor. You'll see this very chair that Grandpa James is sitting in, with this very quilt draped over him."

She turned over the quilt and showed them the small dotted stains on the back.

"Any guesses what these stains are?" Savannah Mae asked. She received only blank stares. "They are 140-year-old blood stains." A gasp filled the room.

"How do you know that?" a woman in the back asked.

"We had a quilt appraiser evaluate it. She said that blood stains like these are not unusual in old quilts like this one. Remember, in those days, quilts had a more utilitarian purpose."

"Do you know who made the quilt?" a woman in the front asked.

Emma told them that they thought that Lillian, James's wife, had likely made the quilt. She held up a photo of Lillian, the one from the hallway wall.

"See our red hair?" Savannah Mae pointed to Emma and herself. "There are many redheads in our family, and it all started with Grandma Lillian. It's too bad you can't see it in this old black-and-white photo. From what we understand, she had the brightest red hair of all."

Several women got out of their seats to more closely inspect the quilt and the photos.

"What a treasure you two have," said a woman dressed in jeans, cowgirl boots, a cotton Western-style shirt, and pearls. Her French-twist hairdo belied her country outfit. "To be able to connect this quilt with your family heritage and how this quilt was used must be very rewarding to you both."

Emma and Savannah Mae nodded. Savannah Mae bent over and whispered to Emma that she had let the chef in and that he was in the kitchen, getting started.

"Are y'all ready to learn how to make your own family heirloom?" Savannah Mae asked. The women clapped. "Please get out the fabrics you brought. There are ironing boards set up around the room, and the irons should be hot by now. Feel free to iron your fabrics, and when you're done, in the top drawer of your rolling cart, you'll find your Dresden-plate fan template, quarter circle, and background template for cutting out the pieces for each block." She pointed to the cutting tables topped with very large cutting mats. "While you're doing that, I'll place an instruction sheet next to each of your sewing machines."

A woman raised her hand. "I forgot my rotary cutter," she said, her face red; she was obviously a little embarrassed. "I can never remember to bring it to retreats."

"No worries, we have some new ones in that bin over there," Savannah Mae said, pointing to a plastic bin along the wall. "You're welcome to buy yourself a new one. You can never have too many rotary cutters, right?"

"Right!" the woman said.

While Savannah Mae was speaking, Emma slipped out and scurried up the ramp to the kitchen, finding the chef busily unpacking supplies and food for the week of meals.

"Hi, Tony!" Emma greeted the chef, who looked up at her, smiled, and went back to the dish he was making.

"What's for lunch?" she asked cheerfully.

"Did you get the schedule I sent you?

Emma nodded. "Sorry, I've been a little distracted with setting up this first retreat."

"I can imagine. It's probably like opening a restaurant."

"I've never opened a restaurant, but maybe. It's been challenging."

"Put all that behind you, Emma. Lunch today is farm-to-table."

"And what exactly would that be? 'Farm-to-table' encompasses a variety of dishes."

"We'll be starting with a crustless quiche filled with ripe cherry tomatoes, eggplant, and zucchini. Because there's no crust, the student you told me about who has celiac will be able to eat it worry-free. On the side will be roasted carrots in a creamy light yogurt sauce and a vinaigrette-based French potato salad. They will have a choice of freshly baked artisan French bread or soft gluten-free challah rolls. For dessert, I've made a raspberry peach gluten-free crumble."

"For tomorrow, I'm planning a cold salad spread: The first one will be a Caesar salad with roasted pepita seeds and gluten-free sourdough croutons, the second will be avocado halves stuffed with salmon salad, and the third will be a cubed watermelon tossed with goat cheese, spinach, berries, and pecans. The fourth will be gluten-free spiral pasta, cubed roasted chicken, chickpeas, Kalamata olives, and feta cheese in a Greek vinaigrette. Dessert is a strawberry rhubarb pie, made with a gluten-free crust."

"Tony, that sounds fantastic. Thank you for remembering the student who can't eat gluten."

"No problem, every day I have at least one customer at the restaurant who can't eat gluten."

She pointed to a cabinet. "The plates and glasses are up there. Flatware is here, and napkins are in the next drawer. The covered butter dish is over there on the other counter. Please set the table for twelve people. Put the bottled drinks in the ice bucket sitting on the far kitchen counter and cover them with ice you'll find in the freezer. There's a long buffet table against one of the dining room walls that you can use for laying out everything."

"Gotcha! Thanks, Emma."

When she led the students into the dining room at noon, everything was laid out beautifully on the buffet table. Chef Tony stood off to the side, still wearing his chef's coat. The women tittered around the table. One woman looked at the chef.

"Is everything gluten-free?" she asked.

He nodded. "Yes, except for the French bread. The challah rolls are celiac-safe."

"All the dishes are vegan, aren't they?" another asked.

"They're vegetarian, though not strictly vegan," he answered.

"I hope they're keto-friendly," a third woman remarked.

"I think you'll find plenty of options," he said, smiling at the woman.

Everyone raved over the food. Later, for dinner, Tony made Caprese salad from fresh tomatoes and basil, chicken piccata, gluten-free pasta Alfredo, Italian bread, gluten-free crackers, and a trio of gelato choices: chocolate, pistachio, and coconut. The women retreated to the parlor, happy and content.

Emma was in the kitchen, helping Tony clean up and put away food, when his phone rang. She barely paid attention until she heard him say, "Oh no! How bad is it? Where is he? Okay, I'll get there as soon as I can."

Not being able to help overhearing his side of the conversation, she looked at him, a worried expression on her face.

"Emma, I am so sorry. My brother's been in a bad accident. I've got to get the next flight out."

"Where is your brother?"

"Seattle."

"I'm so sorry."

"I'm sorry too. I'm not going to be able to cater any more of the meals for this retreat. I hope you understand."

"Of course I do. Family comes first. Leave, I'll finish up."

"What are you going to do?"

"Don't worry about it, I'll figure something out."

Savannah Mae walked into the kitchen just as Tony was darting out the front door. "What's up with Tony? He seemed in a big rush. Isn't he going to clean up?"

Emma told her what had happened.

"Oh no! Now what?"

"I'll think of something."

Early the next day, Bonnie Ada, who was married to Emma's former husband Jack McDonald, came to the rescue. The two women had formed an easy friendship based on respect and mutual interests. After all, Bonnie Ada was Savannah Mae's stepmother, Jack was her father, and Jack and Bonnie Ada's children were Savannah Mae's half brother and sisters. Everyone got along surprisingly well. No one felt strange or awkward; they were simply family.

When she got Emma's call about what had happened to the chef, Bonnie Ada told her not to worry, she would step in. She stayed up half the night preparing her Louisiana specialties. For breakfast, she served chocolate beignets sprinkled with powdered sugar, Creole eggs benedict, and chicory coffee. A few of the students who had come in from Louisiana swooned over the breakfast. At lunch, Bonnie Ada served chicken and sausage gumbo. On the side buffet, students helped themselves to a side of hot rice and hush puppies. For dessert, she served sweet potato pie with a gluten-free crust. Again, the students were delighted with the authentic meal. They noticed that Bonnie Ada had replaced the chef from the day before and told Emma that switching out the chefs and theme of the food every day was a very creative idea.

If only they knew, Emma thought, thanking God for Bonnie Ada.

For supper, Bonnie Ada served jambalaya, shrimp étouffée, gluten-free cornbread, and creole bread pudding with bourbon sauce for dessert. When Savannah Mae saw the bread pudding, she quietly said to Bonnie Ada, "What, no doberge cake?"

"Savannah Mae!" Bonnie Ada exclaimed. "That cake takes two days to make!"

"I'm kidding, I'm kidding, Bonnie Ada. Honestly, we don't know what we would have done if you hadn't stepped in."

Overhearing the conversation, Emma joined them. Bonnie Ada looked at Emma.

"*Chère*, I'm so sorry I won't be able to help you out tomorrow. I have something to do at Honey's school."

Emma shook her head. "Don't worry about it. You've been an angel to help us out today, which reminds me, don't forget to give me your receipts, I'm fully reimbursing you. As for tomorrow and for the rest of the week, cousin Charlene has agreed to come in and cook."

"That's great, *chère*, she's good, really good. In fact, I'm surprised that she hasn't opened up a catering business."

"Agreed. Now you scoot, you haven't been home all day."

"But, all the dishes ..."

"I'll take care of them. You've done more than enough. You saved my derriere."

A deep, guttural, uncharacteristic laugh boomed out of Bonnie Ada. "Ah, *chère*. Anytime."

On the third day, Charlene all but moved into the house. Emma described the food supplies Chef Tony had left, and from that, Charlene planned the menus for the rest of the week. One day, her theme was Mexican food, Asian another, and on the final day, she prepared French recipes, each with accommodations for the woman with celiac disease. From quiche lorraine, croissants, and fresh fruit at breakfast, to French onion soup with a crouton crust and salade Niçoise for lunch, to a dinner of Basque chicken stew, a bacon and onion tart, and glazed carrots, finishing the meal with meringue floating in crème anglais, a rich vanilla custard. The students raved over Charlene's meals. Emma turned to her.

"Cousin, you're hired! Permanently!"

Charlene ran her arm through Emma's and squeezed Emma's hand. "I can't make a quilt worth a darn, but I can cook."

"Understatement of the year, cousin. Love you."

"Love you more," Charlene replied.

After supper, Savannah Mae and Emma asked all the students to gather in the parlor. Savannah Mae ran upstairs and returned to the parlor with Stella, who was carrying something.

"Ladies," Emma addressed everyone. "I'd like to introduce you to Stella Rogers, who I have known since early childhood. Stella and I discovered a mutual love of quilting at a young age." Stella did a cute little curtsy, which made everyone smile. "Stella is one of the instructors here because she is an extraordinary quilter. I mean it. Wait till you see her work. After Savannah Mae and I finished piecing the blocks y'all brought for the quilt top, Stella quilted and bound it."

Stella unfolded the quilt while Savannah Mae stepped forward to hold up the other end. The room erupted in oooohs and aaaahs. All the women stood up and stepped closer to Stella and Savannah Mae to get a good look at the quilt.

"Will you look at that?" one woman declared, pointing to intricate feather designs along the two outside borders. Another woman pointed to the center, which featured multiple birds in flight. On and on went the comments. Although the quilt blocks were all different, Stella had deftly made them all congruent, as though they had been chosen to complement each other, which they did.

Emma coughed into her fist to garner everyone's attention. When everyone looked at her, she held up a six-by-six-inch piece of muslin. Near the top, in perfect handwriting, someone had printed "Gift from the Inaugural Yellow House Quilting Retreat" with the day's date. Emma passed out fine-point felt pens with indelible ink. "And now it's your turn," Emma said, handing the piece of muslin to a woman standing closest to her. "Please sign your name and then pass it to the next person."

"Do we have to sign our real names?" a short woman standing on the side asked.

Emma cocked her head to think on the question. "Well, I suppose not. You could sign with a nickname."

The woman liked that idea. The group passed around the muslin, every one of them happily signing. When the fabric made its way back to her, Emma wondered whether the nickname "Pixie" belonged to the very short woman.

Chapter Eleven

With the first retreat over, Jesse stopped by to say hello. When Emma saw him holding a guitar case, she double-blinked. "You play guitar?"

Jesse nodded.

"What's it for?"

He didn't miss a beat. "Most people use 'em to make music, other people break them over their adversaries' heads."

"Oooh, good comeback, Jesse!"

He blushed a little. "After seeing you every day during the construction and renovation, I've missed you."

"You could have stopped in during the retreat. The women were flabbergasted by what you did in the schoolhouse."

"Naw, way too much estrogen," he said, winking at Emma.

"So why did you bring a guitar?" She wondered aloud.

He nodded. "It feels like our friendship is moving in a good direction, am I right?" His voice was soft, much like a warm quilt on a cold winter's night.

She didn't answer right away. She looked him in the eye, puzzled about where he was going with this. His question hung in the air between them.

"Yes," she finally answered.

"When we had dinner that night after the plumber flooded the house, you asked me how I had been injured in the war, and I didn't want to ruin the evening by telling you then."

"You said you'd tell me another time."

"You made a good point: that good friends share important things with one another, that it builds trust and helps friends support each other."

"I remember."

"Well, I'm ready to talk about it—if you're up for it, because it isn't pretty."

"When is war ever pretty?"

"I figure that you should know a few things about me."

"I take it that the guitar has something to do with it?" He nodded. Feeling a little nervous about the tone of the conversation, she made an attempt to lighten the weighty mood that seemed to be filling the room. "Oh my goodness, Jesse, I get it. You head up a band, and you want me to be your backup singer!"

Jesse shook his head as a chuckle escaped his lips. He took her hand and led her to the parlor. "Let's sit. Bear with me."

She sat close to him, their shoulders and legs touching. "Go on, I'm listening," she whispered.

"When I was in the VA hospital after my injury, I got to witness firsthand the importance of making rooms, especially bathrooms, accessible for people in wheelchairs. I know how important it is."

"Sounds like it was a tough way to learn about the regulations."

"It was. I was one of the lucky ones. A lot of guys who ended up there had such severe injuries that they never made it back to their families. We called the hospital 'God's Waiting Room.' For many of us, the war came home with us."

"Go on."

"It was a constant battle of daily struggles, trying to be brave when all we felt was despair, trying not to let fear consume us, and trying to be strong when all we could feel was weakness. Before my deployment I had my heart set on becoming an animal trainer for first responders, but after the injury and my recovery, they wouldn't take me into the program. Hard as it was at the time, I learned an important lesson."

Emma nodded, urging him to continue.

"It's good to have dreams and goals, but they're fragile. They can be wiped out by an unexpected turn of events; like in my case, they were crushed by enemy fire."

Seeing the sadness on her face, Jesse turned the conversation around. "I used my time at the VA to learn everything I could, and I'm a better contractor because of it."

He took a moment to run a hand through his hair and rub the back of his neck.

"When I was brought to the VA hospital, my injuries were so severe that they didn't expect me to live. I suffered more than physical wounds. I developed PTSD."

Emma leaned in; he was speaking so softly, she could barely hear him. She noticed that his hands had begun to shake.

"I was terrified," he continued. "Of everything, 24/7." He shot her a glance, a dark sadness filling the depths of his eyes. His stomach began to churn, and turmoil rose in his chest. "Which was so atypical for me. I'd never been scared or terrified of anything in my life. At one point, I began to give up the will to live. I couldn't imagine ever having a normal life again, ever going back to the way my life had been before the war. Fear brought me back to my senses."

Emma squeezed his hand, lifting her head to look at him eye to eye. He peered at her, holding her gaze like a lasso.

"Fear? How did fear rescue you?"

"I was afraid to die almost as much as I was afraid to live. In the end, fear won out, but not before battling the worst demons I'd ever experienced."

Emma placed a hand on one side of his face and held it there for several seconds. "Go on."

"The nights were bad, really bad. Nightmares every time I tried to go to sleep. Memories were the most infuriating aspect. For nearly a year, I couldn't sleep, which made everything worse. Faces would appear out of nowhere—faces I wanted to forget. I came to realize that memory banks are sort of like a camera taking pictures of our lives. Images would ripple before me like pages rustling in a breeze. Sometimes, they would fade quickly, while other times, they didn't fade at all. They're like watching a movie on a continuous loop, reminding you of what you've witnessed. On top of that, the sleep deprivation caused me to imagine things that weren't there. The slightest movement, the smallest sound made my heart race, and panic attacks followed."

"Didn't the doctors give you medication to sleep or calm you down?" she asked.

"Oh, they wanted to. I refused. I didn't want to go that route. You gotta understand that many of the guys thought drugs would end their pain. But they didn't. We lived a war of our own making, a war of daily mental skirmishes, wrestling between optimism and despair, tenacity against paralyzing anxiety, and toughness versus weakness. I don't think any of them realized that while the drugs would temporarily numb them from the pain, they would become dependent on the drugs, even on meds that weren't addictive because they put so much faith in the drugs that they didn't realize they were part of the problem, not the solution. Many who couldn't get out of that endless cycle after leaving the VA would seek out street drugs that were much worse than anything they were given in the hospital. Many went on to die by their own hand. Veteran suicide is a huge problem."

"Jesse, did you have nightmares before the war?"

"Before Afghanistan, I didn't appreciate what a nightmare was because up until that point, I'd never experienced one."

"What were they about?"

Jesse bowed his head. "I kept reliving the scene of the ambush." His breathing turned uneven, sounding like thunderous waves breaking along a rocky shore, rough and jagged. "What I saw seared into my memories. Each night, I felt helpless, watching it over and over in my head." He shook his head, trying not to see what he wished he could forget. He sat perfectly still, breathing in rapid, shallow breaths.

Emma looked away. Emotions were welling up inside of her, faster than she could control. She wanted to hide her emotions from him, yet when she reached up and rubbed his shoulders and neck, she knew she couldn't. She cared about him too much to turn away when he needed someone, and that someone was her.

"You don't have to continue, Jesse."

"Yeah, I do. I want you to understand what I went through and why I'm the way I am. After the ambush, while I was passed out, the medics moved in, put me on a stretcher, and loaded me onto a helo. First, I was taken to base camp, then airlifted to Landstuhl Regional Medical Center in Germany. I was in a coma for a week. When I woke up, I was stabilized. They put me on a transport to the VA Medical Center in Houston. It was surreal when we landed; I had thought I'd never step foot on American soil again, not that I was stepping anywhere."

"Did things get easier then?"

"Not really. I was awake most of the time, and the PTSD started to dominate my days as well as nights. What I'd seen, what had happened in that field, scorched my conscience, embedded itself in my brain. Not long after, I began rehab to learn to walk again, and while I was very focused on doing whatever it took to walk, the terror was taking its toll. I wasn't alone. Each and every vet in my ward was waging an internal war with his soul, struggling between dire, crushing despair one moment versus giddy hope the next, trying to be courageous when all we felt like doing was cratering into ourselves. To give up. We were trained to be brave and strong, yet we were afraid of the dark where our deepest horrors lay."

She took his hands into her own. "I can't imagine how you got through it."

"It's hard to comprehend the power of the light, unless you've lived in the shadow of the dark. Despair, hopelessness, and misery bore down, sucking the life out of me. It's like a thousand bricks are piled on your chest. Then, when the darkness lifts and the light takes over, the despair slowly evaporates. It's a staggering feeling, one that's hard to explain."

She tipped her head and stared at him. "How did you go from being in the depths of despair to rising above it?"

"I almost didn't. Had it not been for a doctor who saved me, I swear I wouldn't be alive."

She nodded, encouraging him to continue.

"She placed me in a PTSD program. She didn't just hand me off; she visited me every day, and each time she encouraged me to keep going, not to give up. She told me about patients she had who were in worse shape than me, and how they made it. How they were able to come out of the darkness and turn toward the light, and ultimately how they returned to a normal life. She said one thing that's really stuck with me: that there are cracks everywhere, and I shouldn't ignore or turn away from them because those cracks let the light in through the darkness. It's how the light enters and how healing begins."

"Like you."

"Yeah, like me," he smiled, then it quickly faded. "Plus, she made sure I was assigned to a really great counselor. Ronnie Wines was a veteran who had suffered PTSD too. He knew what I was going through. He taught me ways to deal with the nightmares and the daymares. Ronnie's the reason I brought Millie," he said, patting his guitar case.

"Millie?"

"Yeah, that was my doctor's name. It's my way of honoring her."

"And how does this Millie help you?" she asked, pointing to the guitar case.

"Ronnie taught me that music has a way of healing and providing comfort. I'd seen it myself. Musicians often came to the hospital and played and sang for us. I always felt more relaxed after their visits, so when Ronnie suggested I learn to play the guitar and sing, initially, I doubted my ability. Eventually, I decided to give it a try."

"And?"

"In those moments when I'm playing or singing, my mind wanders, and I escape back to the life I had before the war, to the person I was. I learned that music can mend the heart, where the terror, at least my terror, lives. Someone told me—I don't know if it was Dr. Millie, Ronnie, or who—that music has a way of fostering hope. And as long as there's music, life will go on."

"Jesse, I've long believed that the heart sees hope in what most people would call 'the inconceivable.' I think it operates independently of our brains, even when we can't. I have a theory that the heart knows that love can achieve wonders we mortals would consider unattainable. Funny thing is, a lot of the time it seems like the heart acts randomly, without any logic or sense. Kinda like when you meet someone and there's an immediate attraction, and you know that it's more than physical. It's something deeper; it's your heart and your soul telling you, pushing you, to a person it knows is good for you. Will you play for me? I want to hear how music mended your heart and the hope it's given you."

He bent down and took his guitar out of the case. "There are two songs that I must have played and sung twenty times a day, every day, for weeks and months. They're still my favorites. Here's the first one, "Angels Among Us."

He played it for Emma, who several times had to wipe away tears.

When she had composed herself, she asked him, "What is it about this song that consoled you?"

"The very first time I heard it, I realized that angels were with me that day in Afghanistan. They helped save me. At that moment, I understood that there was something else I was supposed to do in my life, and those angels were sent to protect me and make sure I lived to do it. There's a line in the lyrics about how they come down in our darkest hours and guide us with the light of love. On that field in Afghanistan, it was unquestionably my darkest hour. It felt like that song was written for me."

As she watched him, it became harder and harder to breathe. When he looked straight at her as he was doing now, it paralyzed her and took her breath away. Trying to keep herself composed, she asked softly, "And the other song?"

"One of my favorites by Willie Nelson, "Angel Flying Too Close to the Ground." His son Lukas often sings it as well, and if you've ever heard Lukas sing, he sounds just like Willie as a young man.

Now, I don't sound like Willie or Lukas, but here ya go," he said before he sang all the verses.

"Another song about angels," she observed.

"Yeah. And while there's a similarity to "Angels Among Us," it's that first stanza that says 'If you hadn't fallen, I would not have found you' that gets to me. I interpret that as the angel having found me in that field, as I was dying. It's one of the most beautiful songs I've ever heard."

"You believe in angels, don't you?" she asked.

He nodded. "More than you know."

"And did you before being deployed?"

He looked up and around the room, as though searching for the answer on the ceiling, walls, and furniture. Finally, he turned back toward Emma. "I don't think it was something I had ever thought about. Going through what I did in the war, there is no doubt in my mind that angels are watching out for us."

"Jesse, this is a completely self-serving thing to say, but I like to think that the angels saved you so that one day we would meet," Emma whispered.

"I hope that's true," he pondered, tucking a stray curl behind her ear. "They saved me for a reason; at the time, I didn't know why. I'll tell you one thing. Now, I live every single day as though my life was stolen from the grim reaper, because it was. Though I'm still surrounded by the ghosts of Afghanistan, and I suppose I always will be, now I choose to not let them take over my life. The guilt no longer consumes me."

Chapter Twelve

Faster than a wild mustang sprinting across the grassland, the first day of the second retreat came around. With a little breathing time in between, Emma was relaxed and ready to take it on. Charlene had taken over the kitchen, even making sure that hot coffee and cinnamon scones were ready for when the new crop of students checked in. Stella stood at Emma's side, helping to sign in the ten students. When Stella spotted one using a walker, she said to the woman, "You must be Ella Beck." She looked at the younger woman next to her. "And you must be Deena Beck, her daughter."

The women smiled. "Let me guess, the walker gave us away?" Ella grinned.

Stella beamed back. "Our resident cat told me," she said, pointing up the stairs to Sophie supervising from the top step.

"Ooooh," Deena cooed. "What a beautiful cat. Girl?"

Stella nodded.

"Does she ever sleep with the students? I already miss my cat."

"She actually loves to nap on beds, though she usually sleeps with Emma," Stella pointed to her friend. "However, if you leave your door open a crack, she might wander in and grace you with her presence." Stella led the woman and her daughter to the first-floor guest room set up for students not able to manage the stairs.

Like at the first retreat, the women oohed and ahhed over the little yellow schoolhouse. The room oozed with an air of excitement and anticipation of great things to come. "Look at all the quilts hanging on the walls," a tiny woman said to her equally tiny friend, pointing up toward the rafters.

"Speaking of making quilts, let's get started!" Savannah Mae announced as she walked into the schoolhouse, carrying the quilt she'd made out of Emma's wedding dress.

"This is my daughter, Savannah Mae Sheridan, who will be teaching y'all to make a wedding dress quilt," Emma announced.

"Do you even know how to make a quilt like that, or did you take a quick tutorial online?" asked an unpleasant woman named Terri, chuckling to herself and looking around for agreement from the other students, all of whom ignored her.

Savannah Mae whipped around; it was all she could do not to shoot daggers at the woman. She wondered why a nasty-tempered woman would come to a retreat. What was she trying to prove? Was she bored? Did she have nothing better to do? Was she just incredibly unhappy? Savannah Mae took a deep breath and tried to keep her annoyance at bay by using a reverse strategy.

"Ma'am, perhaps you didn't read the class description," she said, smiling sweetly at the woman. "I am uniquely qualified to teach this class." She held up the wedding dress quilt she had made and explained its history and how it had won Best of Show at the Houston International Quilt Festival. The outspoken Terri bent her head to avoid the stares from the women around her. She made a quick mental note to watch what she said the rest of the retreat. It wasn't the first time Terri's mouth had gotten her into trouble. Savannah Mae directed her attention to the whole class. "Ladies, please take out the fabric from your deconstructed wedding dresses."

Savannah Mae walked around and inspected all the wedding dress fabric that the women had brought, satisfied that everyone had followed the instructions sent to them.

Each day, the students worked on the quilt blocks, oftentimes using their seam rippers to remove errant stitches. One woman appeared to be spending more time ripping out seams than actually sewing. Savannah Mae stood and watched her, trying to figure out what she was doing wrong. Finally, she saw it.

"Sheila, you're not using pins to hold the fabric together."

The woman looked up. "I never have. I don't like to use them."

In as gentle a tone as she could muster, Savannah Mae said, "I understand, but when working with dress fabrics like silk and satin, not to mention lace, they can be slippery and tend to slide around if they're not anchored securely. That's why your seams aren't lining up."

"I don't want to put holes in the fabric," Sheila added.

"Hold on a sec," she said, walking over to the shop area where they stocked supplies. She picked up a package of extra-fine pins and handed it to Sheila.

"I don't know," Sheila said, doubting the pins wouldn't make holes in the wedding dress fabric.

"Here, let me show you. Can I have a couple of those pieces of fabric you trimmed off?"

Sheila handed them to Savannah Mae, who opened the package, pinned the pieces together, and handed the fabric back to Sheila.

"Try sewing the seam now."

Sheila hunched her shoulders and let out a sigh. Clearly, she didn't believe the pins wouldn't ruin her fabric. She sewed the seam, took it out from under the needle, and began removing the pins. She stopped before she had finished taking out the pins, bent over, and carefully examined the fabric.

"You're right, there are no pin holes!" she exclaimed. "Where'd you get those?" she asked, pointing to the package.

"We buy them wholesale. Honestly, you can buy them at any sewing, quilt, or craft shop. You can buy them online too."

"Well, I'll be," Sheila giggled. "Ya learn something new every day!"

Savannah Mae kept watch over Sheila and noticed that she quickly caught up to the other women now that she didn't have to waste time ripping out seams and resewing them. She wondered why Sheila had been so bothered by potential pin holes but hadn't minded the needle holes she kept having to sew over and over. She shrugged and continued walking around the room, examining the students' progress.

By the morning of the last day, all the women had completed at least half of the blocks for their Double Wedding Ring quilts, while others were done or nearly done.

Savannah Mae stood at the front of the room. "Ladies, since most of you are nearly finished sewing your blocks and others have completed at least half of them, it's time to start sewing the blocks together.'

"But what about those of us who are only half done?" a woman in the back asked.

"Then you'll sew together half of the quilt top," Savannah Mae answered. "You'll be sewing them together in rows, three ring blocks to a row. So, if you've finished six blocks, you'll have enough to sew two rows, and I'll show you how to sew those two rows together. When you've done that, you'll see that your quilt top is half done. You'll be able to easily finish the top at home."

"And if we've finished all twelve blocks?" another woman asked.

"Then you're ready to sew the whole top together. You should be able to get that done today."

Some of them asked whether they could take a second class where they could finish their quilts under Savannah Mae's supervision.

"You could," Savannah Mae answered, "although instead, you could come to one of our open-sew days. It costs a fraction of the price of a weeklong retreat."

"How much is 'a fraction'?" Deena Beck asked.

"For a whole day, $25," Savannah Mae said.

"Oh, heck yes, that's a lot less expensive. Does it include lunch? The food here is awesome!"

"I'm afraid not. If you wish, you can bring a brown-bag lunch or order one of Charlene's lunches. It's pretty reasonable. Runs $12 a person; you have to preorder on the website."

"That's what I'm gonna do," Deena announced. "Maybe she'll make barbecued brisket tacos with spicy black beans and grilled veggies. A friend was here for the first retreat and told me that her brisket tacos are better than in most area restaurants. She said it would be worth driving over here just for them." Several women nodded their heads in agreement.

"Duly noted," Savannah Mae said. "I'll let Charlene know," she said as she continued walking around the schoolhouse, delighted to see the progress everyone had made. She made a mental note to tell her mother that coming up with the quilt retreat idea had been pure genius.

The third retreat came quicker than the second one had, or so it seemed. Emma looked at the calendar and counted up the days between the first and second one and the days between the second and third that was about to begin. The number was exactly the same. But unlike before the two previous retreats, Emma was finally feeling like the learning curve of running a quilting retreat was behind her. She was looking forward to the third one, confident that it would go as smoothly as one of Charlene's banana cream pies. She wasn't the least bit nervous this time.

Once again, her best friend, Stella, was there to help check in the students. Stella looked at Emma, who winked. "We got this," Stella said confidently.

"We sure do," Emma agreed. "I don't think there's anything we haven't encountered. Should be easy-peasy from now on."

Like at the previous retreats, the women were lined up at the front door long before Emma was going to open up. Emma looked at Stella. "Maybe the ads should say that we're starting at 10:00 a.m. so that the students will show up at nine o'clock instead of eight, the way they're doing now." Stella shrugged and beckoned the women inside.

They'd checked in the first six students when a tall, imposing woman with a massive bouffant hairstyle stepped up.

"I'm Mrs. Reginald Atherton. Is there a private bath attached to my room?" she asked in a booming voice, not unlike her stature.

Emma looked up from the laptop. "What is your name?"

"I told you. I'm Mrs. Reginald Atherton."

"I beg your pardon, I heard you the first time, Mrs. Atherton. We need your first name and your driver's license or government-issued identification to confirm you are who you say you are."

"Why, I never! Do you think I'm lying? Why do you need all that?"

Stella stepped forward. "Mrs. Atherton, we ask all of our guests for their full names, which includes their given names, as well as their identification for security reasons."

"Security? Whatever for? Have you had trouble here?" she asked in an uppity tone.

Stella took a deep breath and smiled gently. "Of course not. We just make sure that everyone is who they say they are for the protection of all our guests. You included. Now, may we please have your first name and your identification?"

The woman snorted. "Well, all right. My name is Lavender, but I am to be called 'Mrs. Atherton.' I am a member of the esteemed Atherton family. I'm sure you've heard of us." Emma simply cracked a small smile while Lavender Atherton dug into her purse and pulled out her driver's license. Emma checked it, thanked the woman, and handed back her identification.

"Does my room have a king or queen bed? I requested a king," Lavender Atherton stated.

"Mrs. Atherton, you have a twin bed, the same as all the rooms. Every room has two twin beds because there are two students in a room."

"A twin bed? That's unacceptable! Are you saying that I have to share the room with someone I don't know? That's also unacceptable! I requested a room to myself."

"Mrs. Atherton, when you filled out the online registration form and requested a king bed in a room to yourself, I emailed you back immediately that we do not have single rooms nor do we have any rooms with king beds. I asked if you still wanted to register for the retreat, knowing you would be sharing a room with another student and sleeping in a twin bed."

"I don't recall that email. I didn't get it."

"Yes, Mrs. Atherton, you did, because you emailed back and said that you would share the room and sleep in the twin bed."

"I didn't. You're mistaken. I would never share a room with a stranger nor sleep in a twin bed."

Emma was growing weary of the woman. She pulled up Lavender Atherton's email and turned the laptop around to show it to her. "See?"

"Well, I don't recall doing that. Can't you just give me a room to myself? Someone can push the two beds together for me."

"I'm sorry, Mrs. Atherton, we can't. We're fully booked. Now, do you want to stay for the retreat or forgo what you paid for the week and not attend the retreat?"

"What? If you're not going to accommodate me, I want a full refund!"

Again, Emma turned around her laptop and showed Mrs. Atherton the registration form she had filled out and signed, acknowledging that she would lose her entire fee if she did not cancel fourteen days before the retreat. Mrs. Atherton's face bloomed red.

"All right, fine! I'll stay, but you should know I'll be sending a letter of complaint to the person running this retreat as well as the homeowner."

Emma grinned wide. "Mrs. Atherton, save your stationery. This is my business and my home." She handed her a room key. "Your room is on the second floor at the end of the hall. Leave your sewing machine and supplies in that corner over there to take to the schoolhouse. Please be back down here in 30 minutes, when we will take everyone to the schoolhouse."

Mrs. Atherton pursed her lips. "I don't suppose you have a bellboy or anyone to carry my luggage?" She had two large suitcases and a makeup case in addition to her sewing machine case and supplies bag.

"No, we don't. Nor do we have an elevator." A moment of awkward silence passed.

The woman looked at Stella. "Aren't you the maid? Can't you carry my belongings upstairs?"

The only reason the woman missed seeing Stella's indignation was that her smooth cacao-colored skin hid the incensed redness creeping across her face, but if Mrs. Reginald Atherton had paid attention, she would have noticed Stella pressing her full lips together. Mortified, Stella turned to Emma, her amber eyes blazing.

Emma stood up, infuriated herself, but conscious that she needed to maintain her composure. "Well, bless your heart!" she smiled sweetly. "Stella is not the maid. As a matter of fact, she is one of the most gifted quilters in Texas, and we are fortunate she took time off from her job as a nurse practitioner to teach this retreat."

"I didn't mean any offense," the woman said, trying to backpedal.

Emma and Stella stood fast. Lavender Atherton looked from one to the other. "Okay, I'm sorry. Now, can someone help me with my luggage?"

Emma told her that there wasn't anyone to help and kindly suggested that next time, she bring less luggage. Lavender walked over to the stairs and hauled one case at a time upstairs.

The next person in line stepped up, shaking her head. "Geez, was she for real?"

Emma smiled and moved on. "And what is your name?"

"Linda Mayfield."

Emma looked at the register and back up at Linda. "I have only one twin bed left and ..."

"Lemme guess, it's rooming with the esteemed Mrs. Lavender Atherton." It was all she could do to keep from bursting out laughing.

"Uh, yes," Emma said. "I'm glad you're amused by it."

"I used to work in the hotel business for a high-end property that catered to the very wealthy. Most of the guests we had were very nice, very gracious. Every once in a while, though, we had people like her. I'm used to the Mrs. Athertons of this world. I just didn't expect anyone like her to show up at a quilting retreat. Quilters aren't usually so uppity. Don't worry, I can manage her." Linda pointed upstairs. She turned to leave, then turned back. "By the way," she added, pointing to Emma and Stella, "you two handled her perfectly." She chuckled, turned, and went up the stairs.

The last guests to register were two local women, Connie Sinclaire and Isabel Allnutt, who proudly stated they had been best friends for nearly as long as they'd been alive. Stella and Emma looked at each other, knowing it was their story too.

Connie and Isabel could not have been more different. Connie was short, a little plump, and wore her blond hair straight to her shoulders. She had an adenoidal voice that sounded like her speech came through her nose. Isabel was the polar opposite, extremely skinny with a high-pitched voice; she sported a deep tan that she said came from running five miles every day. She pulled her thick black hair into a bun the size of a hamburger at the back of her head. The two women told Emma that they did everything together and loved going on retreats to enjoy a little girlfriend time away from home. They even wore matching pink T-shirts printed with "Besties for Life."

Emma and Stella finished the registrations quickly and then checked on Charlene, who had brought out scones made with local Nacogdoches blueberries and coffee for when the students came back downstairs. After the registration debacle, the rest of the first day went smoothly. They didn't hear one more word from Mrs. Atherton but noticed Linda Mayfield walking around with a Cheshire cat grin plastered on her face. Stella noticed Linda's odd expression and pointed it out to Emma.

"What do you think that's about?" Stella asked.

Emma shook her head. "Who knows? Just as long as she and Mrs. Atherton get along, I don't much care."

Chapter Thirteen

The third retreat could not have gone more smoothly. Emma felt that not only had she finally mastered How to Run a Quilt Retreat 101; she was also having fun, just as she had imagined when she first came up with the idea. The students seemed to be having a good time too. Everyone reveled over Stella's Spiral Lone Star quilt designed by Jan Krentz. Between the pattern, fabric choices, and exquisite quilting, the students recognized that they were learning from a woman who was truly a gifted artist, not just a quilter. Though challenging, each day Stella broke down the components, explaining how it would all come together at the end. A couple of students asked Stella whether they could just give her all their fabric and she could make the quilts for them. Stella tried hard not to laugh, especially when she realized they were serious. She assured them that they could do it, one step at a time.

On the fourth morning, one of the besties, Isabel, did not come down to breakfast. Charlene asked Connie whether her friend was sleeping in or just not hungry.

"Oh, I don't think so. She was getting ready when I left. She said she would be down in a few minutes. I'm sure she'll be here soon. She was really looking forward to the pecan pancakes."

After ten minutes, Isabel still hadn't shown up. Emma asked Connie to go up to their room and check on her friend. "She won't have any time to eat before class starts if she doesn't get down here soon," she told her.

"Sure," Connie responded. She got up from the table and headed for the stairs. Charlene began clearing the dishes and the buffet sideboard.

Suddenly, a blood-curdling scream resonated throughout the house. Everyone froze. They all looked at one another, apprehension etched on their faces. Emma and Stella bolted up the stairs, searching for the source of the scream that continued like a broken record. They found the door to the besties' room open and saw Connie standing over Isabel on the floor, a silk scarf tied around Isabel's neck. Isabel's eyes were open, staring off to the side. Connie continued screaming. Stella bent down and placed her fingers on Isabel's neck, then her wrist, checking for a pulse. She looked up at Emma, shaking her head.

First, Emma stepped over to Connie and wrapped her arms around her, holding her and rubbing her back to calm her down and get her to stop screaming. Emma looked over at Stella and mouthed, "Call the police." Stella nodded, took her phone out of her pocket, and dialed 911. Meanwhile, Emma slowly moved Connie out of the room and into the hallway. Connie pulled back and looked at Emma, who saw that whatever eye makeup Connie had applied that morning had run in gullies down her face.

"Connie, what happened in there?"

"I-I-I don't know. When I left to come downstairs, she was fine, she was getting dressed. I came up here to find out what was taking her so long like you asked, and I found her like that!" She pointed toward the room and started crying all over again.

"Okay, okay, calm down. You need to have your wits about you for when the police get here."

"The police?" she whimpered. "Why?"

Emma thought, *What a strange thing to ask. There's been a murder here. Or at least something that looks like a murder. Of course we would contact the police.*

She decided that Connie must be in shock and not thinking clearly. One thing she knew for sure was that she didn't want to take her downstairs and upset the other students, who were already scared. Oh heck, she was a little scared herself. But she couldn't think about that right now. Instead, she led Connie up the stairs to the third-floor sitting room. She sat her down and handed her a box of tissues she got out of a cabinet. Then, she took out her phone and texted Stella.

> Brought Connie up to the 3rd floor sitting room to avoid upsetting other students. I'll stay with her till police arrive.

A minute later Emma's phone buzzed with a text.

> Got it. Am downstairs calming everyone. Waiting for police. Told everyone to stay on 1st floor. Closed and locked door to Isabel's rm.

It didn't take long for the Waxahachie police to arrive and let the whole neighborhood know something was amiss. Their sirens wailed all the way from the station. Five squad cars pulled up in front of the house. The officers got out of their cars, unholstered their pistols, and ran up to the house with their guns drawn. All the neighbors stood on their front porches, their mouths hanging open. Stella heard them arrive and stood in the open doorway. The police rushed in and looked around. A man who appeared to be in charge stepped forward.

"We got a call about a body found in this house. And you are?"

"Stella Rogers. I'm one of the instructors here and friend of the homeowner, Emma Clayburne Jenkins. I called you."

"Where is the homeowner?"

"She's in the third-floor sitting room with Connie Sinclaire, the student who found the body, trying to calm her down. She's acting very strange. Emma thought it may be because she's in shock."

He scrawled what Stella told him in his notebook. She couldn't help noticing that the officer's hands were shaking. She wondered whether he might not have much experience with murder cases or was nervous.

"And the deceased?" the officer asked her.

"She's in the room on the second floor that she shared with the woman who found her."

"What's the name of the victim?"

"Isabel Allnutt."

"Has anyone touched the body or moved anything in the room?"

"When we heard Connie's screams, Emma and I ran upstairs and found Connie standing over Isabel's body. I'm a nurse, so immediately I kneeled down and checked her for a pulse at her neck and then wrist. She didn't have one. Emma took Connie upstairs to isolate her until you got here, and I left the room, locking the door behind me, and came down here to wait for you."

"Good work." He looked toward the parlor and noticed everyone crowded in small groups. "Who are all those women in there?"

"Students who are here for a quilting retreat. They've been here all week."

"A quilting retreat? What's—oh never mind, you can explain later. Can you take us up to the room with the victim?"

Stella nodded. The lead officer told all the uniformed officers to stay downstairs, get the names and contact info from all the women, and not let anyone leave. He waved to someone in plain clothes wearing a jacket that had "Medical Examiner" embroidered on the back. The ME stepped forward, carrying a medical bag, and followed the officer and Stella upstairs.

Stella unlocked the door and let the officer and ME into the room.

The officer pointed to the scarf around Isabel's neck. "Is the scarf exactly as you found it?"

"Yes, sir," Stella nodded.

"Did you touch or handle it in any way?"

"No, sir."

"So, the room, the body, and everything around it is exactly as you found it?"

Stella nodded.

"Were you here alone with the body?"

"No, I told you, the best friend, Connie Sinclaire, found the body and started screaming. Emma and I ran upstairs to find the source of the screams. We heard it coming from this room, entered, and discovered Connie standing over the body."

"Good, good," the officer said. "Had she touched the body?"

Stella shrugged. "I have no idea. She didn't while Emma and I were in the room, but she could have before we arrived."

"You said that Emma is with the friend now. Where are they?"

"Upstairs in a sitting room."

"Please take me up there. They and everyone who was in the house, including you and the homeowner, need to come to the station to be interviewed."

"Of course," she responded.

The officer turned to the ME. "Joe, if you'll get started here, I'll go upstairs with Mrs. Rogers." Joe knew the routine and was putting on his examination gloves before the officer finished speaking.

When Stella and the officer reached the third floor, they could hear Connie wailing from down the hall, where they found the door open to the sitting room. They walked in, and the officer introduced himself. He told both women to come downstairs, as everyone would have to come to the station for questioning.

"Why?" Connie wailed. "I didn't do anything."

The officer could see that Connie wasn't going to be very cooperative. "Because this is a suspicious death, and everyone who was in the house needs to be interviewed, and we do that at the station."

"You're going to interrogate me? I'm innocent!" Connie wailed.

"Ma'am, no one is saying you aren't. This is police protocol. It's only an interview to ascertain the facts, not an interrogation."

"It's the same thing," Connie whimpered.

"No, it's not, now come downstairs."

"And if I refuse?"

"Ma'am, don't make this hard on yourself. I really don't want to cuff you."

"OMG!" Connie looked at Emma and Stella. "He's going to arrest and handcuff me!"

Emma stepped forward and placed her hands on Connie's forearms. "Connie, he isn't going to arrest you, and he won't handcuff you if you cooperate. Can you do that? Just go downstairs and go with everyone to the police station, where they will interview everyone, including Stella and me."

Connie looked at Emma like a deer about to be shot. Fear oozed out of her pores.

"Come on." Emma took Connie's arm and led her out of the room, Stella close behind, followed by the officer.

By the time they reached the first floor, the other officers had gotten everyone's names and contact info. They proceeded to escort everyone to the patrol cars, Charlene, Emma, and Stella included. In less than ten minutes, the cruisers pulled into the police station parking lot. They opened the car doors and escorted all the women into the station and into a large meeting room. They all sat there, waiting to find out what would happen next. After what seemed like an eternity, but was only a half hour, a short man wearing a dress shirt and tie and a blond-haired woman wearing a pantsuit entered the room.

"I'm Detective Adam Corbin, and this is Detective Kristin Holecek. We will be interviewing each of you about this morning's events. We will call two names. One of you will follow me to an interview room, and the other will follow Detective Holecek to another interview room. The rest of you will stay here with Officer Wallace until your name is called. Is that clear?"

Connie spoke up. "I refuse to answer any questions on the grounds that it may incriminate me."

The detective looked at her as though she had just landed from another planet.

"You haven't been asked any questions yet. You don't even know what we're going to ask."

"Well, I refuse anyway."

The detective shook his head. "You shouldn't have anything to worry about if you aren't guilty."

Connie didn't budge.

"Do you want us to lock you up and let you think about it?"

"That's police abuse!"

The detective looked at his partner, then at Officer Wallace. "Where'd you get this woman?" he asked under his breath.

"She found the victim," Officer Wallace said.

"She might be stressed out from seeing a dead body," Detective Holecek whispered to Detective Corbin.

"It's more likely she escaped from an insane asylum," he whispered back.

The detective began calling names in pairs and leading the women to the interview rooms, making sure to not call Connie Sinclaire's name until the end. First, they called Emma and Stella. Detective Corbin took Emma, and Detective Holecek took Stella.

"Was there anyone on this retreat who knew Mrs. Allnutt, someone who may have wanted to do her harm?"

Emma blinked a couple of times. "I have absolutely no idea. The only two people that I was aware of that knew each other were Isabel and Connie. They both told me they'd been best friends since childhood. That's why they wanted to room together."

"Did you hear them arguing or getting into a fight?"

Emma shook her head. "Quite the opposite."

"How's that?"

"We heard them laughing, constantly chatting, sitting together at meals. They were inseparable, in a good way."

"What's 'in a good way'?"

"Detective, they're best friends. Obviously, they enjoy each other's company."

"And you don't find that strange?"

Emma couldn't understand what he was getting at. "Detective, why would I find that strange? That's what besties do, what women do."

"'Besties'?" He raised his brows.

"Yes, 'besties.' You know, best friends?"

The detective's face went blank. "Hmmm, guess I've never heard that term."

Emma thought, *Does he live under a rock? How has he never heard women or girls referring to their besties? It's a common term.*

"Well, that's all the questions I have for now."

Emma nodded and scooted out as fast as she could. She didn't like him, not one bit. He exhibited an austere hardness, devoid of any level of compassion or understanding. Plus, the tense way he held his jaw made him look like he had lockjaw. It wasn't a normal expression, and she was pretty sure he didn't have lockjaw; rather, he was pretending to in order to look like he was tough. The detective struck her as somewhat clueless, and she wondered whether he had learned how to question witnesses by watching TV cop shows. Then, she thought if he hadn't, maybe he should have.

After interviewing Emma and Stella, the two detectives were convinced that neither of them had anything to do with the death.

Finally, only Connie Sinclaire was left. The two detectives decided it would be best if they interviewed her together.

Officer Wallace led Connie into the room. She sat down, nervous and frightened, more than she'd ever been in her life. Her palms were sweating; she wiped them on her jeans. She thought that if the detectives saw that she had sweaty palms, they might think she was guilty. Suspicious deaths were something you heard about on the news. But in the idyllic town of Waxahachie? Never.

The detectives waited to begin and simply watched her. "Why am I here?" Connie blurted out, her face red, stress oozing out of every pore. Her whole body stiffened, as though waiting to be slammed in a fight.

"You don't know why you're here?" Detective Corbin asked.

"No, no. Why am I here being interrogated?"

"Ms. Sinclaire, this isn't an interrogation. Far from it. We're simply gathering facts and trying to find out what happened."

"Oh," she said. "I thought this was an interrogation, and I would be arrested and go to trial and ..."

"Hold on," Detective Corbin said gently, trying to allay her fears. "Why do you think you'd be arrested? Have you done something wrong?"

"Of course not!" she blurted out. "I'm innocent!"

"You do know that the law states that a person is presumed innocent until proven guilty in a court of law, don't you?" He watched her carefully. She was a wreck, and he wasn't sure whether it was because she knew something or was simply afraid. Her eyes went wild, shooting all over the room like those of a cornered, feral animal.

He thought that perhaps Detective Holecek was right—she might just be in shock over finding her friend's body.

"Yes, of course, I know that!" she nearly shouted at him. "I'm not stupid, you know."

"And no one thinks or says that you are. We're simply trying to ascertain the facts. Now, can you calm down enough to answer a few questions?"

"I am calm!" she shrieked at him.

"No, you're not, and if you don't settle down, I will be forced to leave you in this room for as long as it takes for you to cool off until you can answer our questions."

"You're going to arrest me? Oh my God! I haven't done anything wrong! This is abuse! I'm going to call the police," she yelled, pulling out her cell phone.

The detective reached over and covered her hand holding the phone. "Ms. Sinclaire, remember, we are the police."

"Well, then I'll call someone else!"

The detective looked at her with the kindest expression he could muster. His wife always told him that when he employed his well-practiced puppy-dog expression, no one could resist him.

"No one is arresting you. If you can just settle down and answer a few questions, you can be on your way."

Connie leaned back, took several deep breaths, and looked back at him. "Okay," she finally said. "I'll answer your questions, as long as you don't ask me anything about what happened to Isabel."

The detective lost it, breaking out in a boisterous laugh and looking at Detective Holecek, who was trying to suppress a smile. "Seriously? What do you think I'm gonna ask you about? The weather forecast?"

"I don't know," she said, looking nervously around the room.

"Listen, all I'm going to do is ask you about what happened to your friend. Don't you want to help us find out what happened to her?"

Connie melted as far into her chair as she could. "No, no, I don't want to answer any questions!"

Detective Holecek tried convincing her in as gentle a voice as she could. "If the roles were reversed, wouldn't Isabel be willing to answer questions about what happened to you? Isn't that what a friend does?"

Connie didn't move.

"This won't take long," Detective Corbin said, but then, having lost all patience, he added, "If you want to get out of here, I suggest you quit acting like a child and answer the questions."

Connie pouted, sat up in her chair, and said, "Okay."

"Do you agree to answer all of Detective Corbin's questions and not just the ones that suit you?" Detective Holecek asked.

She looked around the room again and back at her. "All right." She turned toward the lead detective. "Just watch yourself. Don't try to entrap me."

Detective Corbin burst out laughing. "You're really a paranoid piece of work. Let's get started. I'm going to warn you only once. Answer the questions honestly and truthfully, and you'll have nothing to worry about. We just want to find out the circumstances around your friend's murder."

"Don't use that word."

"What word?"

"'Murder.'"

"Why?"

"She wasn't murdered."

"And what would you call someone who was strangled to death and is no longer breathing?"

"I-I-I don't know, but it wasn't murder."

"And what do you think it was?"

"I don't know. I think she just died."

"With a scarf tied around her neck so tightly that it cut off her airway and killed her? I'm sorry you're having so much trouble understanding this. Unless a person hangs themselves, which Isabel did not do, it's pretty hard for a victim to strangle herself. She didn't just die of natural causes. She was murdered by someone in the house."

Connie pursed her lips. "Fine! Ask your questions."

For the next hour, the detectives repeatedly asked her questions. On the first or second repetition, she clammed up or pled the fifth to prevent incriminating herself.

The detective finally sighed and said, "I'm not asking you any questions that incriminate you."

"Yes, you are. You asked me where I was before I found Isabel."

"I know that you were downstairs having breakfast because Emma and Stella told me you were. Remember what I said about being honest and truthful? Is it so hard to say you were downstairs having breakfast?"

"Well, maybe not," she admitted.

"Okay, where were you before you found Isabel?"

"You already know that I was downstairs having breakfast."

"Yes, I know it because others told me, which is hearsay. I need to hear it from you."

"Fine! I was downstairs having breakfast. Happy now?" she snarled.

And so it went for another hour. Exhausted, disgusted, and annoyed by Connie Sinclaire, Detective Corbin finally ended the interview. He decided that he was dealing with either a conniving psychopath or someone incredibly stupid, or maybe both. He stood up and glanced back at her.

"Don't leave the Waxahachie city limits."

"Why not?"

"Because I may have further questions."

"I've already answered all your questions."

"No, you haven't, far from it. Like I said, don't leave the city limits."

"And what if I do?" She shot him a scornful look.

He'd reached his limit. He whirled around. "I'll arrest you so fast you won't know what happened." He and Detective Holecek stepped over to the door. Detective Corbin opened it, slammed it shut behind them, and returned to their desks, where Detective Corbin held his head as if he were trying to keep it from exploding. A few moments later, Connie emerged from the interview room, looked over at the detective, and smirked at him.

Detective Holecek, who was sitting at her nearby desk, leaned over. "What do you think that was about?"

"I think that bat-crazy woman is trying to give me a heart attack. My grandfather used to have an expression for someone like her."

"What's that?"

"The porch light's on, but no one's home."

Back at the house, the ME collected every bit of crime scene evidence he could find. Then, he supervised Isabel being transported in a body bag on a gurney to a waiting ambulance.

At the station, Detective Corbin walked downstairs to the ME's office and found him at his desk. "Find anything?" he asked.

"You mean besides the fact that she was likely strangled to death by a silk scarf and might have died of anaphylaxis? I also found what looks like some paint embedded in her hair on the back of her head. It may match a statuette I found in the closet and bagged. Can't tell you anything else right now. Hopefully, I'll know more when I conduct the autopsy and take physical samples."

When Emma and Stella returned to the house, they entered the schoolhouse, where they found all the other students packing up their machines, supplies, and quilt projects. Connie was there too. A couple of the students told Connie how sorry they were about Isabel, but the others ignored her, packed as quickly as possible, and all but rushed out of the building. When everyone was gone, Emma and Stella searched the schoolhouse and bedrooms, looking for any items the students might have left behind. The room where Isabel's body was found was taped off with Crime Scene and Do Not Enter signs. All Emma and Stella could do was look over the tape into the room. The silk scarf was gone, having been collected with other evidence from Isabel and Connie's room.

Emma saw Stella scratching her chin. "What's up? Got an itch?"

Stella shook her head. "No, I was just thinking. I heard about a case not long ago where the police in another city were able to identify a killer from fingerprints and DNA the killer left on clothing."

"They can do that? DNA, I can understand. But how on earth can they get fingerprints from fabric?"

"Apparently, they can. In fact, in that case, they were able to get the fingerprints off of silk."

"Did you say 'silk'?" Emma asked.

"Yeah, silk. Can you believe it?"

"I'm no forensic scientist, so what do I know? All I can tell you is that the scarf that strangled Isabel was silk."

Stella slapped a hand over her mouth, then dropped it. "Oh my gosh, Emma, you're right! We should tell the police."

Emma laughed. "Don't you think they already know that? They're probably testing the scarf as we speak."

"I hope you're right. Listen, I'm exhausted. This whole thing has really worn me out. Will you be okay if I go home?"

"Of course, go!" Emma turned her toward the door.

Stella turned back around. "I told Charlene to go home after the police released everyone. She was really upset."

"I'll bet she was. We all were. You get out of here. I'm gonna go see if there's anything in the fridge. I am oddly hungry."

"Charlene told me she had prepped all of today's meals. They're in the fridge, so all you have to do is heat up a portion. Or if you're really hungry, there're twelve servings of today's lunch and supper."

"Thanks, but I'm not *that* hungry. Think I'll call Jesse and see if he wants to come over and eat."

"I was gonna suggest you do that. You shouldn't be alone in this big house tonight."

Emma reached over and gave her a big hug. "Thank you. I sure wouldn't have gotten through today without you."

"Ditto, sweetie," Stella said, then she turned and left.

Emma first called Savannah Mae after Stella left to tell her what had happened at the retreat.

"Oh, Mama, that's horrible! Are you okay?"

"Yes, honey, I'm fine. The worst is over, though I admit, I was pretty rattled in the beginning. Thank goodness Stella was here."

"Mama, can you drive?"

"Of course."

"Then put Sophie in her carrier, pack an overnight bag, and come stay with us. With a murderer loose, you shouldn't be alone in that big house."

"Savannah Mae, I'll do no such thing. I'm fine. Charlene prepared a lot of dishes to serve today and tomorrow that she left here. I'm going to call Jesse and ask him to come over and eat if he's hungry. Then, I'll pack up a bunch of food for him to take home. There's more than he or I can eat. Will you stop by today or tomorrow and pick some up too?"

"Sure, but I'd feel better if you came here."

"You and Travis are more than welcome to come over and eat with me or us, if Jesse is available."

"Oh, I wish I could. Travis has a function at the law firm later today, and we're both supposed to dress up and be there."

Emma smiled, imagining her daughter in a dress that would have the men gawking at her and the women shooting jealousy shivs her way. She certainly had gotten the best of both her and Jack.

Next, she called Jesse and briefly explained what had happened.

"I'll be there as soon as I can. Lock the doors." His voice was serious and full of worry. "And don't answer the door unless it's me, Stella, or your family." He hung up quickly, grabbed his keys, and limped as fast as he could to his truck. His normal 25- to 30-minute drive took 12 minutes. He was sure he was going to get stopped and receive a ticket, but not a police officer was in sight. He pulled into Emma's driveway, slammed on the brakes, and quickly hobbled up the stairs. Emma saw him coming through the sidelight. She opened the door as he rushed in. Jesse threw his arms around her and held her tight, burying his head in her neck. After a long time, she pulled her head back and looked up at him. She couldn't miss the worry lines etched on his face.

"Hey, I'm okay," she assured him.

"Yeah, but it could have been you who was targeted. I don't know what I'd do if I lost you."

A rush of warmth flooded her whole body. "That's very sweet, Jesse. Seriously, I am fine. Listen, there's a ton of food in the fridge that Charlene prepared. I'm starving. Have you eaten supper yet?"

"Uh no ... how could you eat given what happened?"

"Because I'd barely had a bite of breakfast when the screaming started, and after that too much was going on to even think about food. You up for a meal?"

"Sure, I haven't eaten much today either."

Jesse followed her into the kitchen and leaned into the fridge as she showed him their options.

"What do you think? Sweet and sour pork with fried rice or chow mein, or lasagna, salad, and home-baked Italian bread?"

"You pick. Anything is fine with me. Hey, are there any of her desserts in there?" he asked, looking around inside the fridge.

"You mean like her banana pudding with vanilla wafers?"

"That's what I'm talkin' about," he said, laughing quickly.

Emma pulled out the lasagna, took a knife, and cut two ample servings. "While I heat this up, would you please go to the pantry and get out a bottle of zinfandel?"

"Sure 'nuff." As soon as he turned toward the pantry, Emma placed the lasagna servings in the microwave, took out the salad and salad dressing, and sliced the Italian bread on a cutting board. She put everything on plates on the kitchen dining table, along with the butter dish. Jesse came back with the wine, opened it, and poured it into two wine glasses. Emma set the table while Jesse took the plates with lasagna out of the microwave when it beeped. They sat, and Jesse reached over to hold Emma's hand. He suggested saying a short prayer for the meal and keeping watch over Emma.

"You don't usually say a prayer before a meal," Emma observed.

"I do occasionally when the day warrants it, and today it does."

They dug into the meal, not talking much until they'd polished off their bowls of banana pudding and vanilla wafers. Jesse sat back, patting his stomach.

"Okay, tell me everything that happened today. Don't leave out a single detail."

They moved to the parlor and sat on the comfy couch, placing their wine glasses and the bottle of zinfandel on a table.

It took the better part of an hour for Emma to relay the events because she kept remembering earlier facts later in the story and had to backtrack.

"The only part I don't know much about is the interview that the detectives had with Connie at the station. Then, later, when Stella and I got back here—it took a while for one of the officers to drive us—we found the students in the schoolhouse, packing up. Connie was there and had an odd look on her face."

"'Odd' how?"

"I can't really describe it. I don't know the woman, so it could be a normal look for her. To me, she looked off-center, like she wasn't all there."

"What do you think that was about?"

Emma shrugged. "Have no idea, and my brain is too exhausted to speculate."

"Emma, you shouldn't be alone tonight."

"That's what Savannah Mae said too."

"Are you going to stay with them tonight?"

She shook her head. "No, this is my home, and I'm not going to run away and hide like a scared puppy."

Jesse watched her, looking for a thread of fear or uncertainty. He saw none. "Then I'll stay here with you."

Emma's brows shot up. "Pardon me?"

"I don't mean in your room," he quickly said. "I'll sleep here on the couch. If anyone is going to break in, they're probably going to come through the front door, kitchen door, or the one from the porch. I sleep real light. I'll hear anyone trying to enter."

"Jesse, you don't have to stay over. I'm fine, and I will be tonight too."

He laid his hands on her shoulders. "Emma, I believe you. Who I don't trust is the murderer, and until we know who that is, and that person is arrested, you shouldn't stay here alone. I'm staying with you. Here"—he pointed to the cushions—"on this couch."

"And I can't talk you out of it?"

Jesse shook his head.

"Okay then," she said, standing up. "Do you want to borrow my pink nightgown or the yellow one?" she asked with a straight face.

He broke out in a grin. "No, thanks. They're not my colors. I'll sleep in my clothes. Can you spare a pillow and a quilt?"

"Coming right up." She turned and ran upstairs to the linen closet. Sophie accompanied her and then descended the stairs and jumped on the couch with Jesse. "If the quilt isn't warm enough, Sophie will keep you nice and toasty."

Chapter Fourteen

The next day, Detective Corbin phoned and asked Emma whether Isabel's belongings were still in the house. She told him that they weren't, that before she and Stella had been taken to the police station for questioning that they watched the ME remove them.. Detective Corbin showed up ten minutes later, with an officer. They asked to see the room; she took them upstairs. The officer and the detective held up the police tape to enter the room where they dusted for fingerprints.

"You didn't mention you'd be dusting for fingerprints," Emma commented from the hallway.

"Didn't I?" the detective responded, not looking away from where he was dusting. "It's routine."

"Are you going to take my fingerprints?"

Now the detective turned, raised one brow, and looked suspiciously at her. "Should I?"

"I would think you'd want them because this is my house and my fingerprints are everywhere, including this room."

"Good observation." He turned back to where he was dusting.

"I also have a housekeeper who comes in after every retreat and cleans the whole house. Wouldn't you want her fingerprints too?"

He turned back to her again. "You never mentioned that before."

"You didn't ask."

"Fine!" he said, getting irritated with Emma. "Please ask her to come down to the station and ask for me. I'll print her myself. Even better, come down with her, and I'll print both of you at the same time."

A few weeks after the murder, Emma hadn't heard anything from the detective and thought that she should have gotten at least a phone call. She stopped in at the station and asked to see him. He came out to the waiting area and ushered her back into an office.

"What's up?" he asked.

"That's the question I was going to ask," Emma responded.

"Why?"

"Well, it's been several weeks since Isabel Allnutt was murdered in my house and that long since you dusted for fingerprints and took my and my housekeeper's fingerprints."

"And?"

"And I was wondering if you've learned anything."

"Like what?"

"Like, have you come up with a suspect?"

The detective sniggered. "You really don't know how police investigations are conducted, do you?"

Emma felt her face turn red. "Only what I watch on the cop shows."

"Well, it doesn't work that way in real life."

"Okay, enlighten me then. When can I expect to hear any kind of progress on the case?"

The detective sucked in an obvious lungful of air. "Look, I know you're concerned because it happened in your house. But since you're not the next of kin, you don't get first dibs on relevant information. The woman's husband does."

"That's understandable," Emma quipped. "I still want to be kept informed. I'm running a business in my house that has dried up completely because ladies are afraid to take classes until this case is solved."

"Why?"

"Word is going around the quilting community that there was a murder in my house. Before the first retreat, I had fully booked the first four retreats and had a six-month waiting list for the rest of the year. All the students who were booked and had prepaid for the fourth retreat have canceled and asked for a full refund, which I have done. I started calling the people on the waiting list, and not one of them wants to come now."

"That's unfortunate, but not surprising."

"Ya think?" Emma felt her face flushing. "I'm on the verge of losing my business if this murder doesn't get solved real quick. Nobody wants to come to a retreat in a house where an unsolved murder occurred."

"Sorry, but a murder investigation is not something that can be rushed. There are protocols to follow, leads to be checked out, all sorts of things you wouldn't understand."

"Try me," Emma said, standing her ground.

A woman in a police uniform cracked open the door. "Detective, if you're done here, can I have a moment with you? In my office."

When she left, the detective looked at Emma. "When the chief wants me, I gotta go." He escorted Emma out to the front and found the chief in her office next to the bullpen. Her door was open.

"Come in," she waved him in. "How's the investigation going on the Allnutt case?"

The detective nodded. "I think I've narrowed it down to one suspect."

"Oh, really? Who would that be?"

"The caterer, she's a cousin of the homeowner. Her name is Charlene Montrose."

"And why is she a suspect?"

"Right now, it's a gut feeling. I think it's her."

The chief crossed her arms over her chest. "So, what does your gut say? What's your evidence?"

"She was more upset than anyone else who was there. Then, when I dusted for fingerprints, I found her prints all over the kitchen, dining room, and banister."

"And why is that evidence?"

"Because her fingerprints were everywhere."

"She prepared all the meals, correct?"

"Yes, ma'am."

"Of course her prints would be all over the kitchen and dining room! She was catering."

"Yeah, but why would her fingerprints have been on the banister unless she was going upstairs to murder the victim after serving the food?"

"You said she is related to the homeowner, correct?"

"Yes, ma'am."

"Check with the homeowner. Since she's related, she might have been staying in the house, and her fingerprints were on the banister because she was going upstairs. Is that where all the guest rooms are located?"

The detective nodded.

"Did you find her fingerprints in the room where the body was found?"

"No, ma'am," he acquiesced. "Chief, there's more."

"Like what?"

"She's got a real attitude. And she was extremely nervous during the interview. I think she's covering up something."

"What could she possibly be covering up?"

"I don't know yet. I need to dig deeper."

The chief shook her head in disbelief.

"Are there any other suspects?"

"Well, there was one student who was suspicious, but I think she's too stupid to have done it. She's a real crackpot."

"Detective, it doesn't sound like you have much of anything. Keep digging and don't dawdle. I'm getting calls from neighbors who live around that house. They're nervous. You need to solve this case as soon as possible. If you can't, I'll pull you and assign someone else."

"Yes, ma'am. I won't let you down."

"Make sure of it and please close the door when you leave."

Frustrated that she'd gotten nowhere with the detective, Emma came home and sat on the back porch to nurse an iced tea when her brother, Keith, walked up the driveway and around the corner of the backyard, carrying something. He saw her first and called out to her.

"Hey, Emma!"

She turned and saw him, a big grin spreading across her face. "Keith! Long time no see. To what do I owe this brotherly visit?"

"Just checking in on you, sis." He walked up the stairs and sat down on a chair, placing the bag he was carrying on a table between them.

Emma pointed to the bag. "What's this?"

"Just a little something I made for you. Here." He handed her one of the two forks he took out of the bag.

Emma looked at him quizzically. "Okay, so it's something edible."

Keith nodded.

"I'll go get some plates," she said, starting to stand up.

"No need," he said.

As she sat, Keith took out a homemade pie. Emma grinned like a kid about to open a birthday present. "What kind is it?"

He smiled, keeping the mystery to himself. "Dig in and figure it out for yourself."

"Are you serious?"

"Yep, take a bite, dear sister, and tell me what you think it is."

Emma knew her brother's fondness for baking pies. He'd won countless blue ribbons at the county fair. She scooped a bite off the edge to make sure she got an ample bite with his prize-winning flaky crust. As soon as the forkful passed her lips, she closed her eyes, savoring the sweet-sour taste of the pie. She opened them to see Keith watching her intently.

"Raspberry rhubarb pie!" she squealed like a little girl. "You remembered it was my favorite when we were kids."

"Sure do. Figured if anything could cheer you up, this could."

"You nailed it, Keith. This is sooooo good. Why did you bring two forks?"

"You can't eat this whole pie by yourself."

Emma laughed. "No? Try me." She grabbed the pie just as Keith's hand holding the fork jetted across to get a bite.

Keith's face fell. "Really, I made you this pie, and you won't share it with me?"

Emma broke out in a laughing fit like she did when she was a girl and would play a practical joke on him. Keith was always a sucker for Emma's teasing. She placed the pie back on the little table between them. Keith dove in and took a big bite with his fork. Not to be outdone, Emma took an even bigger mouthful. And on it went, each of them trying to outdo the other. When they'd devoured nearly half the pie, they both sat back in their chairs to catch their breath and digest what they'd eaten.

"Oh, Keith, I'd forgotten how much I loved this pie."

"I didn't, and I must say you now look a lot happier than when I got here. So, what's up? Why are you in a funk?"

"This may take a while. Are you thirsty?"

"Always."

"I'll be right back. Now, don't go eating any more of **my** pie until I get back."

"Yes, ma'am." He saluted her and, the second she went inside the house, snuck another bite.

She returned a few minutes later, carrying two champagne glasses filled with a light-colored bubbly liquid.

"Champagne?"

Emma beamed. "Close. Prosecco."

Keith took a bite of pie and washed it down with a slurp of prosecco. "Perfect! Okay, now, tell me what's going on, Emma." He sat back in the chair, waiting for Emma to tell her tale.

By now, she had every frustrating detail of the afternoon at the police station memorized. After Keith heard it, he leaned forward.

"I have an idea, but I need to talk to some folks first about it. I'll get back to you."

"You know where to find me, I'm not going anywhere."

"And just to show how much I love you, I'm going to leave the rest of the pie here with you."

"That's good, because I was going to fight you for it if you tried to take it."

"See ya, Emma."

"See ya, Keith."

Keith wasn't gone five minutes before her phone rang. It was Jesse.

"Since you don't have a retreat going on right now, you up for some of the best seafood that'll ever cross your lips?"

"Oooh, that sounds lovely. What do you have in mind?"

"Have you been to Atkins Seafood?"

Emma thought for a minute before responding. "Nope, don't think I have."

"Do you like seafood?"

"Love it. When I lived in Georgia, I must have eaten fresh-caught seafood three times a week. Couldn't get enough of it. There certainly wasn't a seafood restaurant in Waxahachie when I grew up here."

"Then you're in for a nice surprise."

"There's only one problem."

"What's that?"

"My brother was just here. He brought me his homemade raspberry rhubarb pie."

"Why is that a problem?"

"We ate half of it. I'm not hungry."

"I have a solution. There's an architectural salvage warehouse I've been wanting to visit to pick up some ideas on a new job I'll be starting. We could walk around there, and you might work up an appetite."

"Oh, I'd like that. I might find something to put in the house."

"Chances are good you will. Pick you up in half an hour?"

"I'll be waiting on the front porch swing."

Thirty minutes later, Jesse pulled up in front of the house and whisked her off to an architectural salvage warehouse in town. They walked inside, and Emma stopped in her tracks; it was more than she could have imagined. The interior was huge, as large as a warehouse club. They slowly walked through row after row of lighting fixtures, antique carved doors, Tiffany-style stained-glass antique windows, arched cathedral and farmhouse window frames, wall pediments, intricate corbels, dozens of wall scones, and things Emma could not even identify.

"Oh my goodness, Jesse, look at that!"

He turned around and saw her pointing at a very large cast-iron skeleton key. He took out his digital measure to figure out the dimensions: It was fourteen inches long and five inches wide.

"Isn't that amazing?" she cooed over the massive key.

"I don't know, Emma, it's too big to open any of your doors. Besides, I doubt it will fit in that little purse you carry around. You're gonna have to start using a really big tote bag." He turned away so she wouldn't see him smiling.

"You're such a brat, Jesse!" she said, playfully slapping him on the arm.

"Emma, seriously, why do you want it? It has no function."

"You are such a man. I like it, and it doesn't need a function if I like it."

"What are you going to do with it?"

Emma jutted out her chin. "I'm going to have a contractor friend of mine hang it on one of the walls in the reading room."

"And who would that be?"

She raised her eyebrows and cocked her head sideways. "Would you please take one of them down?"

Seeing she was completely serious, he reached up and removed one from a higher shelf. He held it across his two open hands, palms up, and bowed his head. "M'lady, your key."

She took it from him. "This sure is heavy. It really is made of cast iron."

"You should put it where you can get to it easily. If any burglars break into the house, you can hit them on the head with it, and they'll probably stay passed out until they wake up in jail."

"That, or I'll accidentally kill 'em."

"Yes, that too."

They continued wandering through the rows and rows of stuff. In one row, Emma spied a box full of miscellaneous crystals that at one point probably hung on chandeliers. She began rifling through the box.

"Whatcha doin'?" Jesse asked.

"I've been wanting some of these. I had no idea where to find them."

"What are you going to use them for?"

"I'm going to thread them with the heaviest thread or yarn I have and tie them onto the lowest tree branches around the property."

"And that would be because ...?"

"Because when the sun rises and sets, the rays will hit the crystals, making them shimmer like magic. Wait and see. It'll be dazzling."

"I'll take your word for it," he said, lifting the box of crystals and putting it into the basket.

They kept walking up and down the rows until Jesse stopped in the middle of a row of doorknobs. Emma came up beside him.

"Is this what you were looking for?" she asked.

"Sure is. I have a client who wants me to return her house to how it looked when it was built in 1890. She asked me to replace all the cabinet knobs and interior doorknobs with vintage glass. These are exactly what she wants. The centers are mercury glass stars."

"That sounds like a lot of replacing."

"It is, and I told her that I doubt they'll all match, but if they're all made with the antique glass, they'll be close enough."

"Was she okay with that?"

Jesse nodded. "She knows that she doesn't have much choice. It's not like you can go into a big-box home improvement store and order a few hundred antique glass knobs."

"Are you going to buy everything they have here in stock?"

"I will, yes, just not today."

"Why not? I mean, as long as we're here."

"Because I'll have to load them all into the back of my truck, and they could get stolen while we're having dinner. It's better to come back and buy them when I can take them straight to the client's house."

"That's true. By the way, you achieved your goal of coming here."

"Finding the glass knobs?"

Emma shook her head. "Walking all around this place has definitely worked up my appetite."

"Okay, let's go then."

"Not before I buy my key and my crystals," she said, pointing to the iron skeleton key in the basket and box of crystals. "I really love that key," she added, looking at it like it was a highly sought-after treasure. She steered the basket toward the checkout stand.

She left the key and box of crystals on the floorboard of Jesse's truck when they pulled in front of Atkins Seafood. She got out and stood in front of the restaurant's large window, staring.

"Something wrong?"

"Nothing," Emma responded. "I must have driven by this place dozens of times. I don't know how I missed it. Let's go in, the smell is killin' me."

Jesse held the door open for her, and once they were inside, a hostess took them to a booth in the back. In the booth right next to the one where they were being seated sat Aunt Thelma and Aunt Ruth. The three sisters did a double take.

"Sweet sister," Ruth began, "what are you doing here?" Thelma nodded her head in agreement.

"I'm pretty sure the same thing y'all are doing here—getting my seafood fix, courtesy of this handsome man here," she responded, waving her hand toward Jesse.

"Introduce us to your date, Emma," Thelma asked. "We haven't met your friend."

Emma thought, *Date? He isn't a date.*

After making introductions, Ruth and Thelma invited Emma and Jesse to sit with them. Emma and Jesse exchanged glances, shrugged, and stepped forward to join them. Thelma and Ruth rearranged their seats to sit on one side together, leaving the other side of the booth for Emma and Jesse. They slid in comfortably and picked up the menus. Emma spent one minute looking at hers.

"Okay, I'm ready to order. How about you?" she asked her sisters and Jesse.

"How could you have read the whole menu that fast?" Jesse asked.

"As soon as I saw a couple of things I love, I was done reading."

"And what would they be?"

"Oysters on the half shell and a lobster roll."

Jesse slightly turned his head and looked at her sideways. "You're going to eat raw oysters?"

"You bet!" I used to get 'em all the time in Georgia. Love 'em!"

"I've always wondered something about oysters, and now I finally know someone to ask. First, Thelma and Ruth, do you love them too?"

Ruth and Thelma laughed. "Not as much as our dear sister," Ruth said.

Jesse looked at Emma. "I have a burning question to ask you."

Emma nodded, encouraging him to go on.

"How can you look at a slimy, gelatinous thing like an oyster and say to yourself, 'That looks delicious, think I'll eat it'?"

Emma howled. "I wasn't always a fan of oysters. Early in our marriage, my husband took me to a seafood restaurant near where we lived in Georgia. He ordered a dozen oysters on the half shell and challenged me to eat one. We were always daring each other, and honestly, when he goaded me to eat an oyster, I was prepared to lose because, like you, I couldn't fathom how a person could look at a hideous oyster and suck it down."

"So, who won the challenge?" Jesse asked.

"I did, of course." She shrugged, proud of herself.

"How did you mentally put the sliminess aside and eat it?"

"Larry showed me that when you first try a raw oyster, you should doctor it up with horseradish or hot sauce or garlic butter or lemon juice or cocktail sauce or any kind of sauce you like. I've even had oysters with pesto."

Jesse's mouth hung slightly open as he slowly nodded his head. "Well, Mrs. Emma Clayburne Jenkins, you are braver than I."

"It's not a matter of being brave, silly. Once you taste one topped with your favorite sauce, you'll be hooked."

A smile spread across Jesse's face. "I've eaten some pretty weird stuff in my life, never oysters, and I don't plan to start eating 'em now."

Emma burst out in a big grin. "That settles it, then."

Jesse furrowed his brow. "Settles what?"

"I get all the oysters and don't have to share any with you," she said happily. "Ruth and Thelma, what are y'all going to order?"

"Crab cakes for me," Ruth said.

"Probably today's fish special," Thelma answered. "I usually order it blackened. Ever since Paul Prudhomme, that chef in New Orleans, popularized it, that's the only way I eat fish."

Out of the corner of one eye, Emma saw someone approaching their table. "Oh, here comes the waiter."

After they ordered, their food came quickly, or at least it seemed that way. Emma looked at Ruth's crab cakes. "Those look yummy."

"They are," Ruth said. "You should order them sometime."

Emma watched Thelma take a bite of her blackened fish. "How is it?"

"Tender, perfectly blackened, and incredibly fresh. It tastes like it was caught this morning."

"What kind is it?"

"Redfish."

Then, she looked over at Jesse's plate. "I can't believe you ordered a burger in a seafood restaurant."

"It's not just any kind of burger, it's a salmon burger," he explained, taking off the top of the bun to show her a perfectly grilled pink salmon burger studded with flecks of herbs, scallions, and little bits of something bright green.

Emma pointed to the bits of bright green. "What's the green stuff?"

"Not sure, probably jalapeño."

"Who puts jalapeño in a salmon burger?" she asked, wrinkling her nose.

"It's really good. I always order it here." He lifted up his plate. "You wanna try a bite?"

She tossed her head side to side. "Thanks, I'll pass. Did you want to try one of my oysters?" She bit her lip to keep from laughing.

Jesse shook his head. "I'll stick with what I've got. I have an idea. You eat your oysters, and I'll eat my salmon burger, and we'll both be happy."

"Deal!" Emma grinned as she slurped another oyster, letting it course down her throat. She proceeded to slowly savor each and every little mollusk that was hers and hers alone.

Chapter Fifteen

Emma was growing bolder by the day and proving to be relentless. Even though the detective refused to give her any information when she visited him, she called him at least once a day, pretty much hounding him to provide some info on the status of the case. Most of the time he didn't answer, and he never returned her calls. That didn't stop her from continuing to call and leave messages. She figured that she would wear him down and that he would eventually take her call or return one.

Her tenacity paid off. After ten days of her incessant calling, her phone rang, and she had no sooner answered than Detective Corbin said as calmly as he could, "Mrs. Jenkins, because the case is still under investigation, I am not at liberty to share anything with you. You can keep calling me all you want, but it won't change anything."

"Look, why don't you make this easier on both of us and give me some credible news? Then, I'll stop bothering you."

"If I give you something, you're saying you'll stop annoying me?"

"For the short term, yes, until there's new news."

The detective sighed so loudly that it sounded like he was outside and a strong wind was blowing.

"Fine! We got the autopsy report, and it showed two severe injuries, either of which could have caused her death."

"Okay, that's a good start. I assume one was strangulation with the scarf. What was the other?"

"Don't you ever quit?"

"Nope. Keep talking."

The detective let out another hurricane-loud sigh. "The ME determined that the killer must have first attempted to strangle Isabel with the scarf. He thinks that the killer wasn't strong enough to choke the victim to death. He suggested that the killer probably grabbed the statuette he found in the room and hit her hard enough on the head not just to knock her out; the blow likely caused a lethal traumatic brain injury."

"That's helpful. You'd think that a scarf tied so tightly around her neck would be sufficient."

"Maybe the killer had a Plan B when Plan A went awry."

"One more question."

"I thought we were done here."

"Almost. Did the ME test the scarf for fingerprints?"

"You can't do that!"

"Actually you can. Google it. Apparently back in 2011, researchers in Scotland discovered they could lift prints from fabric. Don't you keep up with this kind of stuff?"

"I don't have time because it's wasted by taking unwarranted calls like this!" He slammed down the phone.

At least I got some information out of him, she thought.

Right about that time, her brother, Keith, stopped in again to see her. This time, he wasn't carrying a pie or anything else. As Emma opened the front door and led him into the parlor, he asked, "How's the investigation going? Have the police come up with any suspects?"

"Afraid not," she said in a heavy-hearted voice. "I'm beginning to think that the case is never going to get solved, which means my retreat business is going to bite the dust. Permanently."

Keith laid a hand on one of her shoulders and gave it a squeeze. "Don't lose faith. Remember when I was here, I said I needed to look into something?"

Emma nodded.

"I have a suggestion."

Emma stepped back and looked at her brother, her face showing doubt and discouragement.

"This is kind of a wild idea, but given that the professionals haven't come up with any leads, why not try something off-the-wall?"

She tried to smile. Though her lips turned up at the corners, her demeanor remained melancholy. Keith saw it and ignored her misery.

"So, you know that I'm in a Sherlock Holmes club, right?"

Emma nodded.

"I'm going to call a meeting of the club members and tell them about what happened here."

"And how would that help?"

"Hear me out. We've actually solved a few crimes."

"Like what?"

"Break-ins, purse snatching, shoplifting, that kind of thing. Mostly infractions that don't require jail time, misdemeanors."

"Any murders?"

"Uh, no," Keith admitted. "But that doesn't mean we couldn't solve it. And since the police haven't figured it out, why not let some novices try?"

Emma nodded. "You're right. There's no harm in that. Maybe your group will have better luck."

"That's my girl!" he said, patting her on the shoulder. "I'll get in touch with 'em."

She had no sooner closed the front door behind him than her phone rang. She saw it was Jesse.

"Hey, are you in any better spirits today?"

She tried to smile into the phone, without success. "I could tell you 'yes,' but I'd be lying. I think the police have given up on the case. And now, my brother, Keith, is going to see if his Sherlock Holmes club can figure it out."

"Your brother is in a Sherlock Holmes club?" Jesse couldn't hide his surprise.

"Yep."

"Is it like a book club?"

"Well, maybe, I don't know what all they do. Keith told me that they've solved a couple of crimes."

"Are you sure?"

"He says they have."

"What kind?"

"Infractions and misdemeanors."

"Have they solved anything major, like a murder?"

"Nope. I figure, what have I got to lose in letting them try?"

Over the next two weeks, Keith's Sherlock Holmes club spent hours every week interviewing all sorts of people, including Isabel's husband, hoping to learn even one tiny bit of information that would help them find the killer. That, too, turned into a bust. Despite the many weeks that had gone by, Hank Allnutt was as grief-stricken as the day the police knocked on his door and told him that Isabel had died at the retreat under questionable circumstances. When the club members had exhausted every possible avenue of discovery, they admitted that their search had been futile and walked away from it. Keith was designated to call Emma. She wasn't surprised when he phoned her with the bad news.

"I'm really sorry, Em, we really wanted to solve this for you."

"It's okay, Keith, it was a long shot. Please tell your club buddies that I appreciate all the effort everyone made."

"What are you going to do now? I mean, the house is outfitted for retreats, and you have that beautiful classroom. Seems like a real shame not to use it."

"Don't you worry, Keith. I can easily convert the student rooms in the house back to how they were set up before. As for the schoolhouse, if I have to move my bedroom down there to keep it from languishing, I will. I love the schoolhouse. Jesse and his crew did such a phenomenal job that I cannot, will not, let it go to waste."

"Again, I'm real sorry my club couldn't come through for you. And if you do decide to throw in the towel and need some muscle moving stuff around to convert the rooms back to how they were, you call me. I mean it."

"I promise, Keith. I will."

After she hung up, she went to the schoolhouse and sat in the quilt chair Jesse had had made for her. She looked around and felt her throat tighten. She shook her head. "What was I thinking?" she said out loud. "Like I could make a go of a quilt retreat center when I've never even been to one."

She didn't hear someone knocking on the door. The door slowly opened. Ruth, Thelma, Stella, and Bonnie Ada walked in. Emma was so surprised, she shot up out of her chair and placed her hand over her heart.

"Oh, it's y'all! You nearly scared me to death."

"We did knock, Emma," Ruth stated, and the others nodded in agreement. "You must have been buried in some deep thought and didn't hear us."

"Oh, I was," Emma responded. "Every effort to find whoever killed Isabel has gone to mush. The police, even Keith's Sherlock Holmes club, have all failed. At this point, it looks like whoever did this is going to get away with it, and no one is going to want to come to a retreat at the site of an unsolved murder. I might as well put the main house back the way it was and make plans to use this schoolhouse for some other purpose. Other than moving my bedroom down here, I can't think of what that might be."

"Chère," Bonnie Ada spoke up. "I see that you set up all your machines and supplies down here. Am I correct?"

Emma nodded. "I moved everything down here so I could turn the bedroom on the second floor I had been using for sewing into a student guest room."

"Emma, honey," Stella interjected. "When you first showed it to me, I told you that this is the most astonishing sewing space I've ever seen. You could rent space by the hour or day for people wanting to use it. Please don't give up hope." Ruth, Thelma, and Bonnie Ada nodded in agreement.

"Thank you, Stella. Thank you all. I'm just going to have to muddle through this."

"Agreed, Emma," Thelma said. "Just remember one thing."

Emma looked at her sister. "What's that?"

"You are not in this alone. You have us, and the whole rest of the family." Thelma looked Emma up and down. "It's obvious that you haven't been eating right, or eating enough." Stella, Ruth, and

Bonnie Ada nodded. "You've lost weight, haven't you?" Thelma asked.

"Well, maybe a little."

"Then we're going to do something about that right now. We brought you lunch," Bonnie Ada said, holding up a large brown bag.

Emma shook her head. "You didn't have to do that."

"Yes, we did," Bonnie Ada stated, like a schoolteacher giving a young student no say in the matter. "Let's go up to the big house."

As Bonnie Ada and Thelma began unpacking the bag in the kitchen and transferred everyone's lunch from the carry-out containers to china plates, Ruth set the table. Stella filled up glasses with sweet tea she found in the fridge. Emma saw a card from the restaurant.

"Fern in the Wild?" Emma asked, reading the name of the restaurant where they'd picked up the food. "Never heard of it. What kind of food do they serve?"

"Astonishing food," Ruth said. "I always order their shrimp and asparagus risotto."

"And I usually get the Wagyu steak sandwich," Stella piped up.

Thelma added, "I adore the bobwhite quail and the chicken salad sandwich. It's always hard to pick between the two."

Emma looked at Bonnie Ada. "And you?"

"The sweet and spicy BLT. Never had one better."

"Okay then!" Emma uttered.

"Since you need to put on a couple of pounds, chère," Bonnie Ada stated, "we picked up pasta carbonara for you. It's decadent to a fault."

After Emma finished her pasta, she snuck a bite of everyone else's dishes. "I think I just regained the seven pounds I lost."

"Good!" Ruth quipped. "Okay, it's time to talk business."

"Business? What business?" Emma asked.

"Yours," Ruth, Stella, Thelma, and Bonnie Ada said.

"Why bother? I'm on the verge of losing it."

"Not necessarily," Stella persisted, knowing that Emma was ready to give up and walk away from the retreat business. Stella looked at Bonnie Ada and nodded her head, indicating it was time for her to bring up her suggestion.

"Chère, there is one other option that hasn't been explored for figuring out the killer."

"What could that possibly be?" Emma asked. "Everything has led to a dead end."

Bonnie Ada sat back and looked around the table, finally focusing on Emma. "Not quite everything. Emma, you know that I'm from N'awlins, and all my people go back many generations in the Crescent City." Emma nodded.

"Now, I don't know how much you know about the Creole and Cajun cultures, so bear with me."

Bonnie Ada described the spirituality of the Creole and Cajun cultures, noting the great respect both cultures have for those who have passed. She added that in her family, no one felt like loved ones who had died were ever really gone.

"I grew up talking to relatives that I'd never known in their bodily form. My parents, grandparents, and siblings did too. It came naturally to us."

Emma glanced at Ruth and Thelma and back at Bonnie Ada. "Bonnie Ada, we have spirits in our house too. Ruth, Thelma, Keith, and I grew up with them."

"Really? Then talking to spirits is not unfamiliar to you?"

"Not at all, although they seemed to favor Keith."

"Do they still appear from time to time?" Bonnie Ada asked.

"As far as I know, yes. They've even made their presence known to Savannah Mae."

"Well! This makes my suggestion easier."

"And that is?" Emma asked.

"Hold a séance at the house. Talk to the spirits to find out what they observed in the room where the woman died. Who knows—if the spirit of the woman who died has not left, she may speak to you."

Emma sat back in her seat, thinking and watching Bonnie Ada. After several minutes, she spoke.

"Bonnie Ada, that's not a bad idea. Over the years, we've identified most of the spirits in the house and know them as family members who mean us no harm."

"We've always thought that they must have had good lives in the house and stayed after passing," Ruth chimed in. "Even as children, we were never scared of them."

"Here's what I suggest," Bonnie Ada began. "I'll get in touch with some relatives who have more experience with séances than I. You need an experienced medium, someone who can be trusted. I'll get a recommendation and get back to y'all. How does that sound?"

Everyone nodded their heads. "Sounds like the best idea I've heard yet," Emma said.

A few days later, Bonnie Ada called to say her cousin in New Orleans knew a medium in Dallas with an excellent reputation. She gave Emma the woman's contact info and wished her the best of luck. Emma called the medium and learned that she had a one-month waiting list.

"How does this work? Do I come up with the people who attend? How many people should participate? Is there a website I can review on tips for holding a séance?"

The medium, Louisa Caldwell, chuckled. "You've never participated in a séance before, have you?"

"Is it that obvious?"

"Very, but don't worry about it. There's a first time for everyone. Now, can you tell me a bit about who you want to reach, and why?"

Emma told her everything about the retreat, the murder, the police detective, and the spirits in the house who might have observed something.

"Wow! This sounds like a very interesting case," Louisa declared. "I wish I had an opening sooner. Tell ya what, I'll put you on my waiting list."

"That would be great. Now, how do I get ready?"

"Go to my website—here, I'll send you the link. Click on 'How to Prepare for Your First Séance.' You'll find everything you need to know. Meanwhile, think of at least six and no more than ten people who would participate and hopefully not be intimidated attending a séance. A lot of people say they want to participate, only to find it frightens them, and they bolt out of the room. When that happens, the spirits usually bolt too."

"I don't think that would be a problem at my house. The people who would be attending are family who have lived in the house and know the spirits. The other two people are close friends who are aware of them and not bothered by them at all."

As soon as she got off the phone with Louisa, she texted Stella, Bonnie Ada, Ruth, Savannah Mae, Thelma, and Keith, apprising them of her conversation with the medium. She let them know she'd reserved the next available opening a month out plus put her name on a waiting list in case there was a cancellation. She had no sooner hit 'send' than her phone rang. It was Savannah Mae.

"Really, Mama? A séance?" Savannah Mae blurted as soon as Emma answered.

"Yes, really. The police aren't doing a thing, and the detective won't provide any updates. The autopsy showed that there were two possible causes of death, and then the trail of clues went cold. Keith's Sherlock Holmes club came in and tried to help, to no avail. If I don't try something else, this case will never get solved, and I might as well close up the retreat business."

"But Mama, don't you think having a séance is a bit of a stretch?"

"No, darling, not at all. You know as well as I do that we have a family of ghosts living here. I'm hoping that they saw something, anything, that will help lead us to the killer. I'm at the end of my rope."

"I get that, Mama. I'm just concerned that the medium will be a fraud. Swindlers do that, you know."

"Yes, I do know that. Believe me, I didn't look for mediums on social media or Google. Bonnie Ada suggested the idea. She has a cousin in New Orleans who knows a couple of authentic mediums with very good reputations, one of whom lives in Dallas. That's who I'm hiring."

"What's the person's name?"

"Louisa Caldwell."

"Okay, I'm going to do some research and find out everything I can about her. Please don't pay her anything until I can verify that she's the real deal."

Emma let out a long sigh. "All right. Take your time, her next opening isn't for a month."

Savannah Mae heard the annoyance in her mother's voice. "Mama, please don't be upset with me. I just want to make sure she's honest and an actual medium, with a proven track record, not some scam artist out to take your money and feed you lies."

"And I appreciate your concern, Savannah Mae, I do. If you want to look into Louisa, go ahead. All I ask is that you tell me what you find out."

"Will do, Mama." As soon as she hung up, Savannah Mae dialed her best friend, Maggie Bowen, in California. As an HR specialist who investigated the applicants her company was considering hiring, if anyone could find the dirt on or confirm the credibility of Louisa Caldwell, Maggie could.

Emma was feeling mentally exhausted. She needed to get out of the house, to escape, to do something outside her usual activities. But what? A cloud of uncertainty was hanging over her, affecting her normally upbeat character and outlook. She had rushed into creating the retreat house and setting up classes. Now, she was wondering about the unavoidable repercussions she had created without thinking through all the possibilities that could arise. Then, she realized that even if she had taken an additional year to fully plan for the retreat center, she never would have considered that there would be a murder on-site. Emma decided that she should call Jesse. He might have an idea for a good distraction. Just then, her phone rang. As though he had heard her thoughts, it was Jesse.

She answered the phone by asking, "Are you psychic?"

"What? Why?"

"Because I was thinking of calling you for a suggestion, and before I could dial your number, you called me."

"I'm pretty sure it's just a coincidence, Emma. What kind of suggestion are you looking for?"

"Something to take my mind off the stress of being on the brink of losing my business, and of everything causing it. I was thinking that a good ride on a horse might be what I need."

The answer was so obvious that he smiled into the phone. "Well, you do have a daughter who lives on a pretty nice ranch with a lot of horses. I'm sure she'd set you up on a ride and maybe go with you."

"Ugh! What was I thinking? Jesse, you're absolutely right, except I talked to her a short while ago, and she's got a few other things going on. I don't want to bother her. I need to expel some nervous energy. Any ideas?"

"You want to talk through what's bothering you?"

"Not now, maybe later. I know—water, I need to be around water. It has a calming effect on me. "

"That's doable, but whaddaya say we go to a body of water a ways away?"

"What do you have in mind?"

"It's a surprise, I can't tell you."

Emma laughed. "You and your surprises! Come on, tell me."

"Nope."

"Can you at least tell me if I should wear an evening gown and high heels or something more casual?"

"Definitely something very casual that you don't mind getting wet and can throw in the washer. Same for your shoes. Maybe some old sneakers. Oh, and bring a hat and sunscreen."

"So, you won't tell me where we're going or what we'll be doing except to say that I might get wet and to dress for that, plus wear a hat and sunscreen?"

"Exactly. Be ready in a half hour, darlin.' I'll pick you up." Emma smiled as she put the phone down. He'd never called her "darlin'" before. She liked how it sounded.

Thirty minutes later, Jesse pulled up in front of the house. Emma had been watching for him and stepped out of the house, locked the front door, and walked quickly down the steps. As soon as she got into his truck, Jesse reached over and took her hand in his.

"Ready for an adventure?"

"Always," she informed him, a gleam of happiness sparkling in her eyes.

About an hour later, Jesse pulled up in front of a watercraft rental business next to the Brazos River in Waco. He glanced over at her and felt a sense of pride seeing the look of wonder sweeping across her face.

"Jesse, you nailed it," Emma enthused. "This is going to be a lot of fun!"

"And you don't mind getting wet if you fall in the water or get splattered by a paddle?"

"Why would I fall in the water or get splattered by a paddle? Are you planning to play rough?"

"Who, me?" he grinned, pointing to himself.

"Yeah, you! Game on, Jesse!" She chuckled as she got out of the truck and headed for a small building that appeared to be the rental office. Jesse was right behind her.

In a matter of minutes, Jesse rented a canoe for two.

"For how long, sir?" the clerk at the desk asked him, wide dimples on the sides of his lips, giving him an impish appearance.

Jesse looked at Emma. "You up for a half day on the river? Or do you want to go easy your first time out and do only an hour or two?"

"I'm pretty sure I can handle a half day. I'm no wuss, you know."

Jesse couldn't suppress a burst of laughter. "That you are definitely not!"

After a guide showed them how to properly operate the canoe, they got in, Emma at the front and Jesse behind her. They slowly rowed into the middle of the river. A mild breeze blew toward them, the air warm, a balm to her unsettled soul. Its tender touch on her skin infused her spirit with a quiet serenity. Inches below her, the river's crystalline surface reflected the translucent blue sky and cumulus clouds above. If she allowed herself, she was sure she could curl up in the canoe and drift off to sleep.

"You're not saying anything," Jesse said from behind her. "You okay?"

Emma nodded without looking back. "I haven't been this relaxed in quite a while. This was a great idea."

After a while, he pointed to a place way up the shoreline where they could park the canoe. "Let's aim for over there."

They rowed the boat to the shore. After they landed the canoe, they got out and pulled it up on the shore away from the water to prevent it from floating back into the river. Jesse pulled out a small nylon backpack he'd brought with him. They stood and took in how the gold-colored skies cast a sultry glow on the water. They heard the sounds of animals, and once they sat down, they spied raccoons, white-tail deer, and gray foxes. A squirrel scolded them with loud chittering, making Emma laugh.

"He's more rude than the ones in my yard."

"Probably female," Jesse attempted to say without snickering.

"Jesse Rieger! You take that back!"

"It is a female."

"And how would you know that?"

"See how fluffy she is? She's pregnant."

"Maybe it's just a fluffy squirrel."

"It's 'cuz her belly is enlarged. See how big her nipples are? That's 'cuz she's pregnant and will be nursing her kits when they're born. Hey, look," he added as the squirrel turned sideways. "Now, you can see how big her belly is."

Emma focused and looked hard at the squirrel. She considered that Jesse might be right.

"Plus pregnant squirrels are territorial," Jesse added. "We may be too close to where she's building her nest, and that's why she's yelling at us."

"How do you know so much about squirrels, especially pregnant ones?"

"My parents had a pecan orchard, and there were a lot of squirrels on the property. Ya kinda learn through observation. Tom and I used to play a game counting how many pregnant squirrels we saw. Whoever counted the most would win one of Mom's pecan chewy bars."

"Huh! Whaddaya know?"

A little farther down, Jesse pointed to a small American alligator basking in the sun and a bobcat on the opposite shore. Emma turned to Jesse, her face in awe.

"Aren't they dangerous?"

"Only if you bother them. We'll keep our distance. As long as you don't bother them, they won't bother you. If you enter their space, they'll see you as a threat and will charge to protect their home and possibly family."

"Don't worry, I'm not going anywhere near them."

They stood on the riverbank and watched the water leap over the shoals nestled in the shallow water. Jesse took her hand.

"Let's sit."

As soon as they were settled, Jesse removed a fabric cloth from the pack and laid it down between them. Next, he pulled out a chilled bottle of white wine, a wine opener, and two plastic wine glasses.

"How romantic!" Emma exclaimed.

Jesse didn't say a word, concentrating on opening the wine bottle. He filled both glasses and handed one to Emma.

"Shall we toast something?" he asked.

"To a perfect day," she suggested.

They touched their glasses in a toast, and Jesse reached back into the pack, took out a plastic container, and opened it to reveal a small spread of sliced cheese and salami, two small forks laying on top. Finally, he removed napkins and a third container that held crackers.

"You thought of everything," Emma said.

"I try," he said with a smile.

For the longest time, they sat watching the water and the animals, in no rush to leave. After finishing their snack, he put everything into the backpack and moved closer to Emma, putting his arm around her. She laid her head on his shoulder, where it fit perfectly into the crook of his neck. The warmth of his body infused her with a calm, peaceful feeling. Jesse gently lifted her head, turning her face toward his. They locked eyes and slowly met each other's lips. He ran his hands through her hair and held her face in his hands. When he pulled back, she was beaming, and he took that as a good sign.

"I wasn't expecting that," she whispered. "That was nice."

Jesse bent down and kissed her again, this time with more passion than before.

"What's happening here?" she asked him.

"What do you think is happening?" he asked, staring at her.

"Either you're about to give me your class ring and ask me to go steady, or we're moving beyond friends."

"I never had a class ring," Jesse responded, a slight smile gracing his lips. "I think we're both moving beyond friendship."

"It's about time."

The sun began its descent toward the west, signaling that it was time to row back. They got into the canoe and rowed leisurely to the rental dock. They got back in the truck and headed back to Waxahachie.

Neither of them said a word as they drove back, each immersed in their own thoughts. As the sun dipped below the horizon, the moon hid behind a veil of clouds, shadowing the earth in twilight in that alluring hour of half day and half night. Jesse pulled up in front of her house just as the clouds parted and dissipated. Not realizing that Jesse had parked in front of the house, Emma stared out of the front windshield at the stars beginning to poke through the night sky. It looked like someone had tossed a handful of glitter up into the sky, sprinkling sparkles all across the heavens. She looked around and realized he had brought her home.

"Do you have a job in the morning?" she asked before getting out.

He shook his head. "Finished up a kitchen remodel the day before yesterday. Don't have another one starting for a couple of weeks."

"That's nice to have a break. What do you plan to do? Are you going to take some time off?"

He nodded. "Yeah, I'm fixin' to. Going to Santa Fe."

"I've heard it's incredible."

"You've never been there?"

Emma shook her head. "Are you going alone?"

"I hope not. I have a friend that I'm going to ask to go with me, but I don't know if she will."

Emma felt a lump form in her throat. *He has a friend, a female friend? Silly me, thinking we were going somewhere with this.* She reached for the handle to let herself out of his truck quickly before she became emotional. She jumped out of the truck and stuck her head back inside. "I hope your friend can go with you, because God only knows how much you deserve a vacation. You've been working really hard." She turned and headed toward the steps to her house. She was so caught up in her disappointment that she didn't hear Jesse get out of the truck and limp after her.

"Emma!" he shouted, taking hold of her arm.

She turned around quickly, looking down at his hand grasping her arm and back up at his face, carved with worry lines. The air between them tightened, like a taut string. "What?" she asked sadly.

"It's you."

"What's me?"

"You're the friend I want to go with me."

"Well, why didn't you say so?"

"I was about to when you got out of the truck. I couldn't take another woman. We've become more than friends. I'm crazy about you, don't you know that by now?"

Her face softened. She leaned into him and kissed him lightly. "Come," she said, taking his hand and guiding him toward the steps. "Let's go sit on the back porch, watch the moon rise, and talk about Santa Fe."

Chapter Sixteen

A few days later, in the dawn of early morning, Jesse and Emma transported Sophie to Savannah Mae and Travis's ranch. Before they could ring the doorbell, Savannah Mae opened the door, kneeled down, and cooed at Sophie. "Remember me, sweetie?" Sophie turned around, pointing her back end toward Savannah Mae, who looked up at Emma. "I guess she does remember me, though not in the way I expected."

Travis came up to the door, a jesting look on his face. "Savannah Mae, we could introduce Sophie to the horses and the barn cats and see how they all get along."

Savannah Mae playfully slapped him on the arm. "No way! She's going to live in the house as long as she stays with us."

"Come on," he tried to convince her. "She's a cat. She's gonna smell the other animals on us and will probably be curious." Travis tried to point out a logical reason to acclimate Sophie to the ranch.

Savannah Mae didn't buy it. "Mama, did you bring Sophie's things?"

"Sure did."

She turned to Travis. "Would you mind bringing in her cat box and suitcase?"

"Suitcase?" Travis guffawed. "Are you kidding?"

Emma and Savannah Mae turned and gave him "the look."

Seeing that his friend had just stepped into a semantic cow patty, Jesse told Travis he would help him bring in Sophie's belongings. When the two men got out of earshot of the women, they looked at each other and bellowed.

Fifteen minutes later, Emma and Jesse bid Savannah Mae and Travis good-bye, got in the truck, and headed for the main road. Jesse pulled up a map on the truck's GPS that showed the 654-mile route they would take. Next to the map was an estimate of how long it would take to get to Santa Fe, not including stops for food or gas.

Emma pointed to the screen. "Is that right? Is it really going to take nine and a half hours?"

Jesse grinned. "Naw. More like nine hours, maybe a little less."

"How come?"

"The GPS estimate assumes that I'll be driving at about 67 miles per hour."

"Let me guess—you won't be driving that slow."

"You got that right. Plus, we'll need to make stops on the way, so yeah, I'll be scooting along at lightspeed," he said, grinning like the Cheshire cat. "I've driven this route so many times, the truck could get there on its own."

"I never asked where we'll be staying. Did you make reservations?"

"Nope. We're staying at Tom's vacation house."

"You sure do have a generous brother."

"Yeah, he's a keeper."

"So are you," she whispered quietly, though not so quietly that he didn't hear. She was watching the road and missed the smile that crept across his lips.

As they approached Amarillo, Jesse asked her whether she'd spent much time in the city.

"I can't recall ever visiting Amarillo. Why?"

"Sweetheart, you've been missing a couple of major sights worth seeing."

"Amarillo? Isn't it just a small ranching town in the Panhandle?"

"Nope. They've got a population of more than 200,000 and quite a few interesting attractions."

Jesse pulled off the highway.

"What kind of attractions?"

"Palo Duro Canyon, for one. It's the second-largest canyon in the country, the Grand Canyon being the first, of course. Incredible views. I hiked it years ago, before my injury." He turned and looked at Emma. "Have you done any hiking?"

"Me? No."

"How come?"

"Snakes."

"Ya know, the chances of encountering a snake on a hiking trail is little to none."

"I'll take your word for it. What else is here that's a must-see?"

"The Big Texan Steak Ranch, but only if you're very, very hungry."

"Huh? Why's that?"

"They serve a 72-ounce steak that comes with a shrimp cocktail, baked potato, salad, and a roll. You have to finish all of it in one hour."

"One hour?! I couldn't finish that much food in a week! Why would someone order that?"

"Two reasons. Bragging rights for one. If you finish it in one hour, it's free. And your name will be added to the 72-Ounce Steak

Challenge Hall of Fame. If you don't finish it, you'll have to pay $72."

"That's nuts. Have they had many people take the challenge?"

"Apparently, they have. They've been doing it since the 1960s."

"I gotta check this out online!" Emma pulled out her phone and searched for the Big Texan Steak Ranch. The website came right up. She scrolled until she found the stats.

"Jesse, you won't believe this. Since 1962 when they started running the challenge, 98,207 people have attempted it. And of those, only 10,504 succeeded. Oh wait! There's more. Half of all women who attempt the challenge succeed, whereas only one in seven men does."

"Are you saying you're game to battle it out? We could stop and have lunch there."

"Nope, nope, nope," Emma laughed, shaking her head side to side.

"Okay, then we'll just head on over to the Cadillac Ranch. You won't have to eat anything there."

Jesse caught Emma's blank stare.

"You've heard of the Cadillac Ranch haven't you?"

"Can't say that I have."

"Well, you're in for some fun."

"What exactly is it?"

"Ah, I don't want to spoil the surprise. But you're gonna love it."

They pulled up to a field along the interstate in front of a line of ten half-buried Cadillacs, each on end, nose down, covered in a hodge-podge of colors.

"What do you think?" he asked her.

"Unbelievable," Emma conceded. "Oh, look," she said, pointing to one of the cars. "Someone is spray-painting that car right now. And somebody else is doing it over there."

"And now it's your turn."

"Huh?" She turned toward him and saw him holding a sack. "What's in the bag?"

He pulled out two cans of spray paint, one yellow and one red. "Which one do you want?"

She picked the red. "Is it really okay to paint the cars?"

"Yep. People have been spray-painting them since this exhibit started back in the 1970s."

The biggest grin unfurled across Emma's face. She ran to the Cadillacs and started spray-painting the first car she came to. Jesse spray-painted the next car over. They painted their names and their initials and stick figures of people and animals and anything else they could think of. When Emma could tell she was about to run out of paint, for the last one, she sprayed a big red heart. Jesse walked up and on the inside painted their initials. She caught his eye and curved her lips upward.

"Now, I'm hungry," Emma admitted when she'd used up her whole can of paint. "But not 72-ounces-of-steak hungry."

"I know just the place," Jesse responded. "Tyler's Barbeque serves some of the best 'que in Texas."

They headed over to Tyler's and ordered right away; it didn't take any time at all to receive their food. Once Emma had inhaled a chopped brisket sandwich, slaw, and a Dr. Pepper, and Jesse had downed a pulled pork sandwich, potato salad, and sweet tea, they got back in the truck and continued their journey west to New Mexico.

Several hours later, they pulled into the driveway of Tom's vacation home, shadowed by the soaring Sangre de Cristo Mountains. Emma not only had never been to Santa Fe; she'd never been to New Mexico. Though she had had an idea of what to expect from photos, actually seeing it was a wholly different experience. The serene desert landscape and history-laden pueblo architecture called to her.

She got out of the truck and stood staring at the home. Jesse joined her.

"Is this your first time seeing a pueblo-style home?"

Emma nodded. "What's it made of?"

"It's built of short, pressed, dried mud bricks on the outside. Long ago, people living here realized that adobe could withstand the hot Southwestern weather. This is a traditional New Mexico style that has very thick walls, a flat roof with the rounded edges you see, and the brownish-red color."

"It's not painted that color?"

Jesse shook his head. "Nope, that's the natural color."

"Why aren't there any homes like this in Texas?"

"Texas is too humid. The adobe requires a dry environment. When Tom designed this home, he wanted it to feature the Pueblo Revival style, inspired by the ancient Puebloan peoples. It's one of the most recognizable architectural styles in the state. While there are plenty of pure adobe homes throughout the state, many of the new ones, like Tom's house, are built of both stucco and adobe."

"Why both and not one or the other?"

"The stucco ensures stability and won't wash away in a torrential rain the way an all-adobe house can. Most of these newer homes are built to look like they're made of only the traditional materials, though they comprise a mix of the adobe and new materials, like stucco."

She pointed up to wooden beams protruding from the house. "What's with those beams jutting out of the house?"

"They're called 'vigas'; you'll see the other side of them when we go inside. Traditionally, vigas are the exposed ceiling beams inside that jut through the walls, adding a rustic touch to otherwise smooth surfaces. Their primary function is to support the weight of the roof and carry it to the load-bearing exterior walls. They're traditional in this style of home. When the house is also built with stucco, the vigas aren't really necessary to support the weight of the roof, but most homes built in this style have them because they're traditional. Indoors, you'll see rounded kiva fireplaces and earth-tone Saltillo tiles with lots of area rugs all over."

She pointed to the blue front door. "Is the blue door Tom's idea or traditional to pueblo architecture?"

He shook his head. "No, it wasn't Tom's idea. There's a few theories about the blue doors. The main ones are that the color blue deters evil spirits, and the other one is that for some reason, the blue color keeps bugs away. Let's go inside, there's lots more to see."

"I get the feeling that we're going to be staying in a museum."

"Not really," he said, smiling and opening the front door. When they stepped inside, Jesse pointed to the vigas Emma had asked about outside. "See the vigas? Between them are *latillas*, small wooden supports. They're laid across the vigas, serving as a closed platform for both the ceiling and the roof."

Emma walked all around, touching the walls and examining the *nichos*, niches in the walls to display a carving, statue, or collectible. "Jesse, this home is amazing. Are there a lot of this type of home in Santa Fe?"

Jesse nodded. "This is an extremely popular architectural style, so, yes. Another style you'll see a lot of is Territorial, which borrows from the Greek Revival style. It has a whole different feel to it."

"I love this!" She turned and winked at him. "I can't ever recall having my own personal tour guide."

"Let's put away our luggage. There's plenty to see around town."

They walked out, got their luggage out of the truck, and carried their bags into the main room.

"Follow me," Jesse said, heading toward the back of the house. He opened the door to a bedroom. "This'll be your room. The bed has fresh linens on it, and there are fresh towels in the adjoining bathroom," he said, pointing to the door going to the bathroom. "Oh, and there are hangers in the closet for anything you want to hang up." He turned and left the room.

After he left, Emma began hanging up her clothes and putting her toiletries away in the bathroom. She finished in five minutes and went searching for Jesse.

She found him three rooms down the hallway. She knocked on the door that was propped open. Jesse looked up. "Done already?"

"Yep, I didn't bring that much luggage, so not much to put away."

"I forgot to show you the kitchen. Check it out while I finish unpacking. I think it's my favorite room in the house. I'm particularly proud of the Talavera tile work."

"'Proud,' as in you did the tiling?"

"Sure did," he said, grinning like a proud papa.

"I wasn't aware that you knew how to tile."

"I wasn't either until I did the kitchen."

Emma's mouth dropped open. "Are you saying that this was your first tiling job?"

Jesse nodded and turned around to hang up a shirt.

"Did Tom know that you'd never tiled before?"

Jesse turned back around. "Of course he did."

"You have a very supportive brother."

"I know. As for the tile, we got a great deal on it, and we figured that if I messed up, we'd just tear it out and start over. No biggie."

"And did you?"

"Did I what?"

"Make a mistake and have to tear it out?"

He shook his head. "Nope. Go check it out for yourself. Oh, and if you want to see more, I tiled around the kiva fireplace too."

Emma wandered to the front of the house, walked through the dining room, and stepped into the kitchen. She stopped short; she was taken aback, seeing scads of colorful Talavera tiles covering all the countertops, backsplash, and one entire wall. The other walls were painted a rich golden syrup color, giving the room the striking warmth of a late autumn day. Jesse had covered the floor in fleur de lis–shaped Saltillo tiles rather than the square Saltillo tiles used in the rest of the house.

"Whaddaya think?"

Emma whipped around, her face still exhibiting her surprise. "Seriously, Jesse, you did all this?" She gestured all around the kitchen.

"That depends."

"On what?"

"If you think it's a lousy job, then, no, I didn't. However, if you think it looks good, then, yes, I did it."

Emma chuckled. "Well done, Mr. Rieger, well done! Let's go see Santa Fe. Do you know of a place that serves margaritas?"

"Pretty much every place in town serves them. However, we'll hit one that's on the Santa Fe Margarita Trail. That way, you can taste the best of the best."

Emma stood still, stunned. "A trail? A whole trail? Really?"

Jesse nodded. "Yep. There are several stops."

"Maybe we should get something to eat before we start drinking a bunch of margaritas. I want to be able to remember where we went."

"Don't worry, there's food at every stop. Food like you've never tasted."

"Such as?"

"You'll see for yourself."

They got into Jesse's truck and headed for Canyon Road, home to many of the city's elite art studios. Though it was usually a hard place to find parking, Jesse slid into a parking spot close to El Farol, a restaurant that had been serving patrons since 1835. As he told Emma, it had had plenty of time to perfect the iconic margarita. They stepped inside and looked all around.

"Considering how crowded it is in here, this place looks like it probably knows its way around making margaritas," Emma said.

"Are you still serving the Smoking Bull margarita?" Jesse asked the server as soon as they were seated.

"The Smoking Bull is our most requested margarita," the waiter told them. "It's a combination of smoky mezcal, cilantro, and piquillo pepper agave syrup, then we rim the glass with Chimayó red chile."

"It sounds spicy," Emma pointed out.

"Well, yes, it is," the waiter said. "But even the most hesitant customers like it, and I've never had anyone send it back." Emma didn't look convinced. "Tell ya what," the waiter suggested. "If you don't like it, there won't be a charge. How's that sound?"

"Like a win," Emma responded. "Bring it on."

"I take it that you have been here before?" Emma asked Jesse.

He nodded. "More times than I can remember. The Smoking Bull is Tom's favorite margarita."

"That's quite a recommendation. I can't wait to try it," Emma said.

Despite the crowded room, the waiter delivered their Smoking Bulls in under five minutes, along with a plate of chicken tacos.

"We didn't order tacos," Emma told him.

"They're on the house since this is your first visit to El Farol," he said.

Emma cocked her head sideways. "How do you know that?"

"Because if you'd been here before, I'd recognize you, and you wouldn't have cringed at drinking a spiced-up margarita. You're from Texas, aren't you?"

"Well, yes. And you know that how?"

The man grinned wide. "You've got a Texas accent, and many Texans don't like real spicy food. I'll check back on the two of you in a while."

After he left, Emma looked at Jesse. "I don't know if I should feel insulted or complimented."

"Go with the latter," he advised, picking up his glass and downing a third of its contents. "Now *that* is one fine margarita."

Emma sucked in a breath of air, picked up the glass, and tried not to scrunch her nose as she took a small sip. "Hmmm." Then, she took another sip, a bigger one. Then, a third that was more like a gulp.

"I take it you like it?" Jesse asked her.

"I have never, ever tasted anything like this! I thought I would hate it, and obviously I don't," she said, peering into her glass that held only a bit of margarita at the bottom. "Let's order another round."

"Nope, we've got another place to visit. Eat a few tacos, 'cuz we need to fill up a bit before we drink any more margaritas," he said. They both dove into the tacos, polishing them off as though they were starving. Just as Emma downed the last taco, Jesse took out his wallet and laid a $50 bill on the table.

"Boy, you're a generous tipper."

"He deserves it."

As soon as they got in the truck, Jesse consulted his phone, where he'd listed the places on the trail that looked the most interesting.

"Where are we going next?" She peered over his shoulder to see his phone screen.

"Sazón, one of the finest, most bodacious restaurants in Santa Fe. It's not on the trail, but it should be. Went there the last time Tom and I were in town. You're gonna love it."

Twenty minutes later, she told Jesse that she did love it. As soon as they sat down, he ordered a Sazonrita for Emma and a classic margarita made with aged Don Julio tequila for himself. The drinks arrived, and they each took a sip. She nearly keeled over in rapture. She murmured, "I think I know what nirvana is like."

"We should eat," he suggested.

"Since you're batting a hundred, you order for us."

At that moment, the server returned to their table. "How are your margaritas?"

"The best I've ever had," Emma cooed.

"Are you ready to order?" the server asked.

Emma pointed to Jesse.

"The last time I was here, my brother and I had the Cholula. Are you still serving it?"

"Yes, sir, we are. However, it is the most time-consuming dish on the menu. Are you prepared to wait?"

"Sure. As I recall, it's a one-serving dish. If we split it, we'll probably need something else. What do you recommend for an appetizer?"

"The Xochimilco."

"Is that the corn fungus dish?"

"Yes, sir, *huitlacoche*. It goes very well with our margaritas."

Jesse looked at Emma, whose face had turned pale.

"Fungus? You ordered fungus for an appetizer?"

"Ma'am, it's more like a corn truffle that we serve with miniature tortillas and queso fresco. The dish is very popular in Mexico, and here in Santa Fe too."

"I've had it," Jesse reassured Emma. "It's hard to describe. You've never had anything like it."

"Well, when in Rome ...," she started to say when Jesse turned to the server and said, "We'll have the corn truffles and another order of margaritas while we wait for the Cholula."

"Very good, sir."

After the server left, Emma asked, "Jesse, what is a 'cholula'?"

"That's just the name the restaurant calls their variation of *chiles en nogada*. You've had that, haven't you?"

Emma shook her head.

"Wait till you taste it. The first time I ate it, I gotta say, it was love at first bite."

Twenty minutes later, the server brought the huitlacoche, mini tortillas, and queso fresco, along with more margaritas. After she left, Emma sat staring at the corn fungus. "How am I supposed to eat this?" she asked as she looked up at Jesse.

"The way you'd eat anything," he responded, stabbing a truffle with his fork, putting it into a tortilla, and topping it with the fresh cheese.

Emma watched him eat it. Convinced that it was safe, she put a truffle in a tortilla and topped it with the creamy cheese. She bit into it, chewed and swallowed it, and then ate the rest of it. "Not bad," she opined. "I never would have expected a mushroom to taste like this."

"So, you like it?" Jesse asked.

"I do, though I think it might take a little getting used to. The flavors are very unusual."

"I'm proud of you."

She looked up at him. "For what?"

"You looked like you were going to faint when the server described the dish."

Emma nodded. "I kinda thought I might. It's really not bad at all once you get used to the earthiness."

Jesse looked up and saw their server coming with the cholula. When she set it down on the table, she described it as a poblano pepper stuffed with an unusual combination of lamb, beef, and pork combined with a variety of vegetables and fruits. It was served at room temperature with a walnut cream sauce, pomegranate seeds, and a balsamic jalapeño reduction.

Emma gawked at the dish. The aroma was heavy and intoxicating, making her feel lightheaded, although she realized that might be from the margaritas.

"Ma'am," the server asked, pulling her out of her reverie, "may I serve you?" Emma nodded, watching the server in awe. The server dished up Emma's portion, followed by Jesse's.

After she left, Jesse said, "Pretty spectacular, huh?"

"That's the understatement of the decade. How did you know to try this place and these dishes?"

"Tom and I try different places when we're in town. Sazón is considered one of the finest restaurants in the whole state. The first time we came here, our reaction was the same as yours, and now we always dine here at least once each trip."

She picked up her fork and gingerly stabbed her food. As soon as it settled in her mouth, she swallowed it slowly, savoring every flavor. "Wow!"

"Wow, what?" Jesse asked.

"Just, wow, that's all I got." She proceeded to eat another bite and another after that, washing it down with her margarita. She finished before realizing that she'd scarfed down everything on her plate.

Jesse watched her eat, enjoying the spectacle. "I take it you didn't like it?" he asked, grinning at her.

"Hated it. Can I have what's left?" she asked, seeing he had picked up the serving utensil.

Jesse gave her the last serving, which she dove into as soon as he handed her plate back to her. They ate in silence, occasionally looking up at one another, though mostly concentrating on their food. Finally, Emma placed her fork to the side and pushed her chair back from the table.

"You okay?" he asked.

"I am so stuffed, I don't think I'll eat again for a week."

When they returned to the house, Emma started to head to her room to get ready for bed. Jesse stopped her, took her hand, and said, "Follow me." He led her out onto a back patio, pointed to chairs, and said, "Let's sit."

"Why? I'm actually kind of tired. I was hoping to turn in."

"Bear with me. You won't be in a few minutes. Just sit and relax."

Emma sucked in a big breath, sat, and wondered what he was up to next. After a few minutes, she asked him whether they could light a fire in the outdoor fire pit or turn on some outside lights. "It's kinda dark out here, don't you think?"

Jesse smiled at her, ignoring her question.

As if on cue, the night sky blossomed with the glorious gemstone colors of the aurora borealis. Emma looked all around at luminous shades of pink, purple, green, teal, and blue, in every possible hue.

"What is all this?" She pointed to the skies, still looking all around. "What's happening?"

"I take it you've never seen the northern lights?"

"I've seen pictures, but never in person. I thought the northern lights were only visible in places in the far north, like Canada, Scandinavia, and Alaska."

"That's true," Jesse commented. "When I was a teenager, I saw them once when my family visited an uncle in Juneau. I'd never seen anything like it."

"They're spectacular." She watched in awe, as though witnessing a sign from heaven. "What do you think causes them?"

"From what I've read, there's been a great deal of increased solar activity lately."

"And that causes these light shows? How?"

"Apparently, when the sun discharges massive showers of energy, known as solar storms and flares, it sends charged particles toward Earth. Then, when the sun's particles interact with Earth's magnetic fields, they create these auroras."

She looked over at Jesse. "Huh! How do you know this?"

Jesse shrugged. "Ever since that family trip to Alaska, the northern lights have interested me. I wrote a thesis on them in college."

"You did?" Emma said. "What did you find so fascinating about them?"

"First off, the science is very cool. But it's the various mythologies that are the most interesting."

"Like what?"

"For starters, many early Native Americans believed the aurora was a dance of animal spirits. They saw caribou, fish, and seals in the lights. They claimed the dance of light represented the never-ending cycle of life, which they said proved the powerful link between nature and humans."

"Huh!"

"Then, there's the ancient Greeks and Romans, who connected the aurora borealis with Aurora, the Roman goddess of the dawn, who the Greeks called 'Eos.' They claimed that the lights were her chariot's first light, signaling the sun's approach. This interpretation made the aurora a vessel of renewal and hope."

"I like that, but it's odd. Greece and Rome are quite far south. Are you saying that at one time, the lights appeared much farther south than they do today?"

Jesse shrugged his shoulders "Good question, I dunno know. Coulda been. But then, it is a myth."

"Okay, last question, what was the premise of your thesis?"

"Emma, that was the most interesting part of all. The lights can be seen all over the world. Every group of people, regardless of location, developed myths focused on the same theme, which was to find meaning in the natural wonders."

Emma sat staring, scanning the breadth of the skies; she couldn't get enough of the brilliant colors. Without looking at him, she asked, "Did you know this was going to happen tonight?"

Jesse nodded. "Yeah, I heard about it a few days ago and thought I'd surprise you with the greatest light show you'll ever see." He reached over and took her hand. "I hope it's worth your losing a little shut-eye."

"More than you know," she said, continuing to keenly watch the magical night sky. After 30 minutes, when the lights began to fade, they stood up and walked back into the house.

"Thank you for showing me what was indeed the greatest light show I've ever seen. And a pretty interesting history lesson too." She turned, walked to her room, quickly changed into her nightgown, and slipped into her bed, surprised to find herself enveloped between smooth sheets of silk so luxurious, she drifted off to dreamworld in moments.

Emma awoke the next day to fluid morning light cascading through a large window. She lay there, inhaling the aroma of freshly brewed coffee, then noticed steam rising from a cup of coffee on her bedside table that she figured Jesse had placed there before she woke up. She drank the coffee, quickly showered, and got dressed. After they ate a light breakfast, they got into the truck and headed back toward the center of town. He parked on a small side street, took her hand, and led her toward a chapel on Old Santa Fe Trail. He stopped right in front of it.

"Okay, Mr. Tour Guide, what are we going to see here?"

"You've never seen anything like this."

"And how can you be so sure?"

"Have you ever seen evidence of an actual miracle?" He looked at her, holding her gaze.

"That depends on what you call a miracle."

"Come, I'll show you." He led her into Loretto Chapel. Once inside, he guided her to a spiral staircase and stopped. She looked up.

"Okay, what's so special about the staircase?" she asked.

"There's quite a controversy surrounding this staircase. Here." He handed her a pamphlet. Inside, she found a summary:

Legend states that when this chapel was nearly finished in the late 1870s, the architect died before he could design a staircase to access the choir loft. The Sisters of Loretto, who were the caretakers of the chapel, brought in several area carpenters to build a staircase. All of them concluded that it would be impossible to build a staircase in such a small space. The Sisters made a novena, a prayer they recited nine days in a row, to Saint Joseph, the patron saint of carpenters. According to the legend, on the ninth and final day, a man arrived with his toolbox and offered to build the staircase. He did not give his name and had only one condition: complete privacy when he worked in the chapel.

Emma looked up from reading the pamphlet and started to say something when Jesse stopped her. "What you've read so far is only part of the miracle." He pointed to the staircase. "Look closely at it. See how it's helix-shaped?"

"Yeah. What's unusual about that?"

"Several things. First, the staircase makes two full 360-degree turns with no central or visible means of support."

"How does it stand there? What's holding it up?" Emma asked, turning her head one way and then the other, trying to find a hidden means of shoring up the staircase.

"Good question. It's built entirely of wood, including wooden pegs instead of nails."

Emma peered closely at the wooden pegs, searching for a hidden nail; she found none.

"Here's one of the most perplexing parts. The lumber the carpenter used was an unknown type of wood that wasn't native to the Santa Fe area or the region. A modern analysis was conducted a number of years ago that revealed the wood is a species of spruce. The closest possible locale for this particular type of spruce would have been in Alaska. It doesn't grow down here in the Lower 48. Upon completion of the staircase, according to the story, the man disappeared before the Sisters could pay him. The circumstances surrounding its construction and its builder were deemed miraculous by the Sisters of Loretto, who believed it was Saint Joseph who built it. So, what do you think? Legend or miracle?"

Jesse saw the most quizzical look on Emma's face. "The logical side of me would say 'legend,' but after hearing all the facts you laid out, I have to go with 'miracle.' That's the only thing that makes sense."

"Agreed. Now, here's the kicker: Evidence was found in several old documents a few years ago proving that it was built by a French woodworker, a man named Francois Jean Rochas. The nuns paid him $150 for the work."

"What? If that's true, how did the miracle story come about?"

"It's thought that in the 1960s, it was fabricated to increase tourism to Santa Fe."

Emma's jaw dropped open. "I like the miracle theory better."

"Why doesn't that surprise me?" Jesse asked.

Emma smiled and let it go.

"How about we talk about something else? You up for a little snack?"

"Sure, what kind of snack?"

"French pastry."

"French pastry here in Santa Fe? Where?"

He took her hand and led her to the French Pastry Shop in La Fonda on the Plaza. They went inside and up to the display case, where Emma stared at the sweet offerings. She was dumbfounded at what she saw. Countless elegant pastries she hadn't seen since she and Larry had visited France on an anniversary trip a decade before.

"You have got to be kidding me," Emma declared. "I could never have imagined a French pâtisserie in the middle of Santa Fe."

They ordered crêpes to eat there and picked out a number of pastries to take back to the house. Jesse grinned while watching Emma take a bite of her chicken, mushroom, and spinach crêpe topped with béchamel sauce. He'd ordered a raspberry and chocolate version for himself. Emma quickly devoured hers and noticed that more than half of Jesse's crêpe remained on his plate.

"Aren't you going to finish yours?" she asked, staring at his crêpe.

Jesse shrugged. "I don't know. Why? You want a bite?"

She nodded, reached over with her fork, and scored a big bite. Then, she ate another and another.

"Oops," she said, realizing what she'd done. She could feel her cheeks turning red. "I didn't mean to eat the rest of yours."

His lips curved into a wide grin. "Yeah, you did. It's okay. I don't think I've ever seen you so happy."

They sat drinking their coffee while Emma composed herself. Jesse had been so kind, and how had she repaid him? By eating the rest of his crêpe. As she slowly sipped her coffee, she resolved to do better for the rest of the visit. Oh, but that crêpe was so good; she decided she would try to behave herself, but no promises that she would succeed.

They left the bakery and began browsing in the shops around the plaza, taking particular interest in the Native American artists set up outside the Palace of Governors under a long portico. Emma spied a necklace made of vibrant turquoise and red coral. She couldn't help gazing at it. The artisan held it up to her.

"Try it on," the artisan told her, holding a mirror in his other hand. Jesse helped her clasp it around her neck, took the mirror from the artisan, and held it up for her to see.

"Oh my!" she uttered, turning her torso one way, then the other. "Have you ever seen anything so extraordinary, Jesse?"

"It's probably the finest example of turquoise and coral that I've ever seen. The craftsmanship is outstanding."

She reached behind her neck to take it off. Jesse placed a hand over hers to stop her.

"What are you doing?" she asked him.

"It suits you. Consider it my gift to you."

"Jesse, you've already gone over and above in bringing me here, entertaining me, feeding me, and showing me the magic of the town. I can't accept it."

The artisan, not wanting to miss the sale, offered up a solution. "Sir, I'll sell it to you for 25 percent off. Then, when the lady is in the right mood, you can give it to her as a memento of your trip to the City Different."

A confused look crossed Emma's face. "Why did you call Santa Fe 'the City Different'?"

"Got five minutes?" the artisan asked. "It's an interesting story."

"Sure," Emma responded. "Now, I'm curious."

"When New Mexico became a state in 1912, Santa Fe's city government realized that the economy was declining because the railroad had moved to Lamy. They came up with a way to boost the local economy. They mandated that all buildings be built in the Pueblo adobe style. Twenty years later, in the 1930s, the mandate was expanded to include the Spanish Territorial style of architecture. It's because of the architecture that it is known as the City Different."

"I'm impressed," Emma said. "You're not just a jewelry artisan; you're a history buff too."

The artisan grinned. "Actually, I'm a professor of history at St. John's College here in town. I make jewelry as both a side hustle and a way to stay connected to my roots."

"What are your roots?" Emma asked.

"I am of the Ohkay Owingeh Pueblo. It used to be called 'San Juan Pueblo' until 2005, when we changed our name back to Ohkay Owingeh, which means 'Place of the Strong People' in the Tewa language. It was thc pueblo's original name before the Spanish takeover in 1598."

"That's fascinating." She turned to Jesse and beamed. She picked up the mirror and once again looked at herself wearing the necklace. "Jesse, I truly love it, so even though you've already gone above and beyond, I'll accept it. Whenever I wear it, I'll remember this trip and the story."

Jesse paid, and they headed toward the Museum of International Folk Art. Inside, they found more than 130,000 objects from more than 100 countries, each from differing cultures, constituting the largest collection of international folk art in the world. After walking through several areas of the museum, Emma turned to Jesse.

"I'd need to spend a week in here to see everything."

"Probably more like a month," he responded. "It's the only museum like it in New Mexico, or the world."

"I believe you."

"There's one more you shouldn't miss."

He led her outside, where they walked for a while until they stood in front of the Georgia O'Keeffe Museum. As with everything Jesse had shown her, Emma was in awe of Georgia O'Keeffe's artwork. She caught her mouth hanging open several times and was so embarrassed, she snapped it shut. When they'd seen every inch of the museum, they stopped for lunch at The Shed. Jesse warned her that its chile dishes were quite spicy, to which she said she didn't care because she was in Santa Fe to experience every aspect of the town, spicy food included.

"They have a lot of mild items on the menu. You don't have to eat something that'll sear your tongue off if you don't want to."

"I'm game for whatever."

Just as they finished eating, Emma's phone beeped with a text message. It was from Louisa Caldwell, the medium.

"Contact me," it said. "An opening came up on Thursday evening. Let me know if you want it. I'll wait till tomorrow. If I don't hear from you, I'll offer it to the next person on the waiting list."

Emma turned her phone around and showed it to Jesse. He nodded.

"Let's go back to the house so you can call everyone you want at the séance. Then, let's hit the sack early so we can leave before dawn."

"You don't mind? I know there are other spots you wanted to show me."

He placed a hand on the side of her face and stared at her. "Santa Fe isn't going anywhere. It's been here hundreds of years and will be here for at least another few hundred." He tucked a strand of hair into the bun of hair knotted on the back of her head. "We'll come back another time for the next installment of the City Different."

"All right," she agreed as she stood up and took his hand in hers. When they got into his truck, she texted Louisa: "I'll take the opening on Thursday. Heading home from New Mexico in the morning. What time should the séance guests be at the house?"

Chapter Seventeen

As they headed out of Santa Fe, the early-morning light bathed the adobe buildings in shades of lavender. The streets still hid in the shadows, silhouettes and shapes playing tricks on the eyes. A mystical gray fog hugged the Sangre de Cristo Mountains like a young child who wouldn't let go on the first day of school. A light wind stirred up dust devils that whirled whimsically across the road, and above them, a celestial blue sky beckoned them home. Ahead, they spotted a golden eagle soaring across currents of air, as though leading their journey. It whirled on invisible columns of air, plummeting, then hovering, watching them. The grand bird stayed with them for several miles until it pivoted one last time, turned around, and headed back toward where it had come from, dipping its left wing to seemingly bid them farewell.

Jesse glanced over at her and caught her staring at him. She smiled to let him know she appreciated him. She didn't need to say a word; he knew.

"Are you hungry?" he asked, taking her hand in his.

"A little. I hate to waste time stopping somewhere to eat. How about we dig into the French pastries we got yesterday?"

"I gotta have some coffee to go with them. I'll pull off at the next exit that has food and get a couple of coffees to go. You okay with that?"

She nodded.

After getting their coffees, they headed back out onto the interstate. Despite the vehicles speeding past them, it felt like the world had slowed to an eerie calm. The hours passed quickly, punctuated by unimportant chitchat.

Nine hours after leaving Santa Fe, Jesse pulled the truck in front of Emma's house. Dark, thick clouds hid the moon, bathing the house in an eerie shroud. He got out, opened her door, retrieved her belongings, and headed for the front door.

"Jesse, you're tired. You don't have to carry my things inside. Here," she said, reaching for her luggage, "I'll take them."

He shook his head. "I need to check the house and make sure no one is in there lying in wait for you."

"Really?" she said "Aren't you tired? You've been driving all day. You should go home and get some rest."

"Yes, really. Bear with me," he said, carrying her luggage up to the porch.

"Oh, Jesse, I'm sure that everything is fine."

Jesse set her case on the porch, checked the door, then looked over the front porch sash windows. He walked around to the back porch, Emma right behind him, and found one sash window ajar. "Emma, this isn't fine," he said, pointing to the window.

Emma stared at it. "How did that happen? I'm pretty sure I checked all the windows before we left."

"I'm sure you did. Someone used a credit card to force open the lock."

"A credit card?"

Jesse nodded. "The person slid the card between the window and the frame where the locking mechanism is located," he said, pointing to the spot. "It's a common trick to break into old homes with sash windows. The intruder slants the card downward and applies light pressure to push the lock mechanism inward or upward, depending on the type of lock. Bingo! The window opens without damaging the lock or the window."

"What can be done to fix this?"

"Replace all the windows."

"That's not gonna happen. That would change the character of the house."

"Actually, there are windows available now that look just like the original sash windows, but they're made with a single piece of glass and don't open."

"Huh! I need to look into that."

"I've got some brochures I can show you. But for now, let's go inside so I can check if any other windows or doors were tampered with."

She didn't argue with him. Seeing how easily someone had broken in while she was gone definitely raised her caution meter. "While you're doing that, will you at least let me heat up something to eat? Other than the pastries, we haven't had anything to eat today."

"Sure," he answered. After checking the other downstairs windows and doors and finding nothing amiss, he took Emma's bags upstairs and placed them on the floor of her bedroom. While he was up there, he checked the windows on all the upper floors, then went downstairs into the basement. Satisfied that the house was secure, he walked into the kitchen, where Emma was ladling soup into two bowls.

"Is your pistol loaded?" he asked between spoonfuls of the soup.

"Yes, it always is."

"It may be best to keep it on your nightstand instead of under that floorboard where you hide it."

"Jesse, you don't need to worry. I'll be fine."

"I hope so. I just have an uneasy feeling."

"Like what?"

"For one, someone has been here, someone who shouldn't have been in the house. Didn't you tell me that you and Savannah Mae replaced your security system with a smart monitoring system that Travis installed?"

Emma nodded. "Yeah, he did it awhile ago. I've got an app on my phone where I can watch anything the camera caught. Honestly, I forgot I had it. "

"Let's look at it."

Emma opened the app and pulled up the most recent footage. It showed someone circling the house the last three nights, checking windows and doors and fiddling with the window on the back porch.

She stared at him. "Jesse, have you always had a sixth sense?"

He looked down at her. "It's something you learn on the battlefield."

She couldn't help but notice the steadfast, unwavering expression on his face, one that reflected his moral compass.

"Look, I'm not trying to intrude on your privacy or tell you what to do. I am seriously worried about you staying here alone. You should be worried too."

Emma looked down at her half-eaten bowl of soup and pushed it away. "I am."

Jesse slightly raised his voice to a tone serious with conviction, a tone that conveyed he wasn't taking "no" for an answer. "Your choice: I'll take you to Travis and Savannah's ranch, or I'll sleep on your couch."

"You'd be more comfortable sleeping in one of the guest rooms."

"True, but I'll better be able to hear someone breaking in if I'm on the ground floor, on the couch."

"Okay, I'll go grab a pillow and a quilt for you." She got up and headed up the stairs.

While she went upstairs, Jesse locked up the truck and brought in his luggage. She came back downstairs with the pillow and quilt that she laid on the couch and handed him a key. He looked at her quizzically.

"House key, I figured maybe you'd need it."

He nodded, though he wished it was under different circumstances. He saw how hard it was for her to acknowledge that her life was in danger and yet, she trusted him to be there for her in a worst case scenario.

The next day, upon hearing about someone scoping out and breaking in through a back porch window while Emma and Jesse were in Santa Fe, Savannah Mae and Travis drove over to Waxahachie to have a firm talk with Emma.

"Mama, you're being really difficult about this. You shouldn't stay here alone, and you can't expect Jesse to sleep on the couch until the killer is found."

Emma looked over at Jesse, who was standing back. "Savannah Mae, I didn't—or, rather, don't—expect Jesse to stay over. He insisted. God only knows when the authorities will solve the case. I don't expect him to stay here until that happens."

"Then you're moving to the ranch until the case is solved."

"No, I'm not."

"Mama, I will not let you stay here alone."

"Fine, you can move in here." She looked at both of them. "That includes you, Travis."

Savannah Mae let out a big exasperated breath of air. "Now you know that puts a tremendous burden on us, Mama."

"If you're going to be so adamant about who is going to babysit me, then I get a say in this."

"Well, staying here alone isn't an option, Mama."

"Would you feel better if I hired a private security company to monitor the property with an actual security officer on-site?"

Savannah Mae stopped short. She looked at Travis, then at Jesse, and back at Emma. "You'd agree to that?"

"Didn't I just suggest it? Of course I'd agree to it."

"I suppose that would solve the most immediate problem," Savannah Mae acquiesced. "What company are you going to use?"

"I have no idea. I'll ask around and find the best one in the area that can have a guard on-site 24/7."

Savannah Mae pursed her lips. "That's going to be expensive."

"If it'll make you happy, it will be worth every penny."

"Okay, Mama. Just know that I'm concerned because I love you and don't want anything to happen to you."

"Nothing is going to happen to me, Savannah Mae. I have a cat to protect me. Which reminds me, did you bring Sophie?"

"Yeah, she's in the truck. I think she's ready to move back home."

She looked at Travis, who got the hint and darted out the front door to retrieve Sophie. He was back in two minutes. He set the carrier down and opened the door to the crate. Sophie bounded out and dashed for Emma, stood up, and pawed her leg to be picked up. Emma lifted her up just as Sophie began a loud guttural purr.

"We should go, Mama. We've got a lot to do at the ranch. Is the séance still on for Thursday at seven o'clock?"

Emma nodded.

"Do you need any help checking out security companies?" She turned and gestured to Travis. "Because, you know, Travis used to be in law enforcement. He might have a recommendation."

"Yes, that would be very helpful. Travis, who would you recommend?"

"Tell ya what, Emma, as soon as I get home, I'll text you my top suggestions."

"That'll be fine. I'll be looking for it."

Savannah Mae and Travis left, leaving Emma and Jesse standing in the foyer. "Was that a bit strange?" she asked.

"How so?" Jesse asked.

"She's smothering me."

"Then, she's to be forgiven. It took a long time for her to find you, and she's not about to lose you again. She loves you."

"You're right." Emma let out a long sigh. "So, you want to sleep on the couch again tonight? Savannah Mae isn't going to grant me any peace until I have a security guard on-site."

"It's my new favorite place to sleep," he joked.

After a dinner of coconut shrimp curry and rice, they retreated to the TV room in the back of the house to relax and watch a movie. Jesse had just put his arm around her shoulders when her phone beeped right in the middle of the most exciting part. It was a text from Travis with the recommendations. She showed it to Jesse.

"Good. You've got your work cut out for you tomorrow."

After making fresh blueberry waffles and cheesy scrambled eggs for breakfast, she bid Jesse good-bye the next morning and began calling the security companies on the list that Travis had sent. Only three of the companies were taking on new clients, and of those, only two had the capability to provide twenty-four-hour on-site security and were available to start immediately. She invited the companies to come to the house that day to see the premises and get a better understanding of the type of security she would need. She scheduled the first one, run by Dustin Kolar, for 11:00 a.m., and the second one, owned by Liam Taylor, for 3:00 p.m.

Each showed up right on time. Each man was genuinely concerned about what had happened in the house and said she was doing the right thing in hiring around-the-clock security. They seemed equally qualified and very professional, and they understood the task. She was impressed with both of them, but by the day's end, she found herself leaning toward Dustin. Her gut told her that he was the one she should hire. He was a retired police officer who had spent 30 years on the force, where he had received numerous commendations for his bravery in saving lives. He appreciated that Emma wanted to stay in the house and her desire not to be frightened out of her home, particularly when the investigation to find the killer was going nowhere. She was just about to call Dustin when her phone rang. It was Jesse.

"How'd it go today?"

"Quite well, actually. I interviewed the owners of two companies, and while I wish I could hire them both, I've decided on the one that my gut tells me is the right person for the job."

"Tell me about them."

"That depends on whether you're sleeping on my couch tonight."

"Why?"

"Because if you're staying here, then I'm feeding you supper, and I can tell you about them then. It's our deal."

"Since when? I don't remember making that deal."

"That's because I just made it up. It's the least I can do."

"Emma, you don't have to make me supper. My only interest is in making sure you're safe."

"So, are you staying on the couch tonight or not?"

"Yes, ma'am! What's on the menu?"

"Bourbon chicken with crispy Parmesan new potatoes."

"Did you say 'bourbon'?"

"I did."

"Okay! Looks like I'll be sleeping on your couch again tonight."

The next morning, Emma called Dustin Kolar and offered him the job. He came over at noon with a younger man he introduced as Will Kolar, his son. Dustin would take the first twelve-hour shift, starting immediately, and Will would take the second shift. Emma walked both men through the house as they took notes on their tablets. Dustin promised to text Emma the names and cell numbers of all the guards who would monitor the house on the upcoming days and nights. He also explained that if whoever was on guard needed to come inside, they would call her first. They asked that she keep her phone on and at hand at all times. Emma felt an immediate sense of relief, hoping that now Savannah Mae would stop worrying. She was grateful to have Jesse there, even though she didn't want to burden him with her problems. She called to tell him she had hired someone.

"You hired the Kolar guy?"

"Yeah, he's pulling the first twelve-hour shift, so you can sleep in your own bed tonight, which I'm sure is a whole lot more comfortable than my couch."

"It wasn't that bad. I'm just glad I could help. Gotta go. You call if you need anything."

"Will do."

That night, knowing there was an armed guard on the premises, she felt an unexpected sense of relief. She fell into a deep sleep, never waking up once.

When Thursday evening rolled around and Louisa Caldwell and the people attending the séance arrived, she was relaxed and focused. The guard stood near the front steps, checking their names against a list of guests that Emma had given him.

"What's with the guy packing heat out front?" Keith asked, pointing toward the front door.

"I was told repeatedly that I shouldn't stay here alone, so I hired a security company to keep watch on the house. If the killer does come around, hopefully the guard will deter the person from breaking and entering, in case I'm supposed to be the next victim."

Keith reached over and hugged her tightly. "You know, Emma, you could have asked me to stay with you."

"I didn't want to bother you. This could be a long haul."

"Well, if tonight's séance uncovers anything or anyone, it might be a short haul."

"From your mouth to God's ears, dear brother."

Louisa waved everyone into the parlor to sit on the chairs Emma had placed in a circle. Emma looked around and counted. All seven people she had invited were present: Bonnie Ada, Ruth, Thelma, Keith, Stella, Savannah Mae, and Jesse. Louisa introduced herself and provided some background on her experience as a medium, plus explained what they could expect during the séance. She told them that she had asked Emma to turn off the electric lights, as conventional lighting was not conducive to a welcoming atmosphere.

"Is anyone here afraid of spirits? If you are, I need to know before we begin," Louisa asked the group, looking around. No one raised a hand. "In case anyone is feeling a little nervous, here's a couple of things for you to keep in mind. A ghost is simply a soul who was once a person just like you. Someone who wants their life to have meant something. And, most importantly, doesn't want to be forgotten."

"I never thought of ghosts that way," Stella said just above a whisper. Louisa nodded at her and continued.

"Should any of you become frightened during the séance, please refrain from screaming and running out of the room. Just sit quietly in your chair and close your eyes. I know that this is going to sound strange, but if you scream, you'll scare the spirits and they'll disappear, and I won't be able to get them back, at least not tonight." Louisa looked around the circle; everyone nodded. "Bear in mind that most spirits are not evil; they want to help the living, if they can. This is especially true when there's a family connection, which may be the case in this home. Are there any questions?"

Stella raised her hand, and Louisa nodded, indicating she should speak.

"Will we be able to see them?"

"Excellent question. It's possible, though it depends on the spirits, whether they want to reveal their former earthly forms. Some do, some don't."

In the middle of the circle, Louisa lit several candles she placed on a round table. On a smaller table to the side of her chair, she placed a pad of paper and a pen. She began the séance by asking everyone to turn off their phones and meditate on the spirit world.

"Join hands with the people on each side of you, close your eyes, and relax. Holding hands with those beside you closes the circle and allows all of our combined energy to build up inside the circle."

When everyone had complied, she asked any spirits in the house to join them and to make a noise or give a sign as a response. They heard rustling noises. She explained to the group that rapping worked best for yes-or-no questions and urged them to listen carefully for a noise after each question.

"Spirits, please rap once if you are present."

She had no sooner stopped speaking than they heard a series of raps, presumably from several different spirits.

"Thank you," she said to the spirits. "Please, will each of you rap once so I know how many spirits are with us tonight?" They heard eight raps, each about five seconds apart. "Thank you," Louisa repeated.

"Spirits, are you aware of a death that recently occurred in this house?"

Immediately, the group heard a series of single raps. The group members looked around at each other.

"Spirits, did any of you witness the murder?"

Again, there was a series of single raps, five seconds apart.

"Thank you, spirits. Is Isabel Allnutt with you?"

There was one single rap.

"Are you Isabel Allnutt?"

Again, they heard one rap. Louisa looked across the circle. "Emma, would you like to continue the questioning?" Emma nodded.

"Isabel, we are very upset about what happened to you in my home. Was your death an accident?"

They immediately heard two raps.

"Were you murdered?"

One rap came on the tail of her question.

"Was the person a man?"

Two raps.

"Was the person a female?"

One rap.

"Can you tell us who did it?"

The raps ceased. Louisa signaled to wait. After a minute without any further contact with the spirits, she asked the spirits whether they could offer any further information. Then, as clear as if the person were standing in the room, a spirit asked Louisa to use a pen and write something on a piece of paper that the spirit would dictate to her. Louisa picked up the pen on the table. Her hand no longer in her control, it began to write a message on the pad of paper.

"I was murdered by a woman. I didn't see her face, but I heard her voice."

Louisa waited for more information that did not come. "Isabel, are you still there?"

No answer.

"Are any spirits still with us?"

They heard only one rap.

"Can you provide any further information?"

Two raps. Then, her hand holding the pen returned to the pad of paper. She wrote, "Isabel has left. We spirits of the house cannot tell you anything more. I need to leave and comfort Isabel."

"Wait! Don't go," Savannah Mae called out. "Are you still there?"

"Yes, what is it?" Louisa wrote.

"Which spirit are you? What is your name?"

"I am your great-great-great-grandmother Lillian Clayburne."

"I'm your great-great-great-granddaughter, Savannah Mae."

"I know."

"Did you make the Grandmother's Fan quilt that you used to comfort Great-great-great-grandfather James during the fires of 1882?"

"Yes. How did you know that?"

"We found a photograph taken of him wrapped in that quilt while he was convalescing."

Lillian made one last comment. "I saw that Emma found the quilt in the attic. Emma, my dear, thank you for saving it."

The pen in Louisa's hand dropped to the floor, and all the candles went out on their own.

Louisa told the group they could break the circle. Emma got up and turned on the lights. Everyone else stood up, looking a little dazed and confused.

"Emma, I know you were hoping for a name, which rarely happens in a séance, " Louisa said. "At least now you know it was a woman."

"Louisa, I appreciate your efforts and the information the séance provided. There were over a dozen women in the house at the time of the murder. No men. While the new information does narrow it down, it could have been any of them."

"I'm sorry I couldn't be more helpful," Louisa concluded. "I thought we were right on the cusp of Isabel giving us a name."

"I did too," Emma responded. "It was worth trying anyway."

After everyone left, Emma rearranged the chairs and went into the kitchen, where she found Jesse sitting on a countertop. "Looks like I'm off the hook as a suspect," he said, trying to infuse a little humor into a humorless situation.

"That should count for something. And now I'm back to where I started. Ugh!" she said, plopping into a kitchen chair.

"I have an idea," Jesse suggested. "Let's stream an episode of that old TV show *Murder, She Wrote*."

Emma looked confused. "Why?"

"Jessica Fletcher was always getting into a bind, and when things looked the bleakest, a clue would pop up, and she would solve the murder."

Emma broke up laughing. "I don't know if that's genius or silly. I did watch just about every episode back in the day, and I remember thinking that Jessica was very clever in solving the murders. Sure, why not? You go set it up on the TV, and I'll pop us a bowl of popcorn."

"Don't forget the melted butter," he quipped and headed toward the TV room.

They watched four episodes late into the evening while Emma took notes. When they were tired of watching, Jesse leaned over to look at her notepad.

"Come up with any strategies that might help?"

"Well, I did notice a pattern in all the episodes."

"Like what?"

"First, she ingratiates herself with the local police, something I tried to do, and gets shut down by the detective. Next, the best way to exonerate an innocent suspect is to find the real killer. But that doesn't really apply here because we don't have any suspects. The next thing offers real promise: Did you notice that she obtains a confession by any means available, such as trickery or deceit?"

Jesse cocked his head sideways. "Yeah, she does do that."

"Then, did you see how she often finds herself face-to-face with the person she's pretty sure is the murderer?"

Jesse nodded.

"In a couple of episodes when she's talking to a possible murderer, she calls attention to a lie or an inconsistency in the person's story. Sometimes, she intentionally causes the person to slip up. Also, in each episode, she comes on the scene with backup.

She never confronts the suspect alone. It appears that the backup serves two purposes: to have another person there in case the suspect confesses, someone who can verify the suspect's confession. Having another person there also serves as protection in case the suspect is desperate and tries to harm Jessica."

"You got all that from four episodes?"

Emma nodded. "Hang on, there's more. Did you notice how she's not above lying to or manipulating a suspect, if necessary?"

Jesse nodded again.

"She also lets the conclusion happen naturally, she doesn't force it. In a couple of episodes, Jessica has all the pieces she needs but can't figure out how it all comes together. In those episodes, she deduces what happened when she is discussing another topic with someone and suddenly has a moment of clarity and revelation when she discovers a link that leads to solving the murder."

Jesse leaned back and ran a hand over his head. "I can't believe you got all that just from watching a few episodes."

"Jesse, it wasn't that hard. Actually, it was kind of fun. Unfortunately, none of this is helping to solve this case. I sure wish that Jessica Fletcher was real and I could bring her here to help figure this out."

"Did you talk to any of the students the morning that the murder occurred?" Jesse asked her.

"No, everyone was escorted to the police station. We were all interviewed there."

"Did the detective give you copies of those interviews?"

"No, and I'm pretty sure that he won't. He made it very clear to keep my nose out of it because I am not next of kin. When I pointed out that it happened in my house and that, yes, I deserved to be in the loop, he blew me off. I began bugging the heck out of him."

"How?"

"After he refused to give me any information on the progress of the case, I started calling him and leaving messages."

"How long did that go on?"

"Hmm, ten days I think. Maybe for two weeks."

"Remind me not to get on your bad side."

Emma smirked at Jesse. "Like you could."

"Did all your calls result in anything?"

"Yeah. He finally caved and told me the results of the autopsy."

"And?"

"The ME thinks that initially the killer tried to murder Isabel with the scarf. He surmised that the murderer may not have been strong enough to do the deed and resorted to hitting her on the head with a statuette that was in the room. Apparently, that blow caused a lethal traumatic brain injury."

"That's certainly worthwhile information."

"True, but it still doesn't get us anywhere."

Jesse pondered for a few moments. "You know that I care about you."

"Yes, and I care about you."

"I'm worried about you."

"Why?"

"You're getting into this deeper and deeper."

"Jesse, what choice do I have? Clearly, the police aren't working overtime—or at all—to solve the murder. The longer it goes on, the more it seems like it will end up in a cold-case file. Isabel deserves better than that."

"I agree, but at what risk to you? Call me selfish, but I've finally met a woman who makes me feel not just incredibly happy but alive in ways I'd given up on. I never thought I'd meet a woman who'd overlook my injury and understand my journey back from

PTSD. I'm in love with you, Emma. And now, my greatest fear is that you'll slip through my fingers."

Emma reached over and put her arms around him. "Oh, Jesse, why would you say that? I'm not going anywhere."

"I believe you, I do. But nothing about this case sits right with me. I have a bad feeling that harm is going to come to you, and if I don't figure out what it is or how to prevent it, that I'll lose you."

"Oh, Jesse." She held him tighter and whispered, "I love you, too. More than you know. As much as I can, I promise not to put myself in harm's way."

"I'll hold you to that promise," he whispered back, bent down, and kissed her as though it were the last time, hoping that it wouldn't be.

Not long after, she got an unexpected call from Mrs. Lavender Atherton, who asked about the status of finding the killer and reopening the retreat center. "Call me nosy, if you wish," she said, "but I think you have a nice quilting retreat, and I'd like to see it reopen and succeed."

"So would I," Emma responded. "I'm not sure when that will happen because I'm not getting a lot of assistance from the police."

"What kind of assistance are you seeking?"

"Anything. It took annoying the daylights out of that detective to find out the results of the autopsy, which he finally told me over the phone. Other than that, he's not sharing any information about the investigation, which has left me in limbo."

Even though it pained her to make up a white lie, she told Mrs. Atherton that of all the students who were at the retreat, she had been the most attentive and observant, and Emma wondered if she could share her insights from that morning.

Mrs. Atherton took Emma's comments as compliments. "Yes, that's true. I've always been known for my intelligence and keen eye. I'm glad to hear that you recognize my abilities."

Emma swallowed her pride and responded, "Oh, Mrs. Atherton, your acumen would be invaluable. Can you please make room in your busy schedule to stop by sometime? "

"What for?" Mrs. Atherton asked.

"Since I wasn't privy to any of the interviews at the police station, I have no idea what the police learned and what leads they may be pursuing."

"Didn't you receive a copy of the police report as well as copies of all the interviews the officers did with us that morning?"

"Unfortunately, no. The detective said that because I am not next of kin to the woman who died, I'm not entitled to receive copies of anything regarding the murder. Only immediate family is allowed to see the reports."

"That is ridiculous!" Mrs. Atherton exclaimed. "It happened in your house. Of course you're entitled to copies of everything."

"I wish the detective felt that way."

"What's the detective's name?"

"Adam Corbin."

"The name is familiar, but I don't know him personally. My sister used to be the assistant chief of police before she retired. I vaguely recall her talking about him as her least favorite detective."

"Why's that?"

"What I'm telling you is confidential and not for anyone else's ears."

"I understand."

"I remember Alice saying that he was always looking for ways to elevate his reputation. Apparently he likes to keep information close to his chest so it makes him look important. It sounds like he's still doing that, holding back like he's playing a game of blackjack."

"Well, isn't that interesting?" Emma commented. "It doesn't sound like you know him well enough to ask him to give me copies of everything."

"No, I don't, but I have someone else in mind who may be able to."

"Who would that be?"

"My sister. She worked with him for years. She won't even bother phoning him. She will march right into police headquarters and into the squad room and demand that he hand-deliver the reports ASAP."

"Can she do that? I mean, she's retired. *Would* she do that?"

"Of course she can, and would. She knows the law better than he does. And once an officer of the law, always an officer, at least in the minds of retired law enforcement. Plus, she never took any malarkey from him. This has been a lifelong pattern."

"I can't thank you enough. Being able to review those reports would certainly be enormously helpful."

"Emma, what are you going to do with the information you learn from the file?"

"You mean, do I know what I'm doing?"

"Exactly."

"Actually, no. But given that I've exhausted every possible avenue to get my retreat reopened, I'm willing to try just about anything."

"You do realize that one of the students is the likely killer and that you're putting yourself in danger, don't you?"

"Yes, I do. That's why I've hired a 24-hour on-site security company. Plus, I have a camera on the property that records anyone coming and going from the house. That's how I found out that someone was stalking the property and broke in through a back window while I was recently out of town."

"Well, that's all very nice. I'd like to make a suggestion."

"Go on."

"I want to bring my sister over and have you tell her everything that happened, what you've done so far, and where the case stands now. She may have an idea on how to proceed, cautiously, I might add."

"Do you think she would be interested in helping me?"

"Of course she would. She's a quilter, like us. In fact, she was going to come with me to your retreat, but something came up, so she didn't."

"Mrs. Atherton, you have made my day!"

"Please, call me 'Lavender.'"

Emma smiled into the phone, thinking she'd finally made a breakthrough with Mrs. Atherton. "Thank you, Lavender."

"Think nothing of it. See you soon."

That afternoon, the doorbell rang. When Emma opened the door, she found Detective Adam Corbin standing in front of the door. He handed her a large envelope, nodded, turned around, and started down the stairs. He didn't say a word, which was fine with Emma. She smiled and waved good-bye to him, even though he didn't look back.

Chapter Eighteen

Sunday after church, Lavender stopped by with her sister, Alice Potter. As Lavender had foretold, Alice was extremely approachable and took a keen interest in the case. When Emma told her everything she knew, Alice sat back in her chair and crossed her legs.

"Here's what I'd suggest. First, it would be a good idea to revisit the students and find out what they remember. There may be key things they saw or heard that morning but were so traumatized that they blanked it out when they were interviewed at the station. That happens sometimes. It's been a few weeks since the murder, and now they may well remember some key things they observed."

"And how would I do that?"

"I can help, Emma. Give me a list of the names, phone numbers, and addresses of everyone who attended the retreat. I'll call each of them and ask what they remember."

Emma nodded. "Do you think they'll talk to you?"

"Good question. After I retired and realized that I couldn't sit home all day, even making quilts, I got my private investigator license. When I call the students I will tell them that I'm the former assistant chief of police here in Waxahachie and a licensed private investigator. I think they'll talk to me. I'll call and make appointments to visit each student and interview them individually in their homes, and I'll record the interviews and take copious notes. After I'm done, I'll meet with you to share what I find out and then hand it over to the chief of police."

"That's a lot of work," Emma commented. "Are you sure you want to devote that much time to this?"

"Yes, Emma, mainly because other than my sister here, you should have minimal in-person contact with the students. One of them is the killer. This puts you at risk. I spent my career in law enforcement and can handle myself."

Emma broke a slight smile. "Thank you, Alice. I appreciate your caution."

Alice began making appointments and slowly working her way through the list.

When she was settled in to interview a student in a hot pink caftan, she opened with "As you may know, to date, the police have not yet discovered who killed Isabel Allnutt."

Hot Pink asked, "Are you sure it was murder? I'd heard it was an accident."

"It was definitely not an accident," Alice assured her. "The reason I've been asked to go over the events of the day is to learn what you may have observed that could be a clue to solving the murder."

"What about the interviews we all had with the police that morning? Didn't our answers provide the information you're seeking?"

Alice nodded. "You'd think so, but those interviews occurred shortly after you learned of Isabel's death. You were likely upset, possibly afraid, thinking that because you were on the premises that you may be a suspect."

Hot Pink nodded her head.

As Alice interviewed each of the students, she had them walk her through the events of that morning and recall anything they'd observed in the days, hours, or moments leading up to the death. One by one, she made her way through interviews with everyone who had been present.

The interviews turned up some fresh information. The woman who wore a French twist told Alice that she had been awakened by raised voices coming from down the hall around 3:00 a.m. the night before the murder and recalled that they had ended abruptly.

Another woman who looked to be in her seventies still wearing a hairstyle from her high school years, told Alice that she and her roommate had just come out of their room to go to breakfast in the dining room when they saw Connie Sinclaire and Linda Mayfield descending the stairs. She said the two women's faces were pale, though she didn't know why. They looked shaken. Usually, the woman said, both were jovial, smiling, and laughing. When she'd told them, "Good morning," neither Connie nor Linda had responded, which seemed odd. Alice wasn't real sure what to make of that information, but made a note of it anyway.

After finishing all the interviews, Alice called her sister, Lavender, who said that she, too, had been awakened by the three o'clock argument. She added that her roommate, Linda Mayfield, hadn't been in her bed, and she'd figured she was in the bathroom. The loud voices continued for some time. When they ended, Lavender fell back asleep. She vaguely recalled hearing Linda reenter their room.

Alice set up a video call with Emma, where she relayed her summary of the interviews.

"I can't tell you that any of the students definitively stood out, but it wasn't a total waste of time," Alice said.

"With all due respect," Emma interjected, "it doesn't sound like we're any further along."

"I agree," Alice responded. "Bear in mind that the killer may believe she's off the hook. That happens from time to time. Killers often start taking chances and in doing so draw attention to themselves. It's a common mistake murderers make. I urge you to stay vigilant. The killer is bound to do something stupid and cause their own undoing."

Jesse was standing out of the way while Emma participated in the call. After it ended, she looked over at him and sighed. "More dead ends."

"Not necessarily," Jesse remarked. "The interviews may have shook up the killer, and she may make a lamebrained move."

"Like what?"

"I don't know. Travis may have an idea. Meanwhile, will you be careful?"

"Always." She stepped over to him and threw her arms around him. "Thank you for being my rock."

They stood there for the longest time, holding one another, not wanting to let go. Finally, Jesse left. She walked out the door and down to the mailbox to see if anything had arrived. In it, she found only an envelope with her name handwritten on the front. She opened it and read a brief note.

EMMA, I KNOW THAT YOU ARE WORKING WITH THE WAXAHACHIE POLICE TO SOLVE THE PASSING OF ISABEL ALLNUTT. YOU ARE RISKING YOUR OWN LIFE BY PUTTING YOUR NOSE WHERE IT DOESN'T BELONG. IF YOU REFRAIN FROM COOPERATING WITH THE POLICE, YOUR LIFE WILL BE SPARED. THE CHOICE IS YOURS.

She plopped down on the front step and reread the note, thinking that the killer had just made the first move. She called Alice and read it to her.

"Emma, the police need to see the note and dust it for fingerprints. You and I need to pay them a visit."

"I'm free when you are."

"Okay."

That evening, as Emma sat in the schoolhouse working on a Hunter's Star quilt, her phone rang. The number was from the security company.

"Mrs. Jenkins?"

"Yes?"

"This is Dustin Kolar. I'm on the night shift, watching your house."

"Is everything all right?"

"Yes, technically. Nothing's happened, but I want to make you aware that around seven o'clock, a woman walked by the house and stopped at the front gate, looking all around. I asked her what she was doing. She said she was a friend of yours and that you told her she could come by and look at the roses anytime she wanted. I asked her what her name was, which she refused or neglected to answer. Since we are locking the gate from sundown to sunup, she asked me to unlock it and let her in."

"I hope you didn't."

"No, I did not. I take it that you didn't tell her she could walk around anytime?" Dustin Kolar asked.

"Absolutely not," Emma said

"Any idea who she was? He pressed.

Emma let out a sigh. "Nope. I haven't told anyone that they could walk around the property. You should know that I received a threatening unsigned note earlier today. Needless to say, I'm a little hypersensitive. We should both be cautious."

"Understood. Are you in the house? Have you locked all the doors?"

"I'm in the schoolhouse in the back."

"Ma'am, I'd feel much better if you were in the big house. If you don't mind, I'll come get you and escort you into the house, and I'll check all the doors and windows when you go inside."

"Okay, I'll start locking up here."

Just as Emma shut down her sewing machine and put her quilt top aside, the security guard knocked. Emma went to the door, unlocked it, and opened the door.

"Are you ready?" the security guard asked.

Emma nodded, turned off the lights, followed him out, and locked the door behind them. They walked up the stairs to the back porch and into the house through the door at the back of the house, which was unlocked.

"Ma'am, given that note you told me you received, you really need to keep every door locked."

Emma nodded, not at all liking this new turn of events. She went into the kitchen to make herself a cup of herbal tea to calm her nerves. The guard went through the whole house, checking doors and making sure all the windows were securely locked. She heard him coming down the main stairs and then stop before he came into the kitchen, holding a folded piece of paper.

"I just found this on that small table at the bottom of the stairs. Did you leave it there?"

Emma took the piece of paper and unfolded it. In the same handwriting as the one she had found in the mailbox earlier, the note said:

> WE'RE SERIOUS! IF YOU VALUE YOUR LIFE, STAY OUT OF THIS.

She handed it to the guard.

"Ma'am, this is alarming. That note wasn't there when I went up the stairs, which means that someone is in the house. This is a blatant threat to your life. I'm going to call the police to come do a thorough sweep of the house."

"I have a meeting at the police station tomorrow. I could show them the note then."

"That may be too late. You need to take this as the threat that it is, ma'am. While I call the police, is there anywhere else you can stay tonight or someone you can call to stay here with you tonight?"

"Yeah, I'll call someone." She heard Dustin calling the police station as she dialed Jesse.

"What's up, Emma?"

"You up for a pajama slumber party at my house tonight?"

"Huh?"

She started to explain the reason for her call, but before she could get halfway through, Jesse had hung up and was on his way. She hadn't even had time to tell him that there was probably someone in the house. She thought that while she waited, she should put her handgun in the drawer of the nightstand by her bed. The guard would not let her go anywhere in the house unaccompanied, so he followed her upstairs. She'd been leaving her gun on top of the stand after Jesse's suggestion about not keeping it under a floorboard. She stepped into her bedroom and focused on the nightstand. The gun wasn't there. She ran over and quickly opened the drawer, thinking that maybe she had already put it inside. No gun there either—only a note in handwriting she was beginning to recognize:

> EMMA, YOU SHOULD KEEP YOUR GUN WHERE SOMEONE WITH BAD INTENTIONS CAN'T FIND IT. HOPE YOU DON'T WANT IT BACK BECAUSE NOW IT'S MINE. JUST HOPE I DON'T HAVE TO USE IT ON YOU.

Emma slumped onto the bed. The gun was irreplaceable. She dropped her face into her hands, wondering whether she would survive the night. Then, a flash of anger pulsed through her, emboldening her. She lifted her head. This was the last straw. The killer had stolen the gun her beloved father gave to her, and now she was furious. The killer could threaten her all they wanted, but she wasn't going to tolerate the person stealing a cherished gift from her father. She heard someone coming down the hall. Jesse burst into the room.

"You okay?"

She handed him the latest note and watched alarm tear across his face.

"Where was the gun?"

"On top of the nightstand."

"Not that it matters at this point, but did it have sentimental value?"

She nodded. "It was a gift from my father."

The police had arrived at the same time as Jesse. When he explained who he was and the guard confirmed he was expected, the police allowed him to go upstairs. The officers began swarming the house like mosquitoes on the first warm, humid day of summer. Half the team started in the basement, working their way upstairs, and the other half began on the top floor, working their way down. Every room, including under the beds, closets, bathrooms, even in armoires and bathtubs, was searched. Satisfied there was no one still in the house, they searched outside. One of the officers saw movement inside the schoolhouse and waved over another officer. Emma had been standing on the porch, watching, and when she saw that it looked like the officers were going to break into the schoolhouse, she called to them. The officers turned and looked at her. She waved them over, saying, "Here's the code to get in." The officers searched the whole building, finding only one thing. Holding it in gloved hands, an officer showed Emma a folded piece of paper. She knew what it was before he unfolded it.

> EMMA, YOU ARE WALKING ON A TIGHTWIRE. BE CAREFUL. YOU MIGHT NOT LIKE WHERE YOU LAND.

Jesse was standing in front of her when she looked up. He wasn't sure whether he saw fear or fury on her face.

"Ma'am?" A police officer stepped forward. "I clearly saw someone in here, and that's why we wanted in. Obviously, there's no one here any longer. Where is the other exit door?"

"There isn't one," Jesse and Emma said in unison.

"What do you mean? There has to be."

"My brother designed it and I built this place, and I'm telling you, there's only one way in and one way out, and it's that door," Jesse said, pointing to the door.

The officer looked at him in disbelief. "I'll have to check for myself."

"Be my guest," Jesse said.

He and Emma watched the officer open cabinets, the storage closet, and the bathroom. He walked back to Jesse and Emma.

"This is the oddest thing I've ever seen. I know I saw someone in here."

After the officer left, she said quietly, "I was thinking that maybe one of the ghosts was in here, except that doesn't make sense. Our ghosts aren't mean or vengeful. Whoever wrote that note has it out for me. And it's in the same handwriting as all the other notes."

Jesse saw that Emma was starting to tremble. He wrapped his arms around her until the tremors stopped.

"I don't know what to say or what to think, other than whoever is doing this is really starting to tick me off," she moaned.

Jesse took her hand and led her out of the schoolhouse, turning off the lights as they went, and using her code to lock the door. They walked up the porch stairs and found the door to the house locked. They knocked and knocked until an officer walked down the hallway and let them in.

"Did you find any evidence of someone being in the house, other than all the notes and the theft of my gun?" Emma asked.

"No," the officer remarked. Emma nodded.

"Is anything else gone?" he asked.

"I don't know. I haven't looked for anything else."

"I'll fill out a burglary report. I can't do much about the schoolhouse since we found no evidence of anyone breaking in."

"Obviously someone did," Emma corrected him. "You found a note in there."

"Could it have been left earlier in the day?"

Emma shook her head. "I was in there for several hours and locked it up when I left around seven thirty. You can ask the security guard. He came and got me because he had encountered a woman at the front gate who wanted in, and he didn't want me to be in here alone. When I locked it up, which he witnessed, there was no note."

After the police left, Jesse checked all the doors and windows just to make sure no one could get in. Whoever was gaining access and leaving all the strange notes worried him, and although Emma had been telling him for weeks that there was nothing to worry about, clearly now there was. He was just glad she had called and asked him to come over. Now to figure out the sleeping arrangements. He didn't want to leave her sleeping upstairs without her gun when they couldn't figure out how someone was getting in. He offered to make dinner since she'd had a stressful day. She simply nodded.

"I'm gonna sit in the parlor and relax, if you don't mind. I'm exhausted."

He opened a bottle of wine and set it on the table. Then, he got to work making a batch of rice and stir-frying vegetables and some leftover chicken he found in the fridge. He found a bottle of teriyaki sauce too and stirred a bit into the chicken and vegetable mélange when the rice was ready. He'd already set the table and fed Sophie when he walked into the parlor and found Emma sleeping on the couch. Though he hated to wake her, his urge to feed her was stronger than her will to sleep. He figured that she might not have eaten all day. He gently touched her shoulder.

"Emma, wake up. Emma?"

She didn't stir.

"Emma, the most amazing, most romantic meal ever cooked is on the table. St. Valentine himself made it."

Slowly, he saw Emma move, then finally open her eyes. "St. Valentine was here?" she said, smiling. "And he cooked for me?"

"Yep," he replied, leaning down to kiss her lightly on the cheek. He helped her stand and held her hand, guiding her into the kitchen, where she saw a burning candle on the table and a single rose in a vase. On their plates were rice with chicken and vegetable stir-fry. She sat down, and he poured them each a glass of wine.

"This is lovely, but I hate to admit that I'm almost too tired to eat."

"And break my heart?" he asked, looking crestfallen.

She reached over and squeezed his hand. "I'd never do that."

After dinner, seeing how exhausted she was, he suggested that they go to bed early.

"Good idea, I'll get you a pillow and quilt."

"About that ..."

She turned and looked at him, a question on her face.

"I can't let you sleep alone. Somehow, someone is getting into this house. I couldn't live with myself if I let you sleep alone and found you dead tomorrow morning. I see three options. I can check you into a hotel where you'll be safe, and I'll stay here to keep watch over the house and Sophie. Or you and Sophie can stay the night at my house in my guest room."

"You said there are three options. What's the third?"

"You can sleep down here on the couch, and I'll sleep on the floor next to you."

"That's ridiculous, I'm not letting you sleep on a hard floor."

"It beats sleeping on hard rock in Afghanistan, trying not to get shot by the Taliban."

"This isn't Afghanistan," she announced, "so the floor isn't an option."

"Then I'll sleep on the floor of your bedroom."

"Not any better, Jesse. Look, we're both adults. And I have a big king-size bed. There's plenty of room for both of us. I'm too tired and in no mood for anything romantic beyond your fabulous dinner. And I trust you."

Jesse carried the dishes to the sink and began washing them. She sidled up beside him. "I'll help."

"Naw, you go on upstairs and get ready for bed." He winked at her. "Be sure to wear that sexy flannel nightgown with the frayed hem that no high school teenager in town could resist."

Emma chuckled and headed for the stairs.

The next day, Alice and Emma walked through the police squad room, heading straight for the chief of police's office. The chief stood up when she saw them approach her door.

"Good morning, Alice. Great to see you."

"Good to see you too, Kathryn. If you have a few minutes, there is something you should know about."

"Come in, have a seat," the chief said, beckoning them into her office. "Is this about the Allnutt murder?"

They nodded. The chief stepped out into the squad room and asked Detective Corbin to join them. As soon as the chief and detective joined Alice and Emma, Alice started by summarizing the crime, which the chief acknowledged being very familiar with. The chief turned to the detective. "Detective Corbin, would you please detail what your investigation has discovered so far?"

The detective went white as a brand-new tablecloth. "Well, um, there has been some movement, though I can't reveal my sources or say what that is at this time."

"That's a bunch of poppycock, Detective Corbin!" Alice spewed. "You don't have anything, do you? This case is two months old, and you have nothing to show for it. Isn't that right?"

Everyone looked at the detective.

"Is that right, detective?" the chief asked.

The detective continued to stammer, trying to stall. He rubbed the palms of his hands up and down on his face. Finally, he said, "Yes, that's correct. Bear in mind that it's a very complicated case that requires kid gloves. Not being able to identify the killer has not been for lack of trying. I do have a suspect that I think could have been the murderer."

The chief crossed her arms over her chest. "Are you still trying to throw the caterer under the bus?"

Emma sat straight up in her chair, her voice revealing shock. "Do you mean my cousin Charlene Montrose?"

The detective nodded. "She showed classic signs of guilt."

"Like what?!" Emma insisted.

"I've already discussed this with the chief."

Emma was furious. "So? If you have something on my cousin, who is no more guilty than a butterfly, you need to cough it up!"

"Can't, it's an open investigation," he said, his arrogant and demeaning tone indicating she wasn't worthy of the information.

Emma looked straight at the chief, imploring her to step in. She got the hint.

"Detective, yes, you shared your hunch with me about the caterer a few weeks ago, and when I asked you what evidence you had to prove your theory, you came up empty. I told you that to make a charge stick, you had to find some solid evidence linking the caterer to the murder. Now, did you or not?"

"No, ma'am, I'm still working on it."

Alice and Kathryn sat there, shaking their heads. "What have you tried?" the chief asked.

"I-I-I made some calls."

"To whom?" the chief asked. "And why?"

Caught between two lies, he caved. "I haven't actually called anyone, though I meant to."

"You 'meant to'?" The chief raised her voice. "This is your only case! What have you been doing for the last two months?"

The detective shrugged his shoulders and looked down at the table. "I've been working on that spate of stolen ATMs with Detective Wallace."

"Detective, you knew this was a high-priority case, and you're brushing it off to work on ATM thefts? Bring me the file, you're off the case. I'm assigning someone else."

"That's not necessary, ma'am, I'll get on the case, I promise."

The chief flipped her hand in the air like she was shooing away a mosquito. "Too little, too late. Bring me the file." She turned to Alice and Emma. "I am so sorry about this. I'm going to pull in Detective Ben Barton. I know I can trust him."

She texted him, and the new detective knocked on the door within minutes. The chief motioned him inside. Just as he entered, Detective Corbin stepped into the room and handed a very thin case file to the chief. In it, she found a cover sheet, a list of key people related to the case, the autopsy report, and the statements taken the morning of the murder. The chief shook her head. "This is pathetic."

After the door closed, she asked Alice to summarize for Detective Barton what she'd learned. Alice provided a thorough update, and then she introduced Emma to furnish further backstory. Emma told everyone about her calls to Detective Corbin for two weeks and how upset he had been that she wanted information on the progress of the investigation. She had told him she would stop if he would tell her the status of the case.

"I think I wore him down, and out of desperation, he told me the results of the autopsy."

The chief began reading the autopsy report and found additional information that showed that Isabel had had an extreme allergic reaction to peanuts. "This actually could have been the cause of death," she surmised.

"Excuse the interruption," Alice piped up. "When I was interviewing Hank Allnutt, the husband, he mentioned that Isabel had an extreme peanut allergy."

"Wait a minute, if an allergic reaction could have caused her death, why did the autopsy list strangulation and a hit on the head with the statuette as the cause of death?" Emma asked.

"Good question," the chief said. "If I were to take an educated guess, I'd say the murderer discreetly gave her some form of peanuts to incapacitate her. It could have been something as simple as the killer putting a couple of drops of peanut oil into a glass of wine or a cup of tea. If that's what happened, her peanut allergy would have kicked in and made breathing difficult. That's probably when the killer used the silk scarf to choke her and maybe used the statuette to finish her off."

The chief looked over at Emma. "Is there anything else?"

"Yes." She went on to tell her about the séance. And then, she told her about the mysterious notes that had appeared in the mailbox, in the house, and in the schoolhouse the day before.

"Yes, I have them here. The officers brought them back to the station after their visit to your home last night."

"The thing is, the handwriting matches, so they appear to be written by the same person. Plus, the house and the schoolhouse were locked up, so we have no idea how anyone got inside to place them in locations where I'd see them."

"Who is 'we'? Who was in the house with you?"

"The owner of the security company I contracted with to provide 24/7 coverage until this case is solved."

"Good move. Who is the owner of the company?"

"Dustin Kolar."

"Good man. Did you and Mr. Kolar find anything else out of the ordinary?"

Emma nodded. "A woman came up to the locked gate and asked him to let her in, claiming I'd told her she could visit the grounds anytime she liked."

"And did you?" the chief asked.

"Absolutely not. I have no idea who it was, and she left before Mr. Kolar could get her name."

"The woman probably wouldn't have given him her real name anyway. And you say all the doors were locked?"

Emma nodded.

"This case just gets stranger and stranger, doesn't it?" She handed the notes to Detective Barton. "Get these tested for fingerprints as soon as you can."

The chief leaned back in her chair. "It's been quite a while since we've had a real live soap opera murder in our midst." She turned to Emma. "You are to be commended for taking this bull by its proverbial horns."

"Ma'am, it wasn't all me by a long shot. Travis Sheridan, my son-in-law; Savannah Mae, my daughter; Jesse Rieger, a friend and the contractor who built my quilting retreat; and Stella Rogers, my lifelong friend, all helped. Lavender Atherton, one of the students, introduced me to her sister, Alice, who stepped in and has been an enormous help."

The chief looked over at Detective Barton. "Detective, what do you think?"

"I think we should hire these folks, they did all the hard work. Meanwhile, I'm going to comb through this file and the autopsy report. Before I can identify a suspect, I need to find out more about the victim."

"I think I can help with that," Emma offered.

Everyone looked at her.

"My daughter, Savannah Mae, has a good friend in California who works in human relations, investigating people applying for jobs in sensitive areas of her company. She has some very impressive skills, starting with intuition. How about we use her to find everything we can about the victim?"

"What's this woman's name?"

"Maggie Bowen."

"Is she certified to investigate, and has she actually uncovered any devious characters in the course of her work?"

"I think so, she has a saddlebag full of certifications, and quite a résumé of people she was able to turn over to the police, people who were on various most-wanted lists."

The chief turned to Detective Barton. "What do you think, detective? Do you want this woman's help, or do you prefer to do all the legwork yourself?"

"I don't ever turn down good offers. First, I'd like to speak with her. Mrs. Jenkins, can you or your daughter email her, introduce me, and ask if she would be available to help with the investigation?"

"As soon as we leave here, I'll have Savannah Mae get in touch with her and get that ball rolling. Do you have a card with your cell where Maggie can call you?"

"Sure," he said, reaching into his shirt pocket. He pulled out a card and handed it to Emma. "My email is on there too."

What a nice change, she thought, remembering how Detective Corbin had done everything he could to sideline her.

The chief looked around the room. "If there's nothing else to discuss, let's adjourn and follow up as soon as more information surfaces. Meanwhile," she said, looking at Emma, "you be vigilant. It sounds like the threats to your life are very real."

"Thank you, I will," she promised.

As soon as Emma got back to the house, she called Savannah Mae and gave her an update on the meeting at the police station, ending with her suggestion to have Maggie do some sleuthing about the victim.

"Hope I didn't overstep there. When I heard what the new detective would need, I immediately thought of Maggie. If anyone can dig up a profile on the murdered woman, wouldn't you say that Maggie can?"

Savannah Mae nodded into the phone. "That was a good call, Mama. When you can, text me the new detective's contact info. After I get it, I'll phone Mags."

Meanwhile, Emma went through her front gate, waved at the security guard on the day shift, and headed for the front porch. She saw a box with a vase of flowers sticking out of the top next to the front door. She turned around to look for the guard. He was already walking up the steps.

"Where'd these come from?" she asked.

"A local flower shop delivered them a few minutes ago."

Emma thought they might be from Jesse but decided to err on the side of caution. She placed the box on a porch table and removed a small envelope inserted in the bouquet. In the now-recognizable handwriting, she read the latest message:

THAT WAS REALLY STUPID OF YOU TO TALK TO THE COPS. YOU THINK I WOULDN'T HAVE SEEN YOU GOING INTO THE POLICE STATION? YOU'RE WALKING INTO A PIT OF VIPERS.

"Secret admirer?" the guard asked.

"Afraid not. Guess I should take these inside and call the detective."

"It looks heavy. I'll carry it in for you," he offered. He picked it up and noticed something moving around near the bottom of the vase. He bent over, trying to get a good look at it. Faster than a lightning strike, the head of a snake with reddish-brown crossbands on a light-colored body thrust out of the box, aiming for his face. He instinctively dropped the box, causing it to fall on its side. A very long snake slithered out and moved down the steps, heading for the front garden. Emma covered her mouth, muffling a scream.

"Oh my goodness, you could have been bitten!"

"That would not have been good. It's a broad-banded copperhead."

"Is it dangerous?"

"You bet it is. Copperheads are venomous. One bite can kill a pet or make a small child real sick."

"You're sure it's venomous?"

He nodded. "In general, venomous snakes have a triangular head. Nonvenomous snakes have spoon-shaped rounded heads. That guy," he said, pointing to the snake slithering toward the gate, "has the classic triangular-shaped head. Plus, once you've seen a copperhead, and I've seen plenty, you never forget what they look like."

Emma let out a lungful of air she didn't realize she'd been holding. "You sure know a lot about snakes."

"Yeah, it's kinda a hobby of mine. I have a boa constrictor at home named Bella. She's real sweet."

Emma's eyebrows shot up. "I've never thought of a snake as sweet, especially a boa. Aren't they dangerous?"

"Not really. They're not venomous or aggressive. They make good pets, actually. I've had snakes as pets since I was a kid. Bella has been with me since I got her as a baby. She was so cute." He whipped out his wallet and pulled out a photo. "See? Wasn't she adorable?" Emma glanced at the photo of what looked like a big worm. "She's about ten years old now. Probably has another ten to twenty years in her."

"Well, I'm sure glad it was you working the day shift today. I would have had a complete meltdown if I had carried that box into the house and that snake came out."

Emma unlocked the door and started to go into the house.

"Mrs. Jenkins, you forgot your flowers," he said, picking up the vase.

"You know, I really don't want them. Would you mind throwing them in the trash can?"

"That's a shame. Would it be okay if I take them home after my shift? My wife would love them."

"Consider them yours. I couldn't have them in the house; every time I looked at them, I'd think of that snake."

"Thanks." The guard set the box aside and proceeded to do a walking surveillance of the property.

Once inside, Emma poured herself a glass of lemonade, took out her phone, and called Detective Barton with the latest turn of events.

"You were lucky," the detective said. "A copperhead could have really hurt you."

"So I hear. Hold on, there's a text coming in from my daughter. She says she talked to Maggie Bowen about researching Isabel Allnutt, and she's happy to help. Maggie has your cell and is going to reach out to you."

"Thanks, Mrs. Jenkins."

"Emma. Please, call me Emma."

Next, she called Jesse.

"Hey, what's up?"

"Just the weirdest day ever."

"How's that?"

"Too long for a phone call. You wanna stop by after work for cocktails and a snake story?"

"Snake?"

"Yep."

"Are you okay?"

"Yeah. Just getting really tired of whoever is trying to scare or kill me."

"I'll see you in a bit."

"Be careful coming in through the front. The snake may still be in the front yard."

"Thanks for the warning. Do I need my shotgun?"

"Maybe. It's a copperhead."

"I'll bring my gun."

Chapter Nineteen

Later that day, Detective Barton was sitting at his desk, reviewing all the paper work on the Allnutt murder, when his phone rang. It was a California number.

"Detective Ben Barton," he answered.

"Hi, Detective Barton. This is Maggie Bowen."

"Hello, Ms. Bowen, how is your research on our victim coming along?"

"Do you have a few minutes?"

"Sure, let me have it."

"I discovered that two of the students at the retreat, Connie Sinclaire and Linda Mayfield, are sisters, and Isabel was married to their brother, Hank. Apparently, Hank and Isabel lived out of state for a while. Out-of-state records show that the police had been called to Isabel and Hank's home on numerous occasions for marital disputes. On one occasion, Isabel was booked on marital physical abuse of Hank and then released when Hank said he didn't want to file charges."

"Wait a second," the detective interrupted. "Isabel was being charged? Not Hank?"

"Yep," Maggie said. "And it gets even more interesting. Isabel was a certified instructor in Krav Maga, a martial arts system used by the Israeli military."

"I'm vaguely familiar with it."

"Just to give you a little background on it, Krav Maga motivates students to avoid physical confrontation. If that's not possible or is unsafe, it promotes finishing a fight as quickly and aggressively as possible. It looks like Isabel was practicing her Krav Maga skills on Hank. And if my hunch is right, his sisters came to his rescue."

"Krav Maga is a pretty sophisticated form of martial arts," the detective said. "Wouldn't Isabel have been able to subdue both Connie and Linda if, in fact, they were the ones who killed her?"

"Kinda depends. Maybe the sisters incapacitated Isabel in some way."

"But that should have shown up in the autopsy report."

"Yeah, it should have."

The detective flipped through the police department reports and found the part of the autopsy report that detailed traces of peanuts found in Isabel's system and her severe peanut allergy.

"You're right, Maggie. She had an acute peanut allergy; the ME found traces of peanuts in her system. Although that didn't kill her, it probably disabled her enough that the killer finished her off with strangulation, followed by the pop on the head, causing a lethal brain injury."

"Well, there ya go, detective."

"Maggie, you really came through for us. If you ever decide to relocate to Texas, you have a job waiting for you."

Maggie laughed. "Don't tell Savannah Mae Sheridan. She's my best friend and has been trying to get me to move to Texas for the last two years."

"Why don't you? It's a great place to live."

"I know it is. I've visited a bunch. There's only one problem."

"And that is?"

"I'm a surfer, so I can't live anywhere without good waves."

"There's plenty of good waves down on the coastline."

"Very true. I've actually spent some time surfing them."

"Then what's the problem?"

"Savannah wants me to move to Waxahachie, and last time I looked, there are no beaches in Waxahachie."

The detective burst out laughing. "You're very observant."

"Savannah Mae was so intent on getting me to move there that she suggested I trade my surfboard for water skis and ski the area lakes."

"That's a good solution."

Maggie wrinkled her nose. "No, it's not. When you're used to surfing the breakers in Malibu, water-skiing just won't cut it."

"I get it. Thanks for all your help, and if you do decide to move …"

"I'll let you know, detective. Just don't hold your breath."

About the same time Maggie was chatting with the new detective, Jesse showed up at Emma's house. After Emma had filled him in on her eventful day, he insisted on taking her out for dinner. "You deserve to be pampered a bit. Where do you want to go?"

"Actually, I could go for a really great burger or chicken-fried steak and fried okra."

"I don't think I've ever seen you eat a burger, chicken-fried steak, or okra."

"I do, though not often."

They pulled up to a small mom-and-pop café along the square, walked in, and plopped down at a table in the back. When Emma saw several framed certificates on the wall proclaiming their chicken-fried steak had won the Blue Plate Award year after year, she ordered it with a side of fried okra. It felt good to eat home-style cooking. It felt even better that someone else was doing the cooking and cleaning up the kitchen. When they exited the restaurant, Jesse headed toward the truck.

"Would you mind if we walk for a bit?" Emma asked. "I've spent too many hours sitting today. I'm feeling a little stiff," she added.

Jesse took her hand in his. They walked for several blocks, stopping in front of store windows to check out the displays. As they came to the end of a block, three people turned the corner across the street: a man, with Linda and Connie on either side of him. The women were holding tightly onto him, laughing and teasing one another. Emma pulled Jesse back into an alcove.

"What's up?" he asked.

"I got a call from the new detective working the case. There's new evidence that those women are our murder suspects, and I think the man they're with is the suffering widower, who doesn't appear to be suffering much."

"Are you sure? Have you met him?" Jesse asked.

"No. I think it's him, though; I saw his photo in the paper after the murder," she said, watching the man stroll with Linda and Connie. "I'm not absolutely sure, but I've got a funny feeling about the three of them."

"Let's get out of here," Jesse said.

After stopping to do a couple of errands, Jesse drove Emma home and walked her up to her door. He stepped inside and checked all the doors and windows. Everything was shut up tightly.

"I don't like that the author of those notes is watching you. I think it's best if I sleep on your couch tonight."

Emma laid her hands on his shoulders. "Jesse, I'm fine. And I have an armed guard outside watching the house. Nothing's going to happen. I'm safe, I really am. Trust me."

"I trust you implicitly," Jesse insisted. "It's whoever is threatening you that I don't trust."

"I'll be fine, Jesse. Honestly, I will. Now go home and sleep in your comfortable bed instead of on my couch, where all you'll have to show for your diligence will be a backache."

He stared at her for several moments, finally nodded, and left.

Emma made her way upstairs to find Sophie sprawled on her bed. She laid her phone on her vanity and kicked off her shoes just as she heard a strange sound coming from her closet. She opened the door, gasped, and stumbled back. Linda Mayfield and Connie Sinclaire stood there, one holding a pistol and the other a sinewy rope.

"How did the two of you get into the house?" Emma asked.

"Oh, you mean how did we get past your guard?" Connie responded in a snarky tone. "It wasn't hard. A man like that is a sucker for a flirtatious female. He got a double whammy with both of us," she said, looking over at Linda and snickering.

Emma took a deep breath and concentrated on trying to anticipate what they planned to do. "So, what are you doing here? Y'all could have come to the front door like normal visitors."

Connie and Linda exchanged glances, grinning. "We're not normal visitors, Emma, now are we?" Linda said snidely.

"What's that supposed to mean?" Emma asked.

"We know that you're trying to frame us, and we thought we'd pay you a little visit to point out that if you continue, you're going to regret it," Linda answered.

"Actually," Connie interjected, "you won't even live long enough to regret it."

Suddenly, just the way she had felt when she discovered that someone had stolen the gun her father had given her—the gun Linda was now holding—Emma felt a surge of strength bolt up her back. She was sick of how these two women had been threatening and trying to manipulate her. She'd had enough.

"Quit bein' ugly!" Emma snapped at them.

"We're not the ones bein' ugly, you are," Linda responded, a snarkiness to her voice.

"I take it that the two of you have been sending me those adorable love notes," Emma said.

"What love notes?" Connie asked, tossing her head from side to side.

"Connie, she means all the notes we've been leaving for her," Linda answered.

"Oh, those. They weren't love notes."

"Duh!" Linda hastened to say. "I swear, Connie, sometimes you're completely clueless."

Connie frowned, pushing out her lower lip in a pout.

Linda ordered Emma to sit down on the chair in front of her vanity.

"Oh for God's sake, you think that you're going to get away with murdering me too?" Emma cried, using reason to point out the obvious.

Linda began tying Emma's hands and feet to the chair.

"Hopefully, we won't have to if you'll just cooperate," Connie jeered at her, attempting to sound tough.

"And what exactly is this cooperation that you want?" Emma asked.

"You're going to call the police and have them drop their investigation into Isabel's death," Connie continued.

"Oh hush your mouth, like that's possible!" Emma lashed out in an irritated tone. The two women did have her gun, and though she knew she should probably be scared and refrain from angering them, she couldn't help herself. The two women were as sharp as a smooth, round marble, which wasn't saying much.

"The police investigate murders. That's their job," Emma explained to the women as simply as possible. "What did you two do? Prepare for this by reading *The Moron's Guide to Murder*?"

"Don't say that word," Connie stammered, her hands planted on her hips.

"Why not?"

"It's not what happened."

Emma shook her head from side to side. "Uh, what would you call it?"

"An accident," Connie and Linda said together.

"It wasn't an accident, and you know it. You killed her. Oops, let me rephrase that—you *murdered* Isabel!"

"Did not," Connie persisted.

"Why did you do it?" Emma asked. "Connie, weren't you and Isabel best friends?"

"Yes, and I loved her like a sister, but I love my brother more."

"Okay, that's enough!" Linda intervened. "Connie, she's trying to trap you into saying something they can charge you for."

Emma's phone rang. It was lying on the vanity table, and she could see it was Jesse. Linda picked it up and turned the phone around. "Tell whoever this is that you can't talk right now and don't give any hints of what's going on here." Emma nodded, and Linda put the phone to Emma's ear.

"Hello?"

"Emma, are you okay?"

"Oh, Jesse, is that you? How nice to hear from you! It's been a long time. I was just saying to my friend Sophie—you remember Sophie, don't you—that I hadn't heard from you in what seems like forever. What are you up to these days?"

The line went dead. Jesse had hung up.

"Who's Jesse?" Linda asked.

"A family friend. He built the retreat schoolhouse."

"Why would he be calling you?"

"How do I know? He hung up."

"Don't play with us, Emma!" Linda nearly shouted, simultaneously biting her nails.

"Well, bless your heart!" Emma lashed out at the half-witted women. Obviously, Linda and Connie had no idea what they were doing, nor did they understand what the phrase meant. She hoped that Jesse had picked up that something was wrong.

In fact, Jesse was down in the front garden with several police officers, including Detective Barton and two EMS employees who were taking care of the security guard, who was suffering with rope burns and an ill-placed gunshot wound to his left lower leg.

When Jesse had exited the house after checking the doors and windows, he realized he hadn't seen the security guard. He walked around the property until he found him tied up and pulled behind a tall bush, duct tape slapped over his mouth. He removed the tape, and the guard told Jesse about the two women. Jesse immediately called Detective Barton, who said he and a team would be there momentarily. Once the guard was quietly removed from the property, the police strategized on the next steps.

Detective Barton asked Jesse whether he thought Emma was being held by the two sisters.

"Absolutely, I called her phone when I found the guard. She answered but didn't sound like herself. I hung up right away, which I hope she understood meant that I know she's in danger."

"Are there any other doors into the house besides the front?"

"Yeah, there's one off the side of the house that goes into the kitchen. That ramp over there"—he pointed to the ramp he'd built for wheelchairs—"goes right into it. There's also a door from the back porch into the back of the house."

"Do you have a house key that unlocks all the doors? I'd like to make as quiet an entrance as possible."

Jesse handed him the house key in his pocket.

"Thanks." The detective turned to his officers, and they figured out their strategy. He turned to Jesse. "Where is the room where they might be holding her?"

"I don't know for sure, but it's likely her bedroom on the third floor, in the back half of the house."

The detective waved to the officers to begin unlocking doors and entering the house. Slowly and silently, they entered and cleared each room. They reached the third floor and could hear voices down the hall, undulating between loud and so soft that they couldn't make out what the women were saying. The police advanced silently until they reached the room. They did a silent countdown from five to zero, then threw open the door. Linda and Connie had been so confident that nothing would stand in the way of eliminating Emma that they'd placed the gun and extra rope on Emma's bed. When the police entered, the weapons were out of reach. Linda started moving toward the bed.

"I wouldn't do that if I were you," Detective Barton warned. "I will shoot you if you make one more move." Linda stopped and hung her head low.

"Hands behind your back, both of you," the detective ordered, his voice hard and emphatic. Both women did as told, and officers moved in to cuff them. As the officers took them into custody, another officer untied Emma's hands and feet and extended a hand to help her stand.

"Are you hurt?" the officer asked.

"Only my pride," Emma admitted, just as Jesse burst into the room. He wrapped his arms around her and held her tight—suffocatingly tight. "Jesse?"

"Yes?"

"I can't breathe," she said in a muffled voice.

He loosened his embrace, stood back, and stared straight at her, scrutinizing her for any signs of fright or terror; he found none. "You are one brave woman," he said, marveling at how she had kept her cool and hadn't allowed the incident to upend her. If it had, he knew that this wouldn't have been such a happy ending. All the officers began leaving the room with Connie and Linda.

Emma reached up and placed one hand along the side of his face.

"Jesse, you know how you told me about your past? Well, I've never told you about mine, about my family's."

"Why tell me now? What does that have to do with what happened here?"

"A great deal. Now is as good a time as any to tell you that I come from a long line of strong, dauntless women who, when we believe in something, don't let anyone or anything get in the way of our resolve or perseverance. It's a trait that has been passed down in all the females of the Clayburne family line. I'd lost mine for a while, and with what happened here, I can tell you that it's back, in full force. I have it, as do my sisters, and Savannah Mae, though I'm not sure she's aware of it. We are determined in ways that other women are not. With this resolve comes stubbornness, which some think is a fault. It is not. It is part of the tenacity we are all born with that forms the strength of our character. It's why we don't back down and little scares us."

"Are you saying that's why you weren't fazed by anything that occurred in the house?"

"Yes, Jesse, that's exactly what I'm saying."

They heard a nearby cough and looked over to see Detective Barton standing in the doorway, an officer with him.

"If y'all are done, we need to interview both of you."

"Of course," Emma replied with a nod.

"Mr. Rieger, if you will go with Officer Gonzalez, I'll interview Mrs. Jenkins up here."

Jesse followed the officer while Emma sat down in an antique rocking chair to answer the detective's questions. Sophie came out from under the bed and jumped into her lap. Emma could feel her shaking, and she was pretty sure it wasn't the temperature that was making her tremble. She began petting and massaging Sophie, who finally stopped shuddering and began purring. Before concluding the interview, Detective Barton asked Emma whether she recognized the gun on the bed.

"Yes, my father gave it to me when I was a teenager."

"I need to take it for evidence, but I assure you, it will be returned to you after the trial. If the sisters decide to plead guilty, I can return it to you sooner."

Thirty minutes later, Emma joined Jesse in the kitchen.

"I hope you don't mind. I called Travis and Savannah Mae, who called Stella, your sisters, and your brother. Just to let them know that you're okay and safe."

"Thanks," Emma said. "You saved me a bunch of phone calls. What do you think will happen next?"

"They'll be booked into city jail and then arraigned in front of a judge."

"This has been such an annoying ordeal. I am so exhausted, I think I could sleep for a week. First, though, I need to resurrect my retreat business."

Jesse walked over and wrapped his arms around her again. "Couldn't that wait until tomorrow? I have a better idea."

"What? Back to Santa Fe?" Emma winked at him.

"I was thinking of something closer, like Georgie Boy's."

Emma pursed her lips and wrinkled her brow. "Hmm, I have been meaning to go there."

"Do you like ice cream?"

"Of course. Who doesn't?"

"I can't believe you've never stopped into Georgie Boy's. They serve the best ice cream in Waxahachie."

"I guess I've been a little preoccupied with everything going on over the last year."

"Well, my dear, you are about to meet the intersection of sweet decadence, sinfully rich cream, and flavors you've never imagined."

"Such as?"

Jesse looked up and comically scratched his chin as though in deep thought. "I'm not gonna recite the whole menu. But you'd be missing somethin' real special if you didn't order George Likes the Bananas or Don't Tell Wendy."

"Are you serious? Those are actual names of ice cream flavors?"

"Yep. Pretty wild, huh?"

Emma took Jesse's hand. "Mr. Rieger, lead the way. I've never met an ice cream flavor I didn't like."

"You ever made ice cream?" Jesse asked as they headed toward the front door.

"No," she shook her head, "never have."

"That's a shock."

"Why?"

"With all the cooking and baking you do, I woulda thought that ice cream would be part of your skill set."

She stopped and looked keenly at him. "Have you ever made ice cream?"

"Yeah, I have. My folks made ice cream when I was a kid. Tom and I would help and made a real mess of it, but we had fun. We grew up with it, and I make it whenever the mood strikes. You know what?"

Emma cocked her head sideways. "Can't even begin to guess what's going on in that handsome head of yours," she said with a smile.

"We could have made some when we were in Santa Fe. Tom has a state-of-the-art ice cream maker in the kitchen. Sorry I didn't think of it."

"In that case, you can woo me with your homemade ice cream here. I'm pretty sure that your ice cream–making skills are probably as good as your construction artistry."

"Deal!" He took her hand and led her out the door. "For now, let's hit Georgie Boy's. I'll pick up ingredients later and make some ice cream that'll make you fall head over heels in love with me."

Emma stopped and turned toward Jesse, searching his face. "How is it possible to fall head over heels in love with someone you already love?"

Jesse bent slightly, cupped his hands around her face, and kissed her so deeply, so passionately, that her knees began to buckle. She'd never been kissed like that, laced with a soft gentleness she couldn't describe. He pulled back, continuing to lock gazes with her.

Over the months he'd gotten to know Emma, she had brought a special kind of luminance into the darkness that had consumed him since his injury. Until he met her, he'd thought he'd been doing well and had conquered the mental and psychological pain wrought by the war. It was in the quiet moments, like these, that he realized he hadn't, not entirely. Because now, he was different, the demons no longer dancing at the periphery, threatening to consume him with haunting memories. There was only one thing, one person, responsible for their absence, and that was Emma.

"I love you, Emma Clayburne Jenkins," he suddenly said, taking her hand in his.

As she smiled, a glow unlike any he'd seen before emanating from her eyes. "Love you more, Jesse Rieger."

The next day, Jesse stopped in to see Emma before heading out to his new job site.

"How'd you sleep last night, knowing you were finally safe?"

"'Like a baby' doesn't begin to describe it." She tried to look behind him. "What are you holding back there?"

"Close your eyes."

"Another one of your surprises?"

"You bet." He brought around a vintage-looking heart-shaped piece of barn wood. "Open your eyes."

"How sweet."

"Turn it over."

She saw a simple phrase burned into the wood: "Until We Are Ghosts." She looked up at him and felt her eyes start to water. Emma threw her arms around him, holding him tight. He bent down and lightly kissed her, turned, and left. She placed it on a shelf so she could see it every time she walked into the kitchen.

The next day, the local newspaper and a television station in Dallas ran the story about the killers at the quilting retreat center being found and arrested. By late morning, Emma's phone began ringing from quilters who had canceled their reservations, asking to rebook. She directed everyone to the website and checked her email, discovering that twice as many people had reached out to ask about future retreats, wanting to know which dates were available and which quilts would be taught. By the end of the day, Emma had scheduled several women from the third retreat to come in and finish their retreat week. And by the next day, she had rescheduled everyone from the fourth retreat who had canceled. That one, she knew, was going to be extra special: Savannah Mae had agreed to teach the basics of designing and creating an art quilt, a talent that had won her numerous awards over the years. She called Savannah Mae, Charlene, and Stella with the good news and asked about their availability for the retreats.

"Oh, Mama!" Savannah Mae cooed into the phone when she heard about the retreats being rescheduled. "This is the best news ever, well, almost."

"I agree." Emma slowly let out a big breath and then paused. "Wait, what do you mean by 'almost'?"

"Are you sitting down?"

"I am," she answered cautiously. "Do I need to be concerned?"

"No, I think you'll be happy," Savannah Mae said, smiling into the phone.

"Savannah Mae, spill it! You're worrying me."

"Okay, okay," Savannah Mae turned and looked at Travis, who was standing next to her. They smiled tenderly at one another as Travis ran his arm around her waist. "As Travis is fond of saying, hold your horses. Are you ready?"

"Of course I'm ready!"

"Mama, you're going to be a grandmother!"

"What?! Really?"

"Yes, really. They're due in April."

Silence filled a lull in the conversation.

"Savannah Mae, what do you mean by 'they'? Who are 'they'?"

"Twins, Mama. I'm having twins, one boy and one girl."

Emma dropped her phone just as she began yelping with an exuberance she hadn't felt since the day she'd learned that she was pregnant with Savannah Mae. Euphoria suddenly stole her voice, replaced by tears of pure unabashed bliss. From the floor, she heard a voice coming from the phone.

"Mama? Mama? Are you still there?"

The End

Reader's Guide

The Mercy Quilt

BY JEFFREE WYN ITRICH

1. The main character, Emma, goes through a number of changes during the course of the story. Do you feel that she actually changes, or is it only her circumstances that change? In what ways does she grow, and in what ways does she stay the same?
2. Early on, Emma expresses a lack of confidence, quite unlike her demeanor in *The Wedding Dress Quilt* when she returned to Texas. Why do you feel she experiences self-doubt in this book?
3. Because of her lack of confidence, Emma's family and her best friend, Stella, rally around her, refusing to let her give up her dream of a quilting retreat center. Who do you think provides the strongest influence, and why?
4. At the first couple of retreats, Emma encounters a few hiccups from students and loses her first caterer. What kind of stumbling blocks have you encountered in your own life? If you were in Emma's shoes, would you react the same way?

5. Detective Corbin is seemingly not invested in solving the murder and has something of an attitude toward Emma, who is not in a position to be able to influence his behavior. Have you encountered anyone like this or been in a similar situation? How were you able to handle it?
6. When did you catch on to the identity of the murderer?
7. If you heard that a murder had occurred at a quilt retreat where you had paid for an upcoming week of classes, would you have canceled and requested a refund or gone ahead and attended? Why?
8. Though Jesse appears to be calm and collected, we later find out that he's been battling demons from his time in the military. Do you think he resolves some of his worst issues? If not, what does he still need to work on?
9. Jesse shares his PTSD struggles with Emma. Do you feel she responds appropriately? Does learning a bit about PTSD affect how you might interact with people in the future?
10. Emma and Jesse manage to overcome some of their biggest personal fears. Are they good for each other?
11. We learn that Isabel Allnutt was also a domestic violence abuser. Did that make you less sympathetic toward her as a victim?
12. Do you feel that Linda and Connie were at all justified in their actions?

Emma and Jesse's Favorite Recipes

EMMA'S DIVINE LEMON BARS

CRUST

2 C flour

1 C very cold butter

¾ C powdered sugar

½ tsp salt

FILLING

4 eggs, slightly beaten

2 C sugar

4 T flour

4 T freshly squeezed lemon juice

Additional powdered sugar, sifted to remove lumps

Slice the cold butter and put into a food processor with the powdered sugar, salt, and flour. Pulse until mixture looks like powder. Using a paper towel, lightly grease a 9″ × 13″ baking pan. Press the mixture into the pan with your fingers until you get a smooth, solid layer. Bake at 350° for 15 minutes while you make the filling.

Mix together the eggs, sugar, flour, and fresh lemon juice. Remove the crust from the oven and pour the filling over the warm crust. Return the pan to the oven and continue baking at 350° for 20–25 minutes, until the top is lightly browned. Remove from the oven and sprinkle the sifted powdered sugar over the top while it is still warm.

MORAVIAN SPICE COOKIES

Makes 2–3 dozen cookies, depending on thickness

2 T packed brown sugar
¼ C lard or bacon grease*
¼ C molasses
1¼ C flour
¼ T salt
¼ tsp baking soda
¼ tsp baking powder
⅛ tsp ground white pepper
¼ tsp ground ginger
¼ tsp ground cloves
¼ tsp cinnamon
Pinch mustard powder
Pinch allspice
Pinch ground nutmeg
Powdered sugar (optional)

Mix together the brown sugar, lard or bacon grease*, and molasses in a large bowl. Stir in flour, salt, baking soda, baking powder, and spices. Cover and refrigerate for 4 hours or overnight.

Preheat oven to 350°. Line three cookie sheets with parchment paper.

Roll ⅓ of the dough on a lightly floured board to an even ⅛-inch thickness, as thin as you can get without the dough tearing. Dip the edges of a 3″ round cookie cutter, preferably one with scalloped edges, into a small bowl of flour. Shake off excess. Cut cookies with the cookie cutter and gently place them onto the lined cookie sheets with a metal spatula. Leave ½″ between cookies. Reflour the cookie cutter as needed.

Bake cookies 5–10 minutes, depending on the thickness of the dough. Watch carefully to prevent the cookies from overbrowning. Remove from oven and let cool completely before moving them to a cookie jar. Repeat with remaining dough.

*Bacon grease and lard make the cookies extra crispy, as they should be.

NELLIE'S CHICKEN AND SAUSAGE GUMBO

Serves 8–10

SEASONING MIXTURE

Make this spice mixture first and set aside for later.

2 tsp garlic powder

2 tsp onion powder

2 tsp paprika

1 tsp dried basil

1 tsp dried oregano

1 tsp dried thyme

1 tsp salt

1 tsp black pepper

½ tsp cayenne pepper

GUMBO

3 T vegetable oil

1 lb andouille sausage, sliced

1 large yellow onion, chopped

1 medium green bell pepper, chopped

1 small red bell pepper, chopped

4 large celery stalks, chopped

5 garlic cloves, minced

1 C vegetable oil

¾–1 C flour

6 C chicken stock

3 lb boneless skinless chicken thighs, shredded or chopped

1 lb sliced fresh or frozen okra

3 bay leaves

Salt, black pepper, and cayenne pepper to taste

Cooked rice

Filé powder to sprinkle on bowls of gumbo at the end

4 green onions, chopped (Optional)

Heat 3 T vegetable oil in a large pot over medium heat. Add the sliced sausage and sauté 5 minutes. Remove from the pot and set aside.

Add the chopped onions and cook over medium heat until they caramelize, about 20 minutes. Stir in the bell peppers and celery and sauté for 8 minutes or until the peppers are slightly brown but still fragrant. Stir in minced garlic and cook for another minute; watch to make sure it doesn't burn or get overly brown. Remove the sautéed vegetables and set aside.

Next, make the roux. Add 1 C oil to the pot and heat over medium-low for a couple of minutes. Slowly sprinkle in ¾–1 C flour while continuing to whisk until combined. Keep whisking the roux until it darkens to the color of a very dark chocolate (plan to spend half an hour whisking until it reaches this stage). When it's perfectly dark, stir the cooked vegetables back in and sprinkle in the seasonings set aside earlier. Mix well.

Pour 1 C chicken stock into the pot and mix it with the vegetables, spices, and roux. Add the remaining chicken stock, the chopped chicken, sausage slices, bay leaves, and sliced okra.

Bring the pot to a boil over medium-high heat. This will allow the roux and the okra to thicken the stock. When it begins to boil, reduce the heat to medium-low, cover the pot, and simmer for 1 hour. If your stovetop cooks hot, you may need to reduce the heat to low. When it's done, if desired, adjust seasoning with salt, pepper, and more cayenne. To serve, ladle spoonfuls of cooked rice into bowls, top with gumbo and chopped green onions, and sprinkle with a dash of filé powder. *Laissez les bon temps rouler!*

HOW TO MAKE PIZZA

If you have a pizza stone, place it in the oven and preheat to 475°.

CRUST

1 package active dry yeast

1 tsp sugar

½ tsp salt

2 T extra-virgin olive oil

2½ C bread flour

1 C very warm water

Cornmeal

TOPPINGS

⅓ C savory tomato sauce (best with homemade if you grow your own tomatoes)

½ C each sliced onion and sliced mushrooms and 3 minced garlic cloves sautéed in a teaspoon of olive oil

¼ C roasted red pepper slivers

2 T minced sun-dried tomatoes

Meats of choice (pepperoni, salami, Italian ham)

½ C grated mozzarella cheese

2 T feta cheese crumbles

2 T grated Parmesan cheese

Start by making the crust. Combine the yeast, sugar, salt, and extra-virgin olive oil in a bowl. Stir in the warm water and let the yeast proof. When it starts to bubble, mix in 2½ C of bread flour. Transfer to a large mixer and use a dough hook to thoroughly mix together all the ingredients until it forms a smooth ball. Lay the dough on a clean board. Knead and massage the dough to about 14″ in diameter. Sprinkle cornmeal on a pizza peel and transfer the dough to the peel. Spread a minimal amount of your favorite tomato sauce to the edges of the dough. Then, begin layering the sliced onions, mushrooms, garlic, roasted red bell slivers, sun-dried tomatoes, and your meats of choice followed by the three types of cheeses to serve as a culinary glue to keep all the vegetables and meats secure on top of the crust.

Use a quick jerking motion to slide the pizza from the peel onto the pizza stone once the oven has reached 475°. Bake 15–20 minutes until the cheese is melted and the crust has browned. Remove the pizza from the oven with the peel. Slide the pizza onto a cutting board. Let it rest for 5 minutes before cutting into slices.

BOURBON CHICKEN WITH CRISPY PARMESAN NEW POTATOES

Serves 4–6 people

PARMESAN POTATOES

1 lb fingerling yellow potatoes

Oil

Salt, pepper

BOURBON CHICKEN

2½ lb boneless, skinless chicken thighs, cubed

¼ tsp salt

¼ tsp ground black pepper

1½ T cornstarch or arrowroot

¼–⅓ C oil

2 tsp powdered garlic or 3 fresh garlic cloves, minced

2 tsp peeled and minced fresh gingeroot

1 C plus 1 T chicken stock

⅓ C bourbon

⅓ C low-sodium soy sauce

¼ C packed brown sugar

1½ tsp rice vinegar

2 tsp sesame oil

Crushed red pepper or hot chili powder to taste

2 tsp cornstarch or arrowroot

Toss the potatoes in oil, season with salt and pepper, and transfer to a large skillet. Cook on medium heat, stirring occasionally. Add more oil as needed to keep them from sticking to the pan. Cook for 20–25 minutes.

Toss the chicken with the salt, pepper, and cornstarch or arrowroot in a large bowl. Heat the vegetable oil in a large nonstick skillet over medium-high heat until very hot. Add half of the cubed chicken and cook, turning, until well browned, crispy, and cooked through, about 6–8 minutes. Using a slotted spoon, transfer the chicken to a bowl. Repeat with the remaining chicken.

Turn the skillet down to medium heat. Add the garlic and ginger and cook for about 1 minute. Add 1 C of chicken stock and the bourbon, soy sauce, brown sugar, rice vinegar, and crushed red chili flakes or powder. Whisk until combined. Bring to a simmer, stirring occasionally, and cook down until reduced by half. If needed, add 2 T of chicken stock at a time if the sauce needs more moisture.

Whisk together the remaining 1 T of chicken stock and the cornstarch in a small bowl. Add to the skillet and whisk well to combine. Bring to a boil, then let simmer for 1 minute to thicken. Add the chicken to the skillet and cook for a couple of minutes to warm through and coat with the sauce. Serve with the potatoes to absorb the sauce.

The Mercy Quilt

Finished quilt: 72″ × 108″ **Finished block:** 9″

MATERIALS

Fan background: 2½ yards

Fan blades: 2½ yards of assorted scraps (minimum 5½ ″ x 3″)

Fan quarter-circles: ⅝ yard

Alternate blocks: 3⅜ yards

Backing: 6½ yards

Binding: ⅞ yard

Batting: 80″ × 116″

Template plastic

Mercy quilt templates A, B, and C (see below)

CUTTING

To access patterns A, B, and C through the tiny url, type the web address provided into your browser window, **tinyurl.com/16497-patterns-download**

Print directly from the browser window or download the patterns. To print at home, print letter-size pages, selecting 100% size on the printer. To print at a copy shop, save the full-size pages to a thumb drive or email them to your local copyshop for printing.

Trace patterns A, B, and C onto template plastic and cut out.

Fan background

Cut 48 background pieces with template A.

Fan blades

Cut 288 blades with template B from assorted fabrics.

Fan quarter-circles

Cut 48 quarter-circles with template C.

Alternate blocks

Cut 48 squares 9½″ × 9½″.

Binding

Cut 10 strips 2½″ × WOF.

Construction

Seam allowance is ¼″.

FAN BLOCKS

1. Place 2 blades right sides together and stitch along one long side. Press the seam toward the right blade. Repeat with the remaining blade pieces to create 144 blade pairs.

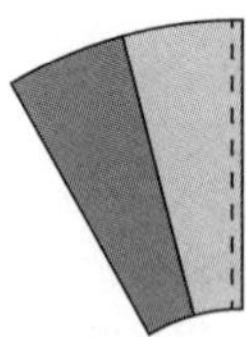

2. Place 2 blade pairs right sides together and stitch along one long side. Press the seam towards the right blade.

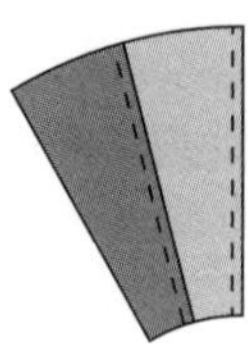

3. Place one blade pair right sides together with the 4-blade unit from Step 2 and stitch along one long side. Press the seam toward the right blade. Repeat Steps 2–3 to create 48 fans.

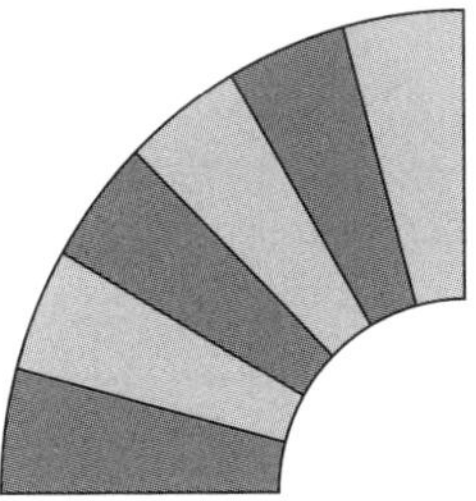

4. Fold a quarter-circle C in half and mark the center of the curve.

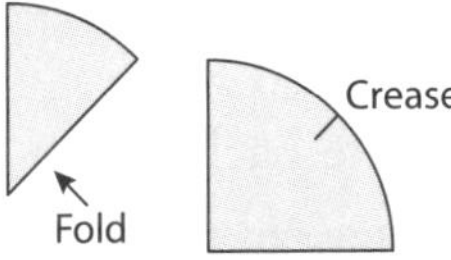

5. Match the center of the C curve to the center seam of the inside curve of a fan and pin. Match the edges and pin densely to ensure accurate piecing.

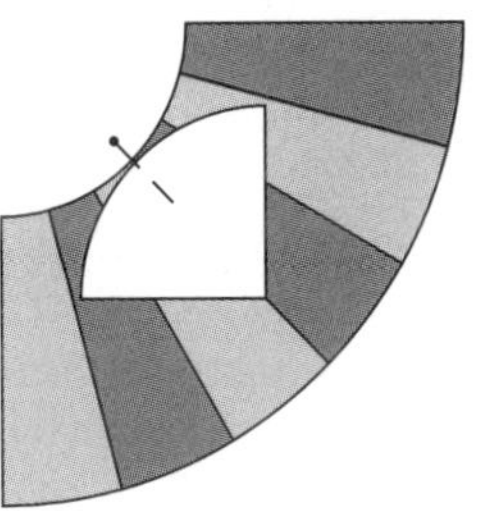

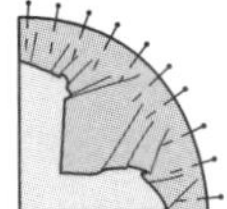

6. Stitch the quarter-circle to the fan. Repeat for the remaining fans.

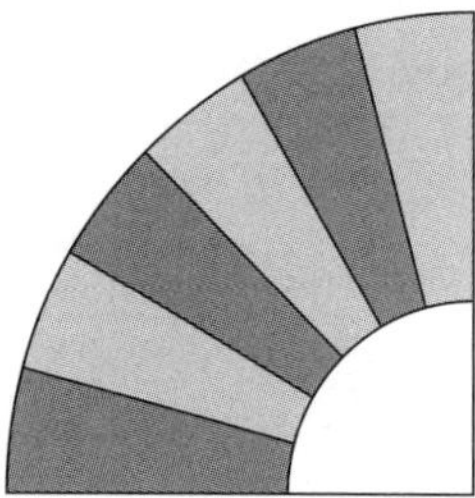

7. Fold a background A in half and mark the center of the curve.

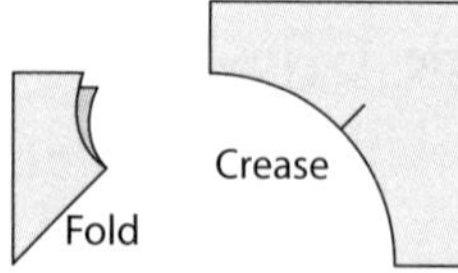

8. Match the center of the background A curve to the center seam of the outside curve of a fan and pin. Match the edges and pin densely to ensure accurate piecing.

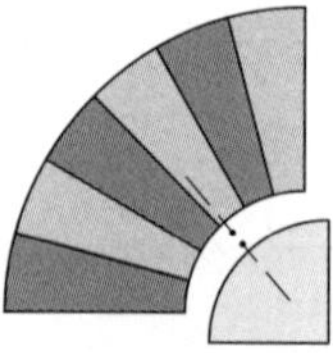

9. Stitch the background to the fan. Repeat for the remaining fans.

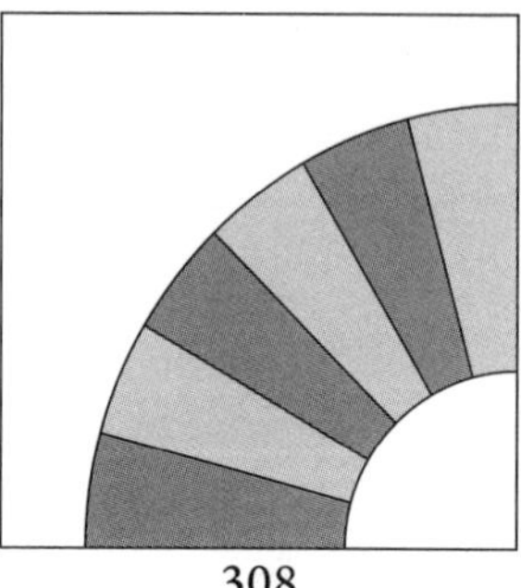

ASSEMBLY

1. Arrange the fan blocks and alternate squares in 12 rows of 8 blocks. Alternate the placement of the blocks in each row.
2. Layer 1 fan block and 1 alternate square, right sides together, and stitch together. Repeat with 3 more pairs of fan and alternate squares. Stitch 4 of these 2-block units together to make 1 row.
3. Repeat Step 2 to make 12 rows, alternating your pressing direction.
4. Stitch rows together and press.

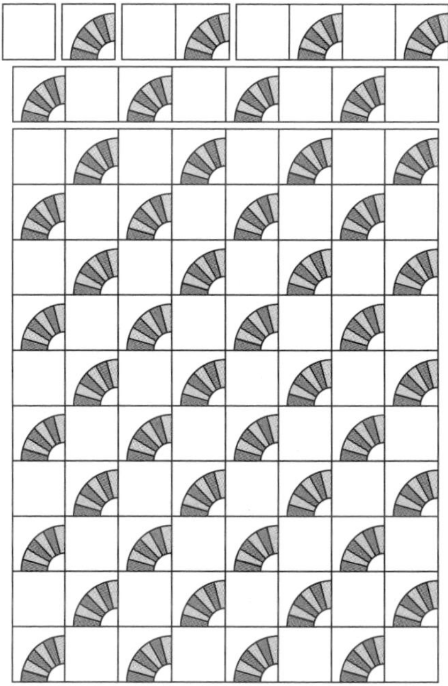

Quilt assembly

5. Layer, quilt as desired, and bind.

About the Author

Jeffree Wyn Itrich was born and raised in San Diego, California. She began writing as a child when she discovered a book filled with her mother's personal writings. The book inspired Jeffree to write. And write she did, filling countless journals with stories and essays.

In school, an English teacher recognized her ability and urged her to follow her literary dreams. She attended the graduate school of journalism at the University of California, Berkeley.

Her first book, *The Art of Accompaniment* was published by North Point Press in 1987, where it was named a Book of the Month Club and a Better Homes and Garden Book Club selection.

She used her journalism education to work in medical communications where she wrote hundreds of articles about medical therapies over a twenty year period. Even with a busy life, she never lost her passion for writing fiction. To date, she has had two novels, one cookbook, and a children's book published. In addition, *Chicken Soup for the Soul* has published seventeen of her stories.

Following her family's roots, she moved to the small town of West, Texas, in 2018. The Wedding Dress Quilt marries her love of quilting and Texas where her family settled more than 150 years ago.

Visit Jeffree online and follow her on social media!

Website: jeffreewyn.writerfolio.com/writing

Goodreads: goodreads.com/goodreadscomjeffreewyn

Pinterest: /jeffreei

Facebook: /JeffreeWyn

Blog: jeffreewynawriterslife.blogspot.com

THE MERCY QUILT DOWNLOAD

To access the pattern through the tiny url, type the web address provided into your browser window. tinyurl.com/16497-patterns-download

WAXAHACHIE, TEXAS, QUILT MYSTERY SERIES